The Edge of Forever

BARBARA BRETTON

Harlequin Books

TORONTO • NEW YORK • LONDON
AMSTERDAM • PARIS • SYDNEY • HAMBURG
STOCKHOLM • ATHENS • TOKYO • MILAN

For Pat and Joi—
who make it all a lot less lonely and a lot more fun.
Where would I be without you two?
And for Robin—for so much.

———————————•———————————

If you wish to be a writer, write.
Epictetus: Discourses II

Published February 1986

First printing December 1985

ISBN 0-373-16138-7

Printed in Canada

Chapter One

Words—both his passion and profession—were failing him once again.

"Joe, I really can't comprehend what you're trying to tell me." The woman on the other end of the telephone line was starting to sound exasperated.

He would try once more to make her understand. "You're a runner, Renee. Maybe this will make it clearer for you." Joe Alessio, aka Angelique Moreau, Alex Dennison and Bret Allen, stubbed out another cigarette in the overflowing ashtray and ignored the accusatory humming of his typewriter. "You remember that scene in *The Graduate* where Dustin Hoffman is running full-out to get to the church before his girlfriend marries another man?"

Renee groaned. "Please, Joseph, have mercy! Not another movie metaphor."

He ignored her protests. "His adrenaline is flowing, he's ready to run in there and sweep her away and—bam! He runs slam into a locked door." He cradled the receiver against his shoulder and pulled another pack of cigarettes out of his desk drawer. "That's what this feels like, Renee; it's like running smack into a brick wall at fifty miles an hour—face first."

"Don't you think you're exaggerating a bit? All writers hit a dry spell now and again."

Joe's laugh held a touch of desperation. "This is more than a dry spell. I stare at the paper for hours and nothing. Not one word. Not one idea. Nothing."

Renee's chuckle was husky but totally female. "I'm an agent, Joseph, not a shrink, but I think even I can diagnose this one. You've got your first case of writer's block."

"Come on, Renee! Give me a break." His voice, rich with the sounds of the New York neighborhood where he grew up, sounded disbelieving. "We both know that's a cop-out. What I'm telling you about is something totally different. There's something wrong with me. Every time I sit down at this damned machine, I go blank. It's like someone pulled the switch on me. I can't write. There's nothing left to say."

"Joe, listen to me. I—"

He could hear the sound of his agent's other telephone ringing across her office, and he groaned. "Renee, come on, this is important. I have to talk to you about the deadline. I can't—"

Her voice was cool and soothing, the tones a psychologist would use on a balky patient. "Just hold on, Joe. I'll let you listen to a little Muzak, and I'll be right back."

Joe's muttered curse was lost as Renee was replaced by a scratchy, saccharine rendition of a Beatles' song that made him want to throw the phone across the room. Instead, he controlled himself and laid it down on top of his desk, where the receiver was nearly buried in a pile of crumpled papers and half-empty packs of cigarettes. He stood up and yanked the corners of his New York Jets sweatshirt down over his taut abdomen, absently flexing muscles that had already been worked to exhaustion earlier that day.

A bottle of Johnny Walker beckoned him from the bar across the room, the writer's classic method of self-destruction. *Choose your weapon,* he thought as he lit up another Marlboro. A red-and-chrome jungle gym, left by the previous owners, glittered in the October sunlight. A breeze gently rocked the swing as if a ghost child were flying skyward. Instead, his eyes traveled from the playground equipment to the swimming pool to the woods beyond—he owned more land now than he ever knew existed when he was growing up in Queens.

Wasn't this what he'd always wanted? He had enough money to move his mother down to Florida, to help his nieces and nephews attend college, to buy one sister a beauty shop and the others a trip to Italy. He had a career with the requisite but unused word processor, the floppy disks virginal as a newborn child; he had a typewriter and tape recorder and all the pens and pencils anyone could possibly need. He had a pile of reference volumes scattered on the bed, on the dresser, on the floor of the bathroom.

He had time. He had the equipment. He had the contract, and God knew, he had the deadline. The only problem was he didn't have the damnedest idea what to do with it anymore.

The Muzak blessedly stopped, and he darted over and picked the receiver back up as Renee's familiar husky contralto said, "Do you know a Fletcher Wiley?"

His body tensed. He could see the muscle in his forearm tighten. "He's a friend of Anna's." It was Anna Kennedy who gave Joe his start with a grant to her artist colony in New Hampshire. He had lived and worked in that protected environment for six months and produced his first novel. "What is it?" He had to force the word out over the block of ice that was freezing his vocal cords.

Renee's sigh was as gentle as the breeze that rocked the swing and its ghost rider outside. "I'm sorry, Joe. She passed away last night."

He saw himself broke and scared, straight out of the army, with his body in the States, his head in the rotting jungles of Vietnam and his heart hanging crazily onto an impossible dream.

"Joseph?" He could picture Renee sitting at her desk, twisting the heavy gold ring she always wore on her right index finger. "Are you all right?"

"Yeah." He cleared his throat and drew the back of his sleeve quickly across his eyes. "Yeah. Strange, isn't it? Anna was eighty-four years old . . . She'd been sick for so long . . . This isn't a surprise, but God—" He broke off to clear his throat again. "It hurts as much as if she'd been cut down in her prime." He hadn't expected that. His acquaintance with death until that moment had been only with the untimely.

"When you love, it hurts, Joe. It's one of the paradoxes of life." Renee talked on softly, giving him a chance to recover his composure, to regain his balance.

"When is the funeral?"

He heard the sound of papers shuffling on her desk. "Thursday morning at the Unitarian Church in Gorham." Renee groaned. "No street address. Damn. I should have asked."

Joe smiled. "Don't worry," he said. "You don't need one in Gorham."

"That small?"

"That small."

"How did a tough city kid like you manage in a little town? Somehow you don't seem the type for Main Street and barbershop quartets."

He thought back to the majesty of the White Mountains, to the lakes that mirrored back the beauty of the land, to the many kindnesses he'd been shown when he understood least how to deal with them. "You'd be surprised," he said. He *had* been—over and over during those six months of healing and discovery. The months made possible for him by Anna Kennedy.

"Do you want me to make plane reservations for you?" Renee's voice cut into his memories. "I'll call up Liberty Travel and—"

"Don't bother," he broke in. "You can't fly directly into Gorham. I'll just take one of those little shuttles out of JFK, then rent a car." He closed his eyes for a moment. "The problem's going to be where to stay. This is the off-season. I might end up camping around a lake somewhere."

Renee laughed. Joe could picture her light blue eyes crinkling behind her owlish glasses. "Not to worry. Mr. Wiley—" He heard the sound of papers rustling. "Ah, yes, here it is. Mr. Wiley said you're welcome to stay at Lakeland House."

The thought of staying in the colony without Anna Kennedy's dynamic presence was a bit unsettling. "I don't know," Joe said. "I'm going to play that one by ear."

"I'm sorry the occasion is an unhappy one, Joe, but it'll do you good to get away."

He grunted, balancing the receiver between ear and shoulder as he lit yet another cigarette. "It's not going to make any difference, Renee." He shrugged. "I can't write now. I won't be able to write when I get back."

"Great attitude, Alessio. You'll go far with it."

He laughed. "I already have," he said. "Don't worry about me, Renee. I'll get by."

"I've never doubted it." She sighed. "I'm not so sure you believe it, though. Remember if you need someone to talk to while you're in the boonies of New Hampshire, call me. That's what you pay me ten percent for."

But of course Renee meant much more than that to him. There had been three people in his life who had influenced him both personally and professionally in ways that were profound and eternal: his father, Anna Kennedy and Renee Arden. Two of the three were dead now, and he shivered, suddenly reminded of the basic fragility of the species.

At least Anna had lived to see his success, he thought after he had hung up the phone, even if his success was pseudonymous. He'd worked hard, damned hard, to make it to the top of his genre, and Anna had appreciated that fact even if she believed he was only skimming the surface of his talent. The Vietnam book he'd begun a thousand times still rested in the bottom of his file cabinet despite Anna's fervent wish that he tackle his memories and lay them to rest. But what he'd needed was fantasy, and he'd chosen to create perfect worlds instead, perfect worlds inhabited by people who played by rules of decency and humanity. Whether the world was the American West, a small planet beyond Neptune or turn-of-the-century Europe, Joe found it easy to bring his fantasy worlds to life on paper.

It had brought him success, and it had saved his sanity. The only cost had been his personal life.

He lit a cigarette and sat on the edge of the window seat and looked out over the yard. "Balance, Joe, balance," Anna had said a few years ago on his thirtieth birthday. "You should be thinking now of expanding your sights."

He had laughed and poured himself another brandy, secure in the knowledge that there would always be time enough to change. "If you're talking marriage, Annie, I'm too young," he said. "Besides, work is my mistress right now."

"Come, now, Joe," Anna had said with a wry smile. "I may be on in years, but I'm not senile." Joe's romantic exploits were well-known around the Kennedy Creative Colony. "I know who you are deep inside, and sooner or later you're going to find yourself very alone."

But he had been having none of it that day. He had a multibook contract and a beautiful redhead waiting for him back in the city, and there in New Hampshire, he had a rerun of *Casablanca*, his dearest friend and some fine Cointreau. He'd managed to push Vietnam to a dark corner of his mind, and marriage seemed as remote as that Asian jungle. "I'll never be alone," he'd said—words he would later regret. "I have you and I have Renee and a hell of a lot of friends back home."

Anna had just shaken her head, and when the time came that she was proved right, she had the class—and the wisdom—to never once say, "I told you so."

Ah, Annie, he thought, resting his forehead against the cool windowpane and staring out at the motionless swing. *Rest well.*

He turned and picked up the phone to book a flight to New England.

MEG LINDSTROM was waxing the rear left fender of the limousine when she found out. As soon as she heard Elysse's high heels tapping across the cement floor of the garage, a sense of loss settled across her shoulders that stopped her in mid-stroke, and a bone-deep chill settled inside her as it had when her sister Kay died. She leaned back on her heels and watched Elysse gingerly pick her way past oil cans and carburetors.

"Have a sudden yen to wax a limo?" Meg asked as her friend approached her. "Or have all your patients suddenly achieved emotional well-being at the same time?" The attempt at humor echoed in the cavernous garage.

"I looked for you earlier," Elysse said. "Were you at the park?"

Meg nodded. For weeks she had been photographing a family of swans that had taken over a small pond next to the Long Island Sound at Sunken Meadow. The uncomfortable feeling intensified.

Elysse was a psychologist whose greatest professional shortcoming was the way her large blue eyes instantly betrayed her feelings. "Meg, something has—"

Meg tossed the chamois to the ground. She knew Elysse would take the long and careful route to cushion her feelings, but there was no need. She already knew. "It's Anna, isn't it?"

Elysse nodded. Meg saw her throat constrict beneath the collar of her silky gray blouse. "Last night," Elysse said softly. "In her sleep,"

Meg sat down on the hard cement floor. It felt cold through the thin denim of her jeans. "Was she alone?" A piece of chrome dug into her backbone, a sharp reminder of life. *Tell me she wasn't alone.*

Elysse crouched down next to Meg and gently touched her shoulder. "No," she said. "Two of her nieces were with her."

"I'm glad," Meg said, "but I shouldn't have postponed going up there. I knew the time was near, but I just couldn't face..." Her voice trailed off.

Elysse moved closer to Meg and hugged her. "You can't blame yourself, Meg. She seemed to be doing well—you spoke to her doctor only a week ago. How could anyone foresee just when it would be?"

The friend and the shrink in Elysse were battling for dominance, and the friend was winning. Meg picked up the hem of Elysse's pale mauve wool skirt, which was poised over an oil slick. "Stand up, Elly," she said softly. "You can't let your patients see you looking like a mechanic."

Elysse ignored her. "Don't turn me away like that, Meg Lindstrom. Talk to me. Tell me how you feel right now."

I feel scared and lonely and suddenly old, Elly. I want to wake up and have this be a dream. But Meg was not a woman who easily bared her soul. "Come on, Dr. Lowell," she said instead. "I can't afford one of your fifty-minute hours."

Elysse's expression alternated between anger and pity. "Meg, I don't think—"

Meg stood up and wiped her hands on a towel draped over a workbench near the limousine. She looked at her friend.

"Not now, Elly," she said, linking her arm through Elysse's. "No lectures. There's too much I need to know." The side door to the garage swung closed behind them. "For instance, when are the services?"

"Thursday morning," Elysse said. "The Unitarian Church in Gorham."

Meg nodded. "I'll need some time off. I'd like to drive up for it. Is Jack home?"

"You don't have to ask Jack." Jack was Elysse's husband. "You own the limousine, you know."

"Yes, but Jack owns the company," Meg said easily. "It's not easy getting a business off the ground." They started to walk toward the cottage Meg rented, situated on a rise behind the main house.

"Meg, please. I think we really should talk about Anna and—"

Meg shook her head. "Not now," she said. "Maybe another time, but not now."

Meg Lindstrom had a long history of postponing painful discussions for "another time." When Meg's journalist sister, Kay Lindstrom, had been killed, Elysse had tried without luck to get Meg to talk about her feelings of loss. When Meg suddenly put aside her own blossoming career as a photographer, Elysse had demanded they talk about her decision. Meg, however, shrugged, made a joke and continued to keep her own counsel.

Apparently nothing had changed.

Meg opened the kitchen door, and Elysse followed her inside. Elysse fiddled around at the stove, setting water to boil for a bracing pot of tea and hunting for some cookies to set out. "When was the last time you went to the supermarket?" Elysse asked, flinging open the cupboard doors and staring at emptiness. "All you have in here is a jar of bouillon cubes and a bottle of soy sauce."

Meg leaned against the doorjamb and smiled at her small and furious best friend. "Why should I shop, Dr. Lowell?" she countered. "You have me up to the house for dinner six nights a week and leave a care package on my doorstep on the seventh."

Elysse found a box of chocolate doughnuts in the equally bare refrigerator and arranged them on a white plate. "I only invite you to dinner five nights a week. Now why don't you pack while I make the tea. You've got a long drive ahead of you."

Meg took Elysse's hand and gave it a quick squeeze, an uncharacteristic gesture for her. "What would I do without you, Elysse?"

Elysse met her eyes for a long moment, acknowledging the gesture and all it meant. Then she laughed. "You'd probably be even skinnier than you are now." She gave Meg a gentle push. "Go pack. The tea will be waiting when you're done."

Elysse watched as Meg left the room, head high and back straight. She knew the effort it took to maintain that self-control, for it was she who had seen Meg through the horrors surrounding Kay's death. The Lindstroms had always made it quite clear that Kay was the favorite child, that it was Kay's achievements and not Meg's that were truly noteworthy. Kay's death, at the height of her promise, froze her forever in time as the golden one. That Meg had just won two prestigious awards went unnoticed.

In the days after Kay's murder, Elysse had held Meg's hand, plied her with hot soup and human comfort and somehow managed to control the urge to grab the Lindstroms and shake them into remembering they still had a very wonderful daughter left.

The teapot whistled, and Elysse busied herself once again with at least providing warmth for her friend's body if not for her soul.

MEG STOPPED for the night in a Holiday Inn outside of Boston. She'd toyed with the idea of pushing on to New Hampshire, but a wave of fatigue overcame her near Braintree, and she decided to take a room instead.

For hours she'd raced one step ahead of her sorrow, unwilling to slow down long enough to let the full measure of Anna's loss overcome her, but now, in that antiseptic hotel room, she had no place to run. Her eyes were caught and held by the small framed photo she'd brought with her and propped up on the bureau opposite the bed.

The sepia tones were a dead giveaway as to when it was taken. When Meg had first arrived at Anna Kennedy's colony, she was so taken by the New England countryside, with its rich sense of history, that she began experimenting with sepia prints, delighting in their old-fashioned feel. The picture she now held in her hand was one of her best. Anna, dressed in long skirt and bonnet, was on the left side of the picture, seated at a spinning wheel. She was surrounded by piles of unprocessed wool. On the right side stood Meg, garbed in one of the fringed and funky disco outfits made of hundred percent polyester that were popular after *Saturday Night Fever* came out. In her hand she held a tiny battery-operated sewing machine. Meg called the picture *American Woman*, and it had won her her first award from the Institute of Photography.

She remembered how Anna had laughed as Meg fiddled with the tripod and fumbled with the timer, getting so tangled up in the wires that one of the dancers had to finally shoot the picture for her. God, how euphoric she'd felt that day, as if the world had been created solely for her to explore and capture with her camera.

But of course that was when Kay was still alive. Kay, media wonder, perfect daughter, the person Meg always wanted to be but never would. It was no wonder the very ordinary Lindstroms had been so entranced with their eldest daughter—she was anything but ordinary. Kay had been blessed with success in the world's toughest market—New York City television news—yet had managed to retain the kindness and generosity she'd always possessed. She made it a point to introduce Meg to the right people, to make sure her little sister had the right equipment and the right contacts. When Kay knocked, doors opened, and she pushed Meg inside. While Meg idolized her sister, she often felt resentful of the help, even though she never refused it.

Winning the grant to study and work at the Kennedy Creative Colony with Anna had lifted Meg from Kay's shadow and thrust her into a world she'd never known existed. Meg's elation knew no bounds. Her horizons had expanded daily, and even if her ambitions were fueled by a degree of sibling rivalry, she had been alive with possibilities, charged through with the need to see and record life.

Now all that remained of that glorious time of possibilities were bittersweet memories, for Kay was dead, and now even Anna, incredible wonderful Anna, was gone forever.

FIRST OF ALL, the heavy wooden door to the church needed oiling. It squeaked loud and clear as Meg tried to slip unnoticed into the church vestibule. The minister barely missed a beat in his ecumenical eulogy, but Meg's face still burned as she stumbled into the last pew next to the radiator. She prided herself on never being late for anything, but her memory of the New Hampshire roads had failed her, and she was halfway to the Maine border before she realized her error and turned back toward Gorham.

She knew the minister must be speaking English, for everyone around her seemed to have no difficulty understanding him, but Meg found him as unintelligible as if he were speaking in tongues. A heavy thick gold light poured in from the high windows and lay over the dark pine benches like rich syrup. It reminded Meg of the sepia portrait she'd tucked into her bag, and her heart ached with memory.

" . . . on the Lower East Side of New York . . . working in the phone company during the day . . . City College at night . . . married Brendan Kennedy, the Pulitzer Prize-winning . . ."

None of this had anything to do with the Anna Kennedy Meg had known. None of this had anything to do with the woman who had single-handedly changed Meg's life during that one brief period when Meg had believed she could spread her wings and fly.

Although it was only October, the heating system was on full blast, and the blistering warmth from the radiator next to her was making her light-headed.

The minister introduced one of Anna's nieces, who was going to read from Anna's prizewinning *Uncommon Press Collection of Short Stories.* The radiator rattled, then kicked into overdrive, and Meg felt the pew tilt sideways and her stomach tilt with it. She grabbed her pocketbook and stood up.

She had to get some fresh air.

JOE COULDN'T BRING himself to go inside the church. The taxi service had dropped him off ten minutes ago, and he'd been loitering at the top of the stairs, suitcase at his feet and cigarette in hand, listening to the slightly nasal tones of the minister that filtered out to him.

All around him the world seemed painfully, vividly alive. The blazing orange-and-yellow foliage made the hurt he'd battled during the plane ride rise up and wrap itself around his throat.

You have to go in, he thought. *You didn't travel five hundred miles to stand on the church steps.* No matter how much it hurt to realize Anna was gone, he owed it to her to go inside. He was about to stub out his cigarette when the massive wooden door squeaked open and a tall slender blonde stepped into the sunlight, frowned and began to tumble at his feet.

Joe grabbed her before she hit the ground. Her body was loose and boneless in his arms, a surprisingly light bundle for such a tall woman, and he easily picked her up and carried her down the church steps, where he sat with her on the grass.

"Oh, God," she said, looking up at him with the unfocused stare of the almost conscious. "I've made a fool of myself."

"No, you didn't," Joe said, holding her by the shoulders as she tried to regain her balance. "It isn't every day I have a beautiful blonde fall at my feet." The remark was meant solely to diffuse her embarrassment, but it hadn't taken more than a second for Joe to realize that she was beautiful—faces like hers were given to only the chosen few.

She pushed against his arm and sat up. Her hair was long and intricately braided, and she flung the plait back over her shoulder as she looked at him.

"I fell at your feet?" Her eyes were a very dark brown streaked with flecks of gold, a strange and exotic combination with the pale blonde hair.

"Is it that hard to imagine?" He smoothed down the collar of her black coat with the back of his hand, smothering a sudden desire to touch the apricot skin of her cheek. "And here I thought I was irresistible."

Her eyes were riveted to his, and he felt himself being quickly judged. "It's not that I doubt your appeal," she said, the frown lines between her pale brows smoothing out. "It's just that I'm not usually the impetuous type."

Joe stood up and held out his hand. She grasped it and got to her feet, straightening out the hem of her skirt and brushing some dried leaves from her stockinged legs.

"Are you all right now?" He'd never seen hair as fine and blond as hers before. It seemed to sparkle with captured moonlight and stars. "Do you need some water or anything?"

"I'm fine. It was just so blasted hot in there that I—" She stopped. "Who am I trying to kid? I couldn't handle it." For the first time, those limitless eyes of her looked away. "I felt as if the walls were closing in on me."

Joe pulled a cigarette out of his jacket pocket. He offered her one, but she shook her head. "You fared better than I did," he said after he lit the cigarette and took a long, comforting drag. "I couldn't bring myself to go inside. I haven't been that scared of anything since I was in 'Nam."

She didn't question his statement, merely nodded her head. They walked toward the stairs. Joe ground out his cigarette on the top step near his suitcase. A low rumble of voices raised in prayer seeped through the church door. *I shouldn't have come,* he thought. He should have honored Anna in his own way, remembered her as she should be remembered, not with pious prayer and anonymous condolences. He wanted to grab his suitcase and leave, but the woman next to him straightened her shoulders and opened the church door.

"We owe it to Anna," she said. Her gaze was so direct that he found it impossible to disagree.

He followed her inside and slid into the last pew beside her. He tried to zero in on the minister's words, but they seemed to grow distorted by the time they reached him.

Next to him, the blond woman rustled in her seat. He glanced over at her and found himself fascinated by the dignity of her chiseled profile, the elegant curve of her long neck, the way her hands rested quietly on her lap.

A man Joe recognized as one of Anna's friends from the days when her husband was alive stepped up to the lectern.

"Anna Kennedy lived the way a human being should live," the man began, his voice rough with emotion but steady. "She embraced every day—every second—as if it were the most precious of gifts, and more importantly, she managed to share her zest for life with many of you who have come today to honor her."

Across the aisle a woman began to cry softly.

"Sorrow wasn't in Anna Kennedy's vocabulary," the man continued. "She loved life too much, and she simply had too much love to give to the writers and artists who came to Lakeland House in droves."

Tears he hadn't shed since his father's death made his eyes sting, and he blinked rapidly to clear them.

"And so we're not here today to sing sad songs or weep for Anna Kennedy's death. No. We're here to celebrate her life."

Joe was about to lose his battle with tears when the incredible, vibrant sounds of the last section of Tchaikovsky's *1812 Overture* blasted forth from the loudspeakers as the mourners began to file their way out of the church.

He thought of Anna, whose idea of quiet dinner music had been this rousing theme meant to lead men into battle, not bouillabaisse. He pictured her at the long dinner table, conducting the crescendo with her sterling-silver salad fork. He'd be damned if he'd mourn her with weeping and sorrow. He glanced at the woman next to him, and a crazy smile spread across his face.

The woman smiled back at him, her face even lovelier than he'd first thought.

"Anna would have loved this," he said.

The woman nodded. "She probably does."

She reached out and took his hand. Her bones were finer, more fragile than he had expected, the skin soft and delicate. And so he sat there until it was their turn to leave, thinking of Anna and trying not to think of the way this woman's hand felt in his.

THE GRAVE-SITE CEREMONY was brief and unbearably poignant. Meg found herself looking at the trees ablaze in fall colors, glancing toward the White Mountains in the distance, concentrating on the rugged face of the man next to her—anything rather than think about what it was that had brought her to that place.

When it was over, she left to walk the quarter mile back to the church, where she'd left her car. The dark-haired man walked with her. She had yet to ask his name; the moment for introduction hadn't presented itself. She liked the way he seemed to understand the value of silence, and she also liked the way he took her hand in his own large one and fell into step with her with no question or pause. And although this was hardly the time to dwell on such things, she also liked the strong, angular bones of his face, the hawklike nose and the beautifully made mouth below. His skin was a light olive with high color around the cheeks; just the slightest hint of dark beard showed. If she had had her camera with her right then, she would have posed him in a thick tangle of woods with a thin shaft of sunlight backlighting his face. He must have felt her eyes on him, for he looked at her, a steady measuring look, then gave her hand a slight squeeze.

She was grateful to have that human hand to hold on to, and she suspected he was just as grateful. Such a shame, she thought, noting the way the sun brought out the green of his eyes and the shiny black of his straight and shaggy hair that had the slightest dusting of silver at the temples. Such a shame that they would part company in a few minutes and this unexpected feeling of warmth and kinship would disappear with no more than a brief good-bye. But this was hardly a social occasion, and he probably had a life of his own to return to, a life bounded east and west with wife and children.

"Are you going to brunch at the house?" he asked.

Meg thought of the clusters of mourners who would be there—wealthy people in furs mingling with perennially starving artists—and shook her head. "I don't think I could handle it."

"Lakeland wouldn't be the same, would it?"

"Not at all." Suddenly she became very aware of the intimacy of what they had shared, and she pulled away, plunging both of her hands into the pockets of her coat. They were standing near her gleaming limousine, and she was about to ask him if she could give him a ride to his hotel when a tall, slim, graying man approached them.

"Well, if it's not the luck of the Irish again." His voice was deep and musical, touched with a trace of brogue. "How about finding you two together like this?"

Meg glanced at the man next to her, who shrugged his shoulders.

"I'm Patrick McCallum, Anna's attorney, and you're Joseph Alessio and Margarita Lindstrom." They said nothing. McCallum looked from one to the other and smiled, his weary face brightening for a moment. "You can't deny it," he said, pulling two photos from his inside breast pocket and extending them to Meg and Joe. "You both might be a little older, but time hasn't done that much damage."

Meg barely recognized the face that looked up at her from the grainy black-and-white photo. It wasn't that she had been that much younger—twenty-six wasn't so far removed from twenty-one, after all—but the look in her eyes was one of such innocence, such enthusiasm, that it was painful to see. Instead, she took the other picture from McCallum's hand, looking from that flat, one-dimensional image to the living, breathing original next to her.

"I can hardly believe this is you," she said, tactfulness going by the boards. "You look so...so—"

"Angry." Joe took the picture from her, glanced at it, then handed it back to Meg. "I was." He pulled a cigarette out of his coat pocket. "Very angry."

Meg brought the photo closer. It wasn't a professional shot, for a professional never would have let his strong-boned face disappear into shadow like that or allow the background to become dominant. No, it definitely wasn't professional, but somehow the anger Joe said he'd been feeling managed to practically singe her fingers as she held the picture. He looked thinner than he did now, less muscular, his denim work shirt open at the neck. Nestled in the thick hair of his chest was a medal of some kind, and below that dog tags. His black hair was long; its straight strands covered his brow and brushed below the collar of his shirt. Most of his face was hidden by a beard and mustache that lacked the lushness of maturity.

He was sitting on a window seat, a lighted cigarette in two fingers of his left hand, which rested on his right knee. His eyes, a brilliant deep green in reality, seemed dark and mysterious in the photo. Through the bay window behind him, Meg could just make out the figures of people playing with a Frisbee in Anna's backyard at Lakeland House.

"I know that room," she said, handing him the photo. "That was the room where the dancers practiced, wasn't it?"

Joe barely glanced at the photo before he handed it back to McCallum, who was quietly observing the two of them. "No," he said, looking back at Meg. "When I was at Lakeland, there were no dancers."

"I thought Anna catered to all of the arts," Meg said, truly puzzled. "When I was there, she—"

"Mrs. Kennedy didn't open her doors to dancers until 1976," Patrick McCallum broke in, putting the two snapshots back in his coat pocket. "If I'm not mistaken, Joseph attended in early 1973, and you were there just a few years ago."

Meg turned to Joe and quickly assessed him.

"I'm not as young as you thought?" Joe asked.

"No," she said honestly. "I thought you were around my age."

"Which is?"

"Twenty-six years and three months," McCallum volunteered. "Margarita was born July sixth and you, Joseph, were born July seventh—a difference of seven years and one day."

Before Meg could respond, Joe broke in.

"The next question," he said, "is how the hell do you know so much about us?"

McCallum's face, lined and friendly as a basset hound's, creased with a smile. "Would you believe it if I said all Irishmen are psychic?"

"Sorry." Meg shook her head. "You can do better than that."

"I was Anna's lawyer," McCallum said, "and I know everything about the people she cared most for."

"I'm flattered," Meg said, "but I don't really see why it—"

"Why it matters," Joe broke in.

McCallum's sigh was long and low. "I hadn't wanted to bring this up until we got to Lakeland House."

"We weren't planning to go back to the house," Meg said.

McCallum stepped between them and draped an arm around each one of them. "Then I'm definitely glad I stopped you both. You have to come back."

"Now wait a minute, pal." Joe pulled away from McCallum's friendly grasp. Meg watched, fascinated, as his deep green eyes darkened and he took on some of the intensity of the younger man he'd once been, the man she'd seen in the photo. "This has been a difficult morning. I don't think either I or—" He fumbled for a second.

"Meg," she said.

His look was one of thanks and apology. "I don't think either Meg or I want to be strong-armed into—"

"Strong-armed?" McCallum released Meg as quickly as if her shoulders had just caught fire. "Strong-armed, is it?" His pale blue eyes were filled with concern. "Good God, but it *has* been a difficult morning, hasn't it?" He rubbed his square chin absently for a second. "Didn't I make it clear? You, Joseph, and you, Margarita, are both *requested* to be present."

"Requested by whom?" Joe still sounded wary.

"By Anna."

"I beg your pardon?" Meg's voice rose an octave.

"I spoke with Anna a few hours before she died," McCallum explained. "She said the will cannot be read except in your presence." He grinned. "Your presences."

"This is the first I've heard of anything like this." An uncomfortable fluttering began in the pit of her stomach. "You would think Anna would have mentioned it in a phone call or a letter or—"

Joe shook his head. "Not Anna," he said slowly. "She delighted in surprises." He looked up at McCallum, who towered over the both of them. "Apparently she still does."

"Now you get the idea." McCallum, satisfied that he was finally understood, draped his arms over their shoulders once again and propelled Meg and Joe back toward the church and the waiting cars. *Anna was right,* he thought as he glanced from the tall, Nordic blonde on his left to the dark and intense man on his right. This would be a very interesting proposition.

Chapter Two

"Lakeland is on the other side of town," McCallum continued, "but then, of course, you both know that already, don't you?" He pointed to a light tan Volvo sedan that was parked a few yards away from Meg's limousine. "I'd be happy to give you a ride."

Joe started to answer, but Meg broke in. "I appreciate the offer," she said, motioning toward the long, sleek luxury car sparkling in the sun, "but I have my own."

Both men turned to look, and she laughed out loud as their jaws dropped in surprise.

Patrick McCallum was the first to recover his poise. "It looks like I should be asking you for a ride," he said with a wide grin.

"You're more than welcome to one," Meg said.

McCallum shook his head. "No, no. It wouldn't do for me to get too accustomed to the good life. I have rich enough tastes as it is." He patted both Meg and Joe on the shoulder. "Give me a minute to get my car started and you can follow me."

"Well," Meg said, turning to Joe, "unless you feel like walking, it looks like you're stuck with me."

"I wouldn't put it quite like that," he said with a smile that was very appealing. "If you think you have room for me—"

One pale eyebrow arched. "I think we can manage." McCallum's car rolled out of its parking spot and sat idling in front of the limousine. Meg waved toward the small suitcase Joe had left at the top of the church steps. "If you just get your luggage, we can get going."

Joe was clearly puzzled. "I thought that's what you paid your chauffeur for."

"That's part of it," she answered, hiding the twinkle in her eye. "Mostly, though, we get paid to drive."

He looked first at the car, then back at her. "I thought this was a chauffeur-driven limo."

"It is. It just happens that *I'm* the chauffeur." She stepped around to the driver's side. "But since this isn't a paid assignment, why don't you get your luggage and I'll start the car. I think McCallum's getting impatient."

Indeed, the attorney had rolled down the window on the passenger side of his Volvo and was intently listening to their conversation.

"I feel like a first-class fool," Joe said when he tossed the suitcase in the back and climbed into the car. "I really thought you owned this thing."

"I do," Meg said, easing the enormous limo out of its spot and falling into place behind McCallum. "I bought it a year and a half ago."

"You own your own limousine service?"

She shook her head and stopped the car at a red light. "No, but I work for a friend's husband as a quasi-partner."

"Why?"

"Why not?" She glanced quickly at him. He was leaning forward in his seat, those intense, beautiful eyes of his focused on her in a way she found as unnerving as it was compelling.

"That's no answer."

"I'm afraid it's the best one I have available on such short notice." The light turned green, and she continued following McCallum.

"No one decides to become a limousine driver on the spur of the moment."

"I hate to ruin your preconceptions, Mr. Alessio, but I did exactly that." Her amusement was turning quickly to annoyance. She would never get quite used to defending her decision—not even to herself. "It's an honest living. I pay my taxes just like you do."

His laugh was husky, a low, amused rumble. "How do you know I pay my taxes? Writers are notorious when it comes to bookkeeping."

"I didn't know you were a writer." She signaled for a right turn and smiled sweetly into his eyes. "I'm afraid I don't recognize your name." *See if you like how it feels, Alessio.*

"There's no reason you would. I write under a pseudonym." He reached inside his coat pocket for a cigarette. "Several, actually." He extended the pack of Marlboros toward Meg, who shook her head. "Do you mind if I smoke?"

"Actually I do." She stopped the car while McCallum opened the large gates to the Lakeland House property and waved her inside. She maneuvered the stretch limo up the narrow, twisting driveway toward the back of the main house. "I'd rather you didn't."

With her peripheral vision she was able to note the amused, curious glance Joe shot at her as he stuck the cigarettes back in his pocket.

"Thanks," Meg said. "It *is* a rotten habit, you know."

Joe sighed theatrically. "Spare me the eighties version of a temperance lecture. I already know all the horrors it can inflict on my unsuspecting lungs."

"So why do you do it?" she asked. "It's like signing a death warrant."

The seat belt strained against his broad chest as he turned around in his seat to stare at her. "You don't mince words, do you, Meg Lindstrom?"

"I try not to."

"I wouldn't think it good business to deprive a paying customer of one of his creature comforts."

Meg gestured toward the enormous rear seating area of the limousine, complete with TV, VCR, stereo, full bar and plush seats. "There are enough creature comforts back there to satisfy an Arab sheikh." She grinned. "Besides, I make it a practice to keep the air vents open and my mouth shut when I have paying customers."

"I'll remember that," Joe said. "Next time I—"

He suddenly stopped as the main house, Anna's house, came into view at the top of the driveway. It was an old white frame building, dating back to the early 1800s, that had once served as an inn and restaurant. Mullioned windows framed with crisp black shutters and pine-green window boxes looked down on the flower beds and rolling front lawn. When Anna and her husband had purchased the property some thirty years before, it had been rotting from within with neglect; it took a lot of money and an equal amount of love to resurrect it and the smaller cottages surrounding it.

From the first second she saw Lakeland House nearly five years ago, Meg had felt as if she'd come home. Even now, on so solemn an occasion, it seemed to welcome her. She glanced at Joe and saw a bittersweet smile on his face. He understood.

Meg maneuvered the car into an empty space away from the crowd of Lincolns and Jeeps and Chevys that were parked closer to the house. She turned off the ignition and unsnapped her seat belt.

"Well, come on, then," McCallum said as they got out of the limousine. "We have an audience awaiting us inside."

An attack of nerves grabbed Meg around her midsection, "An audience? I thought it was just for Anna's family and close friends."

"And that it is," McCallum said, leading them up the cobbled driveway past the bare rosebushes that would be crimson with blossoms come June. "Just an intimate group of Anna's family and twenty-seven addled artists and egocentric writers." Joe's sardonic grin brought McCallum up short. "Present company excepted, of course."

"Of course," Joe answered, holding the side door for both McCallum and Meg.

The big house smelled of perfume and liquor and food, and Meg longed to be outside again, breathing the swift, sharp scent of pine. The living room was through the passageway on their left, and she could clearly hear buzzes of conversation punctuated by the tinkling sound of ice cubes against glass. For a second she expected to see Anna hurrying down the corridor, her plump arms outstretched toward Meg in greeting, and she had to blink for a second to force the image—so clear, so cutting—from her mind.

"Follow me."

Patrick McCallum bounded up the uncarpeted wooden steps two at a time. If Meg had been in her ubiquitous running shoes, she would have done the same thing, but slim skirts and high heels put a definite crimp in her style.

"Why don't you go ahead?" she said to Joe, who waited for her to precede him up the narrow, curving staircase. "I haven't worn heels this high in ages. It will take me awhile to hobble up there."

Joe looked at her with a strangely vulnerable expression on his rugged face that tugged at her heart. He rested one hand against her hip for a moment. She could barely feel its pressure through her heavy woolen coat, but its emotional weight was duly noted.

"Go ahead," he said, giving her a gentle push toward the stairs. "I'll ride shotgun."

She cast him a quick look over her shoulder. "You write Westerns?"

He laughed. "Among other things."

They maintained a light conversation about the demise of the cowboy as hero as they followed McCallum toward the immense library at the opposite end of the second-floor hallway. Joe kept them amused with his list of top-ten Western movies of all time, and when they reached the doorway to the library where Anna had spent so much of her time, Meg almost felt she'd be able to get through the reading of the will without crying. At the very least, she would give it her best shot.

Joe, however, was not faring as well. The lighthearted banter was a mask, a cover for the way his gut had been twisting ever since they drove up the snaking, tree-lined driveway to Lakeland House. Anna hovered over everything; he could hear her voice in the hallway, see her bright blue eyes twinkling at him over a half-written manuscript, smell the pungent aroma of the cup of red Egyptian tea she always kept at her side. It was as if absolutely nothing had changed at all.

But the second he stepped through the door to the enormous library that had been Anna's domain, he knew beyond doubt that everything had. The room looked the same—still the walls of floor-to-ceiling bookshelves, still the heavy leaded windows with diamond-shaped panes of glass, the Turkish carpet beneath his feet. Somehow, though, the spark had been extinguished; the inexplicable something that had made this room so special had disappeared with Anna's death, and it made him want to turn tail and run like a scared kid.

Of course, he was a grown man now and not able to allow himself the privileges of youth, no matter how tempting they might be, so he just followed Margarita Lindstrom toward the two empty leather wing chairs near the center window.

They were all there—or if they weren't, it sure as hell seemed that way. People he'd known during his first time at Lakeland, people he'd met through his continuing association with it. They stopped him with effusive greetings and hyperbolic compliments that would sound false to a deaf man. Each one looked properly sober—despite the glasses of scotch and bourbon near many of them—as befitted the reading of a will, and a trifle expectant, as well. Nowhere but in the eyes of Meg Lindstrom, the limousine driver, did he see anything approaching the sadness he felt over losing one of his dearest friends.

"Joseph, darling." Kiss on right cheek, then left. "We have so much to catch up on." Bettye, the expert in Egyptian art he'd met last year at one of Anna's grand parties, began telling him about the craziness surrounding the exhibition she was putting together for the Freer Gallery in Washington, D.C. Normally, Joe enjoyed her stories, but this time his gaze strayed frequently to Meg.

Unlike Joe, she seemed to have navigated her way to one of the empty chairs without being stopped once. She was sitting perfectly straight, although her back was not touching the chair at all. Her long elegant legs were crossed, and sunlight made the fine texture of her stockings glisten. Her head was inclined very slightly as if she were listening to music far away, and the thick plait of pale blond hair graced her right shoulder. Her strong features were composed; the only clue to her agitation was the way her slender hands gripped the edges of the chair and the intensity that burned in those dark eyes.

"She's beautiful, Joe." Bettye's voice broke into his day-dream. "Have you married and forgotten to tell us?"

"Lakeland's perennial bachelor?" He widened his eyes comically. "Hardly." The truth was, he had yet to be so lucky.

Bettye looked at Meg, then back at him. "Paramour, then? Surely writing those steamy tomes of yours must inspire a few real-life fantasies, Angelique Moreau."

"Sorry to disappoint you, Bettye, but I just met her this morning at the church."

"Perhaps she's one of the newer artists Anna found in Soho last year or—"

"She's not an artist." At least he didn't think she was. "She drives a limousine."

Bettye touched her full lips with the tip of one precisely manicured finger. "An intrigue, is it? A mysterious blond chauffeur shows up at the funeral—"

"Your imagination is running away with you, Bettye." His voice was a shade less friendly than it was moments before.

"You're supposed to be the one with the imagination. Don't you see anything unusual about the fact she seems to know no one in this room?"

Joe glanced toward Meg, who was still keeping her own counsel, then shrugged.

"I've been associated with Lakeland for twenty years. I don't remember seeing her at any of our social functions. She certainly isn't part of the old crowd."

"Maybe that's because she's a good ten years younger than anyone else in here." *Low blow,* he thought, but then she'd had it coming.

Bettye laughed, undaunted. "Have I struck a nerve, Joseph? I don't remember you being quite so bitchy before. Maybe it's writing under those female pseudonyms."

"She told me she's a chauffeur," he said as calmly as he could manage. "As far as I know, that's all she is."

"If you think a woman that beautiful is simply a chauffeur, then you are quite mad, Joseph. She must be an artist's model." She tapped her chin with her index finger. "Yes, that must be it. Look at the marvelous line she has—that elegant carriage, those long, long legs. Surely she must be immortalized a thousand times on canvas. I'm surprised you hadn't noticed, Joe."

But of course Joe had noticed—he'd noticed from the second she came out of the church and gracefully slumped into his arms. This Margarita Lindstrom, chauffeur or artist's model or whatever she was, was the stuff fantasies were made of. His fantasies.

"Look at those smoldering dark eyes," Bettye continued, lowering her voice conspiratorially as she baited him. "That mouth. Where have I seen a mouth quite like that?"

"Ingrid Bergman," Joe said suddenly. "Ingrid Bergman in *Casablanca*."

Bettye's smile widened. "So you have noticed. I'm glad—I'd hate to think all that creative isolation you've been imposing on yourself the last few months had dimmed your discerning eye."

Joe was saved having to respond to that by the approach of another Egyptologist, who, drink in hand, was ready to regale Bettye, Lakeland's princess of the Nile, with tales from Tut's tomb. Joe listened politely for a few moments, then slipped away unnoticed.

MEG HAD PERFECTED the art of watching without being noticed—a talent that came in handy to monitor the limousine's big back seat—and she knew that Joe was keenly aware of her presence across the room as he spoke to the dark-haired woman. When he started toward her, she looked up at him and smiled.

"Thanks for saving me the seat." Joe settled himself in the empty chair next to her.

"No problem." She shrugged, and her black silk blouse rustled. "There was hardly a stampede to sit near me."

Joe smiled back at her. "I was trying to be a gentleman and not mention the fact." He sank a trifle lower in his seat in an attempt to get comfortable.

"You seem popular enough for both of us." She tossed her braid back over her shoulder with a quick movement of her head. "I suppose I just kept a lower profile at Lakeland."

"Doing what?" She caught the sound of above-average curiosity in his voice.

"Would you believe me if I said I was the official Kennedy Colony driver?"

He shook his head. "Afraid not." He leaned closer to her and lowered his voice so the artists returning with their refreshments wouldn't hear. "Bettye is positive you're an artist's model."

She chuckled. "The thought of sitting around being scrutinized by a hypercritical artist sounds worse to me than being caught in Manhattan traffic on a Friday evening."

Joe was about to pursue the topic further when Patrick McCallum stood up and rapped on the desk for attention. "Please be seated," he said. "We'll begin in a moment."

People hurried back to their seats and the high school reunion spirit that had prevailed earlier disappeared. The air was charged with the volatile combination of ego and talent that Meg remembered so well from her stays at Lakeland in the past.

Beside her, Joe unbuttoned his suit jacket and slumped just slightly in his seat, trying to find a comfortable position for his wide shoulders in the narrow wing chair.

If she were to capture him with her camera right at that moment, however, she would have had him shed the coat and vest, loosen his tie and unbutton the collar of his white Oxford cloth shirt. Then she would seat him at the same bay window where he'd posed as a young man. Some of the hunger, the need of the youth was still present just beneath the surface of the man. The camera would find it now just as it had then.

McCallum was well into reading the obligatory opening passages of Anna Kennedy's will. A woman behind her sighed, whether from boredom or sorrow Meg didn't know. There was an interminable passage dealing with her financial holdings, which were divided into real estate, stocks, bonds and two chains of computer stores, of all things, that were household words.

"My God!" she whispered involuntarily. "I had no idea."

Joe leaned in closer to her. "Neither did I," he whispered back.

She shot a quick look at some of the others around her and noted that no one else seemed terribly surprised at the range and extent of Anna's holdings. They either were better informed than she and Joe or much better at dissembling. McCallum stopped to take a sip of water from the crystal tumbler on the desk.

The list of bequests was as endless as it was detailed. Despite a few tears, some of the recipients were smiling into their Kleenex in a way that made Meg want to scream. She had always disliked the greed that accompanied a funeral. When Kay died, it had taken Meg three months to feel even remotely comfortable with her inheritance.

After fifteen minutes more dealing with the distribution of stocks and bonds, McCallum read, "'I now want to deal with the subject dearest to me: the future of the Kennedy Creative Colony.'"

A low buzz of excitement began to ripple through the library, and Meg shuddered despite the warmth from the crackling fireplace just ten feet away from where she sat. She found herself dreading her turn, hating the idea of Anna's love for her reduced to a dollars-and-cents equivalent. Joe Alessio reached over and took her right hand in his and squeezed it.

"That's all right," she whispered. "I'm fine."

"But I'm not," he said, and continued to hold her hand in his. She could feel a tremor running through him that matched the one snaking its way inside her. She was very glad he was next to her.

McCallum read on. With each new bequest, conversation in the room escalated until Meg could scarcely hear herself think. Prints and sculptures, serigraphs and rare books, all found their way to the perfect owner. Anna had noted each one's pet passion and matched gift and recipient with uncanny understanding. Her own sense of unease heightened.

Finally, McCallum reached the end. "Signed and dated August twenty-second, and witnessed by Katie Connelly and James Benino." He took another sip of water and cleared his throat. There was a collective rustle from the crowd; then they stood and prepared to leave the room. Patrick McCallum raised one hand to stop them. "We have one last bequest." He reached into the inside pocket of his suit jacket and withdrew a large cream-colored envelope with Anna's signature embossed in the upper left-hand corner.

Joe removed his hand from Meg's and drew it nervously through his thick dark hair. "What could be left to bequeath?" he asked wryly. "Anna owned more than either of us ever imagined."

Meg looked at Joe and shrugged. "There's Lakeland House," she whispered, not saying how odd it seemed that she and Joe were the only people in the room who had yet to figure in the will.

"I thought that was taken care of in a trust."

Patrick cleared his throat. His blue eyes were twinkling with amusement. Meg swallowed hard as he took a filigreed silver letter opener from the top of the desk and slit open the envelope. Slowly, damnably slowly, he unfolded the letter inside as Meg's palms began to sweat.

An unnatural hush fell over the room as he looked at her and Joe. "I'll spare you all the legal language," he said, never taking his gaze from the two of them. "The phrasing of a trust would tangle the tongue of a linguist. What it amounts to is, Lakeland House was left in trust to Joseph Alessio and Margarita Lindstrom."

He looked at Meg and Joe, who were sitting quite still, staring at him as if he had announced the arrival of Armageddon. "Don't you young people understand?" he asked with one of his hearty laughs as he spread his arms wide. "This is all yours!"

Chapter Three

The room exploded with excitement. People congratulated them as if they'd won the state lottery. The attitude of celebration made Meg physically ill, and from the look on Joe's face, she could tell he felt the same way.

Finally, McCallum closed the double doors behind the last of the merry mourners and perched on the edge of the desk.

"Questions?" His lined face crinkled with his broad smile.

"A thousand," Meg said. "I don't know anything about running a foundation. I can hardly balance a checkbook." She looked to Joe for help.

"What would make Anna think either one of us has the slightest understanding of how to run something like the Kennedy Colony?" Joe asked. "Most writers make lousy business people."

"You don't have to know anything." McCallum reached for the letter he had put back down on the desk. "Anna worked everything out. A few months before her death, the colony made the transition into being part of a larger foundation."

"Don't worry," McCallum said at their looks of surprise. "KCC will still go with the six-month work-interval formula—open only between April and October. The whole enterprise, however," McCallum explained, "would be underwritten and thus able to expand its scope. The two of you jointly own both the buildings and the land Lakeland House rests on. Anna would like you both to oversee the selection of artists who will benefit from the grant structure," he continued. "But most importantly, this is also your home. If the foundation should cease to exist, this property and all buildings on it remain in your joint possession."

Meg's head throbbed. "You still haven't answered Joe's question. What about the physical upkeep, taxes—"

"The parent foundation is responsible. Things are truly all taken care of, dear people. Anna thought of everything." He paused. "But there is one more thing. Were you aware that Anna had been working on an annotated history of the colony?"

They both nodded.

Patrick explained how Anna had set the end of the year as the target date for completion. "Harper and Row is very interested in publishing it, and God knows, the publicity would do us proud. And that, of course, brings me to the last request." He fished another cream-colored envelope from his breast pocket and handed it to Meg.

She unfolded the notepaper. The letter was dated just two days before Anna's death. Her back-slanted handwriting was unmistakable—the descending loops of her g's and y's extended halfway into the line below; the crossbar of her t's flew exuberantly across the page. It proved her indomitable spirit had been with her until the last, and a peaceful warmth settled itself around Meg's shoulders like a caress.

She read: "'My time is almost here, Margarita and Joseph, and you must believe I embrace it as the start of yet another adventure. My only regret is that my history of Lakeland House is not quite completed. I ask your help in doing this, for only you two have understood fully what my life's work has been about.

"'More than any of the others who came to visit, you came to stay. I know you will understand the importance of it all and will open yourselves up to the full meaning of what I'm asking of you both.

"'You two are the children of my heart—you always were, and you will remain so.'"

Meg looked up at Joe, whose eyes had never left her face. "It's signed 'Annie.'"

McCallum had been quietly watching them from where he stood, leaning against the edge of the desk.

Joe closed his eyes for a split second, and a low sigh escaped his lips. "There's nothing more to say as far as I'm concerned. Anna's wishes are my top priority."

"They're mine, as well." Meg turned to McCallum. "Have you any idea how much work is involved in finishing the project?"

McCallum, arms crossed over his chest, nodded. "A month, give or take a week."

A ripple of excitement blossomed inside Meg, whether from the impending work or her impending partner, she wasn't sure. However, she hadn't felt that kind of anticipatory pleasure in a very long time, and the feeling was pure delight.

Joe lit another cigarette. "Can you take that much time away from your limousine?" The words sounded innocent enough, but Meg was certain she detected a note of wry curiosity mingled with them.

"Since it's my limousine," she answered, "it's also my decision." Suddenly that decision didn't seem quite so wonderful. "There'll be no problem." She watched as he took another drag on his cigarette, then stubbed it out in a crystal ashtray on the windowsill. "How about you?" she asked. "Can you take time away from your word processor?"

"Since it's my word processor, I can. Besides," he said with an off-center smile, "I don't even use one. I have a beat-up old Selectric."

They both turned toward McCallum, who was pouring himself another glass of water and adding to it a generous splash of scotch from a decanter beside the desk.

"We'll do it," Meg said. "We want to."

McCallum approached and rested an arm around each of them, much as he had after the services when he'd set this whole crazy afternoon in motion. "I knew you would both be feeling this way," he said, the pleasant scent of scotch barely coloring his breath as he spoke, "but I want you to be sure."

"Of course we're sure." Joe sounded a bit disgruntled to Meg's ears. "We both loved Anna. Do you think we'd let her down?"

"I wouldn't be doubting your intentions, Joseph," the lawyer said, "but I would be wondering about the working relationship." At the puzzled expressions on their faces, he continued, "You'll be working closely together on this. Do you think you'll be able to work toward one goal, with one point of view?"

"Well, of course we will," Meg said, unable to keep the edge from her voice. "We're in this as partners, not rivals."

"Excuse me if I step on anyone's toes," McCallum said, "but Anna said you were both rather, shall we say, volatile individuals."

"That's ridiculous!" Joe exploded. He at least had the good humor to laugh when McCallum pointed a finger at him. "I think both Meg and I can keep our perspectives straight."

McCallum started walking them over to the door to the library. "Take a walk, have some lunch. Talk about it. You two will be connected through Lakeland House for a long time to come. Make sure your relationship gets off on the right foot. You can come back here later and we'll draw up a simple working agreement for this project.''

Because Joe and Meg could think of no logical reason to refuse McCallum's simple request, they agreed. McCallum watched as they disappeared down the hallway to get their coats. He knew Anna had planned on bringing them together to discuss her intentions if she had the time. He remembered how her eyes danced with delight when she spoke about introducing the two of them.

God only knew, they were a handsome pair—she with her pale blond hair and fiery eyes, he with his dark intensity. In her high heels Margarita was a little taller than Joseph, but it didn't seem to matter at all; they appeared to be equal in every other way McCallum could think of. You couldn't help but wonder what a mating of soul and body between two such strong individuals would yield. McCallum rolled his eyes heavenward. If he didn't know better, he'd think Anna Kennedy was trying to do some not-so-subtle matchmaking. But practical Anna Kennedy wouldn't have done that.

Would she?

''Ahh, Anna,'' he muttered to himself as he went back to his scotch and water, ''but it's going to be an interesting month with those two.'' He took a long sip of his drink and smiled.

He was going to enjoy every minute of it.

THE CHILL OCTOBER AIR was a welcome relief after the overheated, overperfumed, overanxious atmosphere inside the house. Joe waited while Meg buttoned up her coat and adjusted the collar; then they set off across the cobbled driveway toward the limousine. In moments he was way ahead of her, and he stopped to allow her to catch up.

"With legs like yours, I'm surprised you're so slow," he said, enjoying the way her shapely knees flashed in and out of view as her coat opened with each stride. "Not that I'm complaining, you understand."

Meg caught up with him and gave him one of those sidelong glances he'd noticed in the library that made her thick lashes cast shadows on her cheeks. "I'd like to know how fast you'd walk in three-inch heels," she said.

Joe started to laugh. "Don't hold your breath. I may write under a female pseudonym, but I'll be damned if I'm going to dress the part."

They were standing in the center of the driveway, and the midafternoon sunlight seemed to be captured in her glittering hair. The play of light hair and unfathomable dark eyes was unusual in itself, but coupled with her strong features, the combination added up in a way that made Meg not a pretty woman but an extremely beautiful one. A couple of fantasies he'd reserved strictly for his novels curled around his brain and made normal conversations a little difficult.

Meg was staring at him, her hands jammed into the pockets of her coat, dark eyes fastened to his. "You write under a woman's name?"

"Don't sound so surprised," he said, a bit defensively. "It's not unusual in my field."

"Which is?" Her eyes were still intent upon his. He would swear she hadn't even blinked. The woman's concentration was something to behold.

"Family sagas," he said. "Those big sprawling multi-generational novels that miniseries are made of."

She laughed, and those dark eyes lit up. "You mean those fat, wonderful books filled with family intrigues and passion and better sex than most normal human beings will ever find?"

"Yes to everything but the better-sex part. I still have hope."

She laughed and linked her arm through his companionably in a gesture that surprised him. She seemed to carry herself with an almost-palpable shell of reserve around her so that this natural, easy action carried more weight than it normally would from someone less cautious. They started to walk again, and this time he made an effort to match his steps to hers.

"Do you have any idea how books like the ones you write influence someone's views on sex?" she asked. "In high school I believed everything I read." She laughed again. "And I mean everything."

"Must have made the real thing a bit of a letdown," Joe said, thinking about the earth-shattering, mind-boggling, transcendental pleasures that abounded in most popular novels. He flashed her his most wicked grin as they neared her limousine. "Was it?"

"I'll never tell." That full, incredibly sexy mouth of hers tilted on one side with a secret smile. "Let's just say I knew more and did less with it than anyone at Mater Christi High School."

"Seems like a waste of a good education to me." He stopped in front of the Lincoln and leaned against the front right fender. "I assume now you've managed to put it to—"

Again those deep brown eyes flashed, and he could almost see the protective shield slide across them. She plunged her hands back into her coat pockets. "Don't even finish that sentence, Alessio. You're treading on thin ice."

So much for repartee. "I didn't mean anything by it, Meg," he said. "It just seemed like the thing to say."

"And you usually just say anything you feel like saying?"

He felt a bit sheepish and a lot foolish. "Unfortunately." He pulled a Marlboro and matches out of his breast pocket, cupped his hand around the cigarette so he could light up, then took a protracted drag. "I think it has a lot to do with being a writer. Words pop out when I least expect them."

She was softening a bit; he could tell by the way her strong jaw seemed to ease and her shoulders relaxed.

"I probably overreacted." She moved a step away from the smoke that now encircled him. "I just find it hard to trust most writers. You can never tell when they're being sincere or when they're just trying out a bit of dialogue on you."

"Is that what you think I was doing?"

"The thought occurred to me."

She waved one hand in front of her face to brush smoke away. Joe, instantly contrite, stubbed out his cigarette. Her observation had been particularly keen, for he often said things just to see if the words flowed easily, to gauge another's reaction, before he committed those words to paper.

"You may be right," he said after a few moments. "I've been guilty of that in the past."

One of her pale eyebrows arched. "But not this time?"

He couldn't help it, but his grin was back. "Not this time," he said. "This time I really wanted to know."

He was back on solid ground again, for Meg's whole body relaxed. "Sorry," she said with a shrug. "I'm still taking the Fifth on that. Personal questions set me back a bit."

"We're going to have a problem then." He leaned forward and smoothed a stray strand of hair off her face. "I always find myself asking them—occupational hazard."

His finger lingered near her cheek for a second, and she seemed to hold her breath, her gold-flecked eyes searching his face for something he couldn't quite identify. He pulled his hand away reluctantly.

She adjusted the collar of her coat, flinging her French braid back. "Then you're going to have to get used to hearing me say, 'Mind your own business, Alessio.'"

They heard a commotion from the side of the house, and Joe saw Bettye and her Egyptologist friend heading down the driveway toward them.

"Let's escape," he said to Meg.

She pulled an enormous ring of keys out of her right coat pocket and twirled them around her finger. "How about a trip to McDonald's?"

He nodded. "Want me to drive?"

She gave him a funny look. "Have no fear," she said. "I'm a professional—this won't hurt a bit."

"That's what my dentist says." Joe got into the limousine and pulled the heavy door closed behind him. "I wasn't implying you were a bad driver. You had a long drive up here, and I thought you might need a break."

Meg began backing the car out of its spot. "I like to drive. Besides, I doubt if you could handle this car."

"I could handle it, Meg." His words came out softer than he'd intended, heavy with other meanings. He wondered if she'd noticed.

She had. As she shifted back into drive, she met his eyes once again. Joe's heart thudded suddenly beneath his heavy coat, and the desire to kiss her passed over him like a summer breeze. The silence became charged with questions and possibilities and an awkwardness that neither one knew how to break. Finally, Meg laughed, high and uncertain, and began to steer the limousine down the narrow curving driveway.

Joe sifted through a pile of cassettes stashed in the glove compartment. "The Beatles, the Stones, Huey Lewis, Frank Sinatra—Mantovani?" He stared at her as if she'd single-handedly shattered all his illusions.

"Don't blame me." She drove the car through the open gates and turned onto the main road. "We have to have something for all tastes."

"I'd ask about their taste in music before I took the job," he said, popping some vintage Beach Boys into the tape deck.

Meg laughed. "Then you'd probably be on unemployment. Let's face it, the folks who can afford limos listen to Mantovani, not Madonna."

"I'll hire you one day, and we'll only play rock and roll."

Meg reached over and turned up the volume so the sounds of surf and summer and sweet, sweet freedom blasted through the sedate car, washing away any sadness or awkwardness that might have lurked there. The scent of her perfume, deep and mysterious as her eyes, lingered in the air, and for a moment it was easy to forget the dear friend he'd just lost and the career that suddenly seemed to be going nowhere, easy to put aside the unfulfilled dream of a home and family to love and simply enjoy the moment— simply enjoy the woman beside him and the sounds of his youth.

Fifteen minutes later, the limousine was angled into a too-narrow parking spot at a McDonald's in town, and Meg was trying to manage a deliciously sloppy Big Mac and fries while every teenager within ten miles stared into the tinted windows and inspected the shiny Lincoln from trunk to hood.

Joe laughed and grabbed one of her french fries. "I don't think McDonald's sees too many limos."

"I don't think this town sees too many limos," she said. "The novelty will wear off in a few minutes."

"You're a good driver, Lindstrom," he said, motioning toward the drive-up window. "I thought you were going to get stuck in there." The distance between speaker and wall had been perilously narrow.

"A compliment for a woman driver?" She clutched her throat in surprise. "I wish I had this on tape."

"A good driver's a good driver. I didn't think it was determined by gender." He seemed a bit embarrassed at being misinterpreted.

"I was only teasing," she said, although that was but partially true. "It's just that I'm so used to people—men, especially—being astounded that I can drive this beast from point A to point B without causing a five-car crack-up that kind words astound me."

"Kind words shouldn't, you know."

She shrugged and ripped open another packet of ketchup and drizzled some on the remaining fries. "Out of practice, I guess."

"I don't believe that." That probing writer's glance of his tried to sneak inside her soul.

"Believe it." She took a sip of coffee from the Styrofoam cup, then wiped her mouth with a napkin. "I'm not terribly interesting, Joe."

"Let me be the judge of that. I'd like to know more about you, Meg."

His intensity unnerved her, and she sought to sidestep it. "All you really need to know about me is that I'm a hard worker, I loved Anna and Lakeland House dearly, and I'm willing to take on this project."

"I don't think that's all I need to know." Joe's voice was light, but there was an undercurrent of steel in it. "Where were you born? Where did you go to school? Do you have any brothers and sisters?" He hesitated for a split second. "A husband? A child?"

Meg finished the last french fry. "You know you can get all of that information from my file."

He smiled at her. "I know," he said. "I'd prefer getting it from you, though."

She wiped her mouth with a yellow paper napkin. "You're about as subtle as a five-year-old, Joe." Actually, she was enjoying his open curiosity. It was a refreshing change from the studied boredom of the wealthy business-men she usually had in her limousine. "You're good at questions; how good are you at answering them?"

He leaned back in the seat and got comfortable. "I'm thirty-three years old. I write under the names of Alex Dennison, Bret Allen and Angelique Moreau. I did the novelization of the last *Star Trek* movie, I know all the theme songs of every TV Western from *Gunsmoke* to *Bonanza* to the return of *Maverick*." His smile widened. "I have all my own teeth, all my own hair, and not enough time to tell you how many people are in my family." He crossed his arms over his chest. "Enough?"

Not even close, she thought. Suddenly she wanted to know everything she could about him. "Are you married?" He shook his head. "Divorced?" Again he shook his head. "Have you ever been in love?"

He threw back his head and laughed. "Many times," he said. "With Isobel and Yvette and Sarah and—"

She stopped him. "Characters in your books?"

He nodded. "How about you, Meg? Have you ever been in love?"

"Afraid not." First she'd been so intent upon her career that there hadn't been time for something so frivolous. Then, when there was time, Meg discovered she preferred keeping an arm's length between her heart and the heart of another.

For once he didn't pursue the topic further. "Where were you born?" he asked, prodding her out of her sudden silence.

"Staten Island. I was—"

"Rich kid?" Joe broke in.

"Not rich, exactly. Let's say comfortable."

He laughed. "From where I grew up in Queens, you were rich."

"It all depends on your point of view," she said, thinking about the lack of attention she'd suffered as a child. "I went to kindergarten and grammar school and high school there and never left the city until I went away to college in Elmira."

"And from Elmira to the Kennedy Colony?"

"That's about the size of it." She shrugged. "I told you it was a dull story."

"Why were you at Lakeland in the first place?" His lazy grin softened his words. "I didn't think they gave grants for creative driving."

Inadvertently, she glanced back at the Hasselblad on the backseat. Joe, ever watchful, picked up on her glance and looked back himself.

"Photographer?" When she hesitated, he said, "You may as well tell me, Meg. I'm going to find out, anyway."

"I was." Maybe it was the stubborn Swedish streak she'd inherited from her father, but she hated questions that demanded she reveal a portion of herself she'd rather keep hidden.

"Was?" He sounded disbelieving. "Is that an artifact in the backseat?"

Her mother's volatile Italian blood took over. "It's a hobby now," she snapped. "And it's none of your damned business."

"The hell it's not." Joe's temper was apparently a match for her own. "In case you've forgotten, we now jointly own a hell of a lot of property. I think we're both entitled to know what we're getting into."

He was right, but she was embarrassed now and retreated into sullenness, one of her least admirable traits and one she could blame on no one but herself. "We're not getting into anything as far as I'm concerned. The foundation will pretty well run itself."

He was turned completely around in his seat, his strong body leaning toward her, those beautiful green eyes angry and cold. "Anna's history won't. Whether you like it or not, we're going to have to work together." He moved away a fraction, an unfathomable expression on his face. "Unless you'd rather back out. I'm sure I could handle it on my own."

"I'm sure you think you could, but writing potboilers hardly qualifies one for detailed work."

"Driving a limousine does, I suppose?"

"Of course it doesn't," she answered, pleased with herself for not letting him see how much his words got to her. "But at least I have no illusions about myself—or my talent."

The insult passed Joe right by. Meg could see him jump into writer's alert, primed for some deep psychological insight into her character that he could use in his work. "Don't you dare ask me to elaborate on that," she warned him.

Joe hesitated for a second. She watched, fascinated, as the cool glitter in his green eyes began to thaw right in front of her. Tiny creases at the corners deepened, and suddenly a smile, a real one, brought his face back to life.

He turned his hands palms up in surrender. "I was just about to ask you why you deny that talent."

"Well, don't." Her anger disappeared as quickly as it had come. "We all have choices to make, and I've made mine." She narrowed her eyes at him. "And if I find that popping up in one of your books, I'll—"

He leaned forward and took a sip from her cup of coffee that rested on the console between them. "You'll what?" he asked. His finger lightly touched the lipsticked imprint of her mouth on the rim of the cup, and a delicious shiver slid through her. "I'd treat you kindly, Margarita."

"I'll just bet you would." She was entranced by the way he was running his finger along the lipstick mark. She became acutely aware of her lips, of their fullness and texture, and involuntarily she moistened them with the tip of her tongue. He noticed everything—as she knew he would— and he grinned.

"You'd be the heroine," he said, his voice low and lazy like his smile. "The woman who founded a dynasty. I'd make you a Viking princess with a castle and—"

"No Vikings," she broke in. "I've always fancied myself as a *principessa* in Renaissance Italy."

"A Lindstrom in Rome?"

"That's just part of who I am," she said. "My mother's maiden name was DeMartino."

"So that's where those dark eyes come from." He leaned back in his seat and crossed his arms over his chest again. The shoulder seams on his trenchcoat strained with the movement. "That's one hell of a combination," he said. "Swedish and Italian—the ice maiden with a heart of fire."

His words caused a tremor to move through her. "You do have a way with the language."

He reached over and touched the long pale braid of hair that rested over her left shoulder. "This would have to go," he said softly. "It would have to spill down your back like moonlight. It would have to be loose so your pirate lover could lose himself in it each night. It would have to—"

"Too bad you don't have your word processor with you." She wanted him to stop weaving this spell around her before she became more entangled. "Sounds like you have your next novel mapped out."

"Don't worry about that." His voice lost that magnetic sexual vibrancy and sounded normal again. "That's about as far as I'm going to get with it."

"Oh, that's right," she said, remembering. "You said you use an old IBM, yes?"

He closed his eyes for a fraction of a second before he answered her. "I can see why you don't like answering personal questions, Margarita. It can hurt."

Joe had seemed so open, so basically uncomplicated, that this revelation surprised her. Impulsively, she reached over and touched his forearm. The feel of the trenchcoat fabric was cool and smooth beneath her fingers.

"Perhaps we need some guidelines," she said lightly. "Sort of our own Robert's *Rules of Order*."

He smiled. "Thou shalt not ask personal questions of thy neighbor?"

She smiled back. "Even if thou art a writer."

"I think we can handle this easily, Margarita," he said, putting his right hand on top of hers. "I'm willing for us to work together if you are."

She nodded. "How difficult can it be? We're both reasonable adults; we both loved Anna and the colony."

"And we both want to turn out the best history of it possible, right?"

"Right," she said. "I say we meet back at Lakeland in seven days and get down to work."

Joe extended his right hand, and they shook on it. His hand was large and warm, just as it had been when she held it during the funeral, but suddenly Meg's hand seemed to be the center of her consciousness. His touch, which had been a source of comfort hours ago, was anything but now, and she pulled her hand away.

The part of herself that needed the touch of a man to spring into life had been long denied. Now her body seemed to vibrate with an urgency that could easily overwhelm her good sense.

A month was not a long time, she thought as she started the engine of the limousine and backed out of the parking spot. She could risk her emotional armor for a month. God knew, she would do anything for Anna, and on the surface, the work of finishing the annotated history seemed straightforward and not fraught with any hidden dangers.

She glanced to her right to check on traffic and caught Joe watching her, his beautiful green eyes both curious and vulnerable. She turned her head away to check the left and to hide the answering look she knew was in her own.

A month seemed suddenly a long time, indeed.

And she wondered what on earth she was getting herself into.

Chapter Four

"I think you should take the typewriter with you, Joseph."
Renee Arden, dressed in a brand-new turquoise running suit
and obscenely immaculate Adidas, stood in the middle of
his office and observed the situation. Renee rarely left
Manhattan, but when she did venture across the Hudson
River to visit Joe at his Princeton, New Jersey, home, she
seemed to view it as a trip to the outback—a trip that re-
quired a whole new wardrobe. "What if the urge to write
suddenly hits you? I don't think you'd know what in hell to
do with a pencil."

Joe was sitting cross-legged on the floor, sifting through
reams of notes and aborted outlines on the new family saga
due on his editor's desk on March first. He'd been spending the better part of his time since he returned from Anna's funeral five days ago trying to make some sense of the
chaos his career was currently in, and he'd been making little
progress. "Give me a break, Renee." He made a self-
deprecating gesture. "The urge to write hasn't hit me in six
weeks. I don't think I'm in any danger." He crumpled up
two pages of dialogue that made him cringe in embarrassment. "I'm going to get a paper shredder," he said, tossing
the paper ball into the wastebasket ten feet away. "If any of
this crap gets out, my career will be ruined."

The crumpled paper missed the basket by easily two feet.
Renee's well-tended eyebrows arched slightly at Joe's poor

aim, but she said nothing, merely bent down and elegantly plucked it up with two fingers and deposited it in the receptacle. "My dear Joseph," she said, "your career *will* be over if you don't have something on Audrey's desk by the fifteenth of February."

Joe muttered a rather vaguely directed curse. "I thought I had until the first of March."

Renee gingerly picked her way through the stacks of books and piles of papers scattered on the floor to the big, fat brown leather couch near the window. "They were so happy with the way *Against All Odds* did on the best-seller list that they're pushing up your schedule." She paused for effect in a way that was as annoying to Joe as it was familiar. "Audrey saw the projected storyboard for an ad during *Good Morning America*'s second hour, and she says it's superb."

Joe stretched his arms overhead in an attempt to loosen the tightly bunched muscles in his back and shoulders. "I know what you're doing, Renee, and I appreciate it, but I think you've been reading too many of those pop-psychology books you peddle. Is this the one-minute-writer approach?"

Renee twisted one of her heavy gold rings and crossed her legs. "Don't be ridiculous," she said. Joe could see the corners of her crimson mouth ready to crack into the smile she was suppressing. "They're calling it the wish-fulfillment technique these days. Dangle a client's number-one fantasy in front of his typewriter and watch those fingers fly." She looked at him, eyes wide behind her owlish glasses. "I've heard it's foolproof."

"I wouldn't bet the farm on it, Renee." Joe stood up. He kicked aside a pile of press clippings with one bare foot and straightened out the legs of his tight, faded jeans. He walked over to the window and leaned against it, absently noting the way the heavy October rain made the swing set in the yard glisten. "Ten percent of nothing is still nothing."

Renee's oath was short and surprising. Despite her tough-talking New York accent and no-nonsense approach, she was never crude, and this outburst startled Joe.

"Don't look at me like that," she said defensively. "I refuse to apologize for it. You had it coming."

"I didn't know you had it in you, Renee. That was quite descriptive." He laughed at the way her face reddened in embarrassment. "And rather inventive, if I do say so."

"That's what I get for reading too many dirty books." She met his eyes, and her delightfully expressive face broke into a smile. "Without you to lean on for my bread and butter, I've had to think about my old age, Joseph. I'll have to take on some more clients—clients who are slightly less respectable than you."

He went to light a cigarette, then thought better of it, stuffing the half-empty pack of Marlboros back in the pocket of his threadbare work shirt. "And what's that supposed to mean?"

Renee took off her eyeglasses and rubbed the bridge of her nose with an impeccably manicured hand. "I'm not getting any younger, Joseph, in case you haven't noticed." She paused delicately, waiting for the polite argument from Joe. He, however, had heard this before and wasn't about to aid and abet. "Be that as it may, I'm not getting any younger, and I have to worry about making sure my IRAs and my money-market accounts are all in order for when I retire."

Joe yawned melodramatically. "What about your T-bills, Renee?" he offered. "You usually worry about them, too."

"Damn it, get serious. I think you're almost enjoying writer's block."

"If you believe that, Renee, then maybe I have the wrong agent."

Renee, elegant and imposing even in sweatpants, stood up and faced him. "Maybe you have at that," she said, her voice crisp and angry. "I've thought you to be many things over the years, Joe, but a quitter wasn't one of them."

Joe leaned back against the windowsill and lowered his head. He wanted to challenge Renee's words, but at the moment quitter seemed to be the best description of himself that he'd heard. Renee touched him gently on the shoulder, and he looked up at her, noting the deepened circles under her blue eyes, the network of lines around her mouth that seemed suddenly more pronounced.

"I'm sorry, Joseph." A slight tremor in her husky voice gave away her emotion. "You're not a quitter."

He made a face. "Maybe I am at that." He dragged his fingers through the thick straight hair that flopped onto his forehead. "Maybe I'm afraid I'm finally tapped out of ideas and I'm going to fall on my face." He shrugged. "That's as good an explanation for this as any I can think of."

"Maybe you're tired," she said. "Maybe you've been pushing yourself too hard for too long. Maybe it's time for you to challenge yourself with something different."

"And maybe it's over." Joe started pacing the room, his muscular body coiled with tension. The thought of tackling the Vietnam book he'd been stalling on for years was enough to send him reaching for the scotch hours earlier than respectable. "No one said this was going to last forever. I might have been dealt a finite number of ideas and I've reached my limit."

Renee's sigh was loud. "Creativity has no limits, Joe. You should know that."

"I used to believe that. I'm not so sure any longer."

"Look, Joe, let me lay it on the line." Renee stepped in front of him, forcing him to stop and listen to her. "They're getting nervous over at Blackwell. Audrey keeps sending up smoke signals that she needs at least a ballpark outline on your next one to keep the boys in sales happy."

Panic, hot and quick, rose in Joe's chest. The thought of facing page after page of blank white paper scared pure hell out of him. "Maybe I'll come up with an idea while I'm at Lakeland House." He forced his usual grin. "After all, you're the one who said the change might do me good."

"We can't wait. You have to give me at least a five-page outline before you go."

"I can't." Joe opened his third pack of cigarettes that day. "I don't have enough of an idea for a short story, much less a six-hundred-page book."

"Joseph, I don't care if you give me a variation on *The Three Little Pigs Plunder the Caribbean*. I must have something in my hand to show Audrey by Monday; otherwise we're in major trouble."

Joe had never missed a deadline in his professional life, and the thought of doing so now disgusted him. "Talk about a no-win situation," he said. "Either I miss the deadline and all hell breaks loose with Audrey, or I hand in a piece of garbage and blow my reputation." He groaned. "I'm damned either way."

Renee put her arm around him and gave him a quick hug. "If you're damned either way, then be damned on the side of the professionals. Give me five pages before you go, Joseph. That's all I'm asking. Give me your private fantasies, your last night's dream, just give me something I can show Audrey. Then you can go to New Hampshire and forget this exists for a month."

Joe doubted he would be able to forget, and he doubted even more that he'd be able to turn out five decent paragraphs, much less five pages, before he left for Lakeland on Friday. "I don't know," he said thoughtfully. "I just don't know."

"Your private fantasies, Joe," Renee urged. "Expand on your fantasies." She arched an eyebrow at him. "I'm sure you still have them despite your newly monastic life-style."

He let his mind run free, and it zeroed in on Meg Lindstrom. He saw her pale blond hair, felt the heat of her dark gaze, knew the way her long legs would feel wrapped around him....

A slow smile spread over his face as some very intriguing possibilities occurred to him. "Fantasies, huh?" He looked at Renee, whose blue eyes were monitoring his every expression for signs of progress. "I think you might be on to something, Renee."

Renee started talking, but her rapid-fire words were fading away from him.

What was it Meg had said—she fancied herself a Renaissance princess? The thought of her in a long dress of black velvet, her long fine hair loose and blowing in the breeze off the Mediterranean, was suddenly doing strange things to both his mind and his body.

So Meg wanted to be a princess? Maybe—just maybe—he'd be able to do something about that. If not, he was sure as hell going to have fun trying.

"Wouldn't you love a nice long walk, Renee?" He put his arm around his agent and friend and began propelling her toward the hall closet where he'd stashed her coat. "There's a terrific path that winds all the way around to the park."

"You're miles away from the park!" Renee protested as Joe helped her into her coat and handed her her leather bag. "I'll be gone for hours."

"It'll do you good." Joe opened the front door wide to the October wind. "You probably haven't breathed clean air in years."

Renee was about to protest again when she stopped and looked up at Joe, her keen blue eyes taking note of everything. "You have an idea for something?"

"I don't know," he said, trying to hang on to the image of Meg that was forming itself in his subconscious. "Maybe." He put his hand firmly at the small of her back and pushed her out the door. Meg, gowned now in robes of golden velvet, was beginning to seem more real to him than the world in which he lived. "Give me an hour," he said, his voice already growing distracted, preoccupied.

Renee, who recognized all the signs, laughed. "Hell, Joseph, I'll give you two if it'll help." She pulled the collar of her tweed coat up around her throat and trudged off into the wilds of Princeton.

By the time Joe shut the door behind her, he was back in the sixteenth century, and Meg was right there with him. He sprinted down the hall to his workroom and prayed the muse would stay with him long enough to get this on paper.

That is, if he still remembered how.

"I THINK I'M GOING to give up the limousine and start my own business," Meg said as she and Elysse took a breather in a quiet pub-style restaurant in Smith Haven Mall.

Elysse looked up at her. "I know I'm going to regret this," she said, "but what business?"

"Shoppers Anonymous," Meg said with a straight face. "Now, don't laugh," she said to Elysse. "I'm serious. I could be the moderator. We'll meet once a week at the community room here at the mall and trade horror stories about overextended MasterCards and closets full of Norma Kamalis."

"You'd be a terrible moderator," Elysse said, glancing down at Meg's one purchase and her three bulging shopping bags. "You have absolutely no sympathy for the chronic consumer. You act as if this shopping trip were a voyage to hell."

"Close." Meg found it difficult to put up with the poking and prodding and endless discussions about her hard-to-fit long legs, narrow hips and broad shoulders that shopping with Elysse usually entailed. "I'm only going to Lakeland House, Elly, not the Riviera."

"We're not talking about buying a major wardrobe," Elysse explained patiently. "I must say I'm getting pretty sick of seeing you in those black work suits of yours and that terrible blue sweater."

Meg looked down at the terrible blue sweater; it was actually a once-nice cashmere that had seen better days. "What's so wrong with this?" she asked, touching the worn softness of a sleeve. "It cost me a fortune, Elly."

Elysse made a face at her best friend. "I'm sure it did," she answered wryly. "College freshmen can't afford very much, can they?"

"I'm greatly offended," Meg said with a laugh. "It's not that old. I'm sure we were sophomores at least when I bought this."

"And we won't go into how long ago *that* was, will we?" Elysse flagged over a waitress to bring the check, and five minutes later they were back in the arcade, heading toward Macy's.

They were chatting about the ridiculously short and sexy black dress that Meg—despite her antishopping lecture—had been seriously tempted by when Meg suddenly pulled up short in front of a bookstore.

"Let's pop in here for a second," she said to Elysse, whose small frame was in danger of toppling over from the weight of the packages she was lugging.

"I never thought I'd say this—" Elysse groaned as she followed Meg into the store "—but right now I don't care if I ever shop again."

"I wish Jack were here to appreciate those words. He's probably been waiting all his married life to hear them."

Elysse grinned as she plopped down the packages on the floor near the psychology section. "Do you think I'd have said it if he were anywhere in earshot? I *do* have a reputation to consider." She leaned against a counter and slipped off one of her shoes. "What are we here for, anyway?"

"You'll see." Meg left her packages next to Elysse's and headed for the back of the store where romances and what was generally considered to be women's fiction were displayed. She flipped through three carousels filled with books until she finally found the racks of family sagas that she'd been looking for. At first she looked for the name Alessio; then she remembered Joe said he wrote under a pseudonym.

Medford...Mitchell...Moreau...Moreau! That was it—Angelique Moreau.

Four glossy, fat Moreau novels with titles splashed across the cover in scrolly embossed script stared at her from eye level in the rack. *Fortune's Daughter, Deny the Conqueror, Inherit the World* and the newest of them, *Against All Odds*, which featured a seminude, supine hero who looked uncomfortably like Joe Alessio himself. This gloriously virile man was leaning over a seductive redhead whose cleavage in her skimpy sarong seemed to mesmerize him. Only a few artfully placed palm fronds kept Meg from learning more about the hero's anatomy than she had bargained for. The whole scene exuded a steamy sensuality, a certain animal lustiness, and given the man's remarkable resemblance to Joe, Meg felt herself both embarrassed and intensely fascinated.

"Good Lord, will you look at that!" Elysse was peeking around her shoulder at *Against All Odds* while holding a copy of *The Dynamics of the Nuclear Family: When Will the Fallout End*. "That woman could give Dolly Parton a run for her money." She took the trade paperback from Meg and read the cover blurb. "Isobel risked everything for the man she loved. An American dynasty of deception founded upon a night of passion!" She looked at Meg. "What gives? I haven't seen you curl up with a good book in months."

"Times are tough," Meg said. "I feel like indulging in a spot of fantasy."

Meg looked at Elysse, expecting an intellectually precise discussion of fantasy. Instead, she saw Elysse's wide eyes grow even wider as she fell under the spell of Angelique Moreau's latest.

"Ahem!" Meg cleared her throat loudly, laughing as her friend finally returned to the real world. "Better be careful, doctor. We wouldn't want you to tarnish your image being caught reading stuff like that."

Elysse grabbed the book by its high-gloss spine and fanned herself with short, rapid strokes. "It must be all that

Hawaiian sunshine. I'm surprised they had time to become a state!"

Meg was amused by the high spots of color on her best friend's cheeks. "Well, well," she said, "and here I thought you'd heard it all."

Elysse slowly shook her head, casting a long, wondering gaze at Moreau's latest. "I thought I had, but it seems Ms Moreau has discovered a few variations worthy of a place of honor in *The Joy of Sex*." She drew a hand across her forehead. "The cover isn't the only thing hot about that book!"

Meg took the book away from her friend and put it with the rest of the Moreau novels she was planning to purchase.

Elysse read off the other titles and whistled. "Ms Moreau must be quite something if you're buying out the store. What's the lady's secret?"

"The lady's no lady," Meg said, laughing. "The lady's a man."

Elysse stared at her. "Care to run that by me again?"

"Angelique Moreau is really Joseph Alessio."

"The same Joseph Alessio you'll be working with at Lakeland House?"

"One and the same."

Elysse grabbed Meg's copy of *Against All Odds* once more and read the author's bio on the back cover. "Angelique Moreau has lived in Spain, a South Pacific island and even once spent a year in Alaska. Her varied experiences have brought a richness and sensuality to her novels that delight all of her devoted readers." She checked the inside cover and the copyright page. "Are you sure about this? I don't see the name Alessio anywhere."

"That's part of the illusion," Meg explained. "Female authors sell better than males in this genre."

Elysse was carefully watching Meg's face. "And what does this man look like? Thinning gray hair and a weak chin?"

Meg pointed to the dark-haired man on the cover of the book.

Elysse's jaw dropped. "You're kidding!" She paused for a second. "Aren't you?"

Meg shook her head. "Afraid not. He's a dead ringer for this guy."

"Hmm." Elysse glanced again at the cover of *Against All Odds*. "Maybe I could borrow your copy when you're finished? There are a few passages I'd like Jack to see—purely from a professional point of view, you understand."

"Sorry," Meg said, "you're going to have to buy your own copy. I'd hate to cheat Ms Moreau out of some royalties."

Elysse plucked another copy off the shelf and seemed mesmerized by the cover. "He really looks like that?"

"He really does."

"And you'll be alone with him for a month at Lakeland House?"

A delicious shiver ran up Meg's spine, and she nodded, not trusting her voice. Elysse scooped up their packages and began nudging Meg toward the cashier in the front of the store, but not before she picked up a copy of Joe's latest for herself.

"Hurry up," she said as Meg put her purchases down on the counter.

"What's the rush?" Meg pulled her American Express card out of her wallet for the hundredth time that afternoon.

"Remember that outrageous black dress you passed up?"

Meg nodded as she signed the charge slip.

"We're going back to Brennan's and getting it for you."

"Don't you think that dress is too—" Meg searched for the word "—risqué for rural New Hampshire?"

Elysse took a final glance at the piratical rogue on the cover and sighed. "Oh, no," she answered. "I have a feeling it's going to be just right." A particularly wicked smile lit up her face. "After all, you'd hate to disappoint Angelique Moreau, wouldn't you?"

AT THAT PARTICULAR moment, Angelique Moreau was in dire need of a shave.

Two days had passed since Renee issued the ultimatum about the outline for a new saga, and two days had passed since Joe saw razor, shower, comb or bed. His desk was littered with half-empty coffee cups, open reference books, closed notepads and enough crumpled sheets of typewriter paper to constitute a fire hazard.

His work on the outline had gone well the first day—so well, in fact, that when Renee finally came back from her walk, he was so far into the fantasy world of Meg and her band of Renaissance pirates that Renee simply called a cab and returned to Manhattan so he could work uninterrupted.

Unfortunately, the muse that had been perched so companionably on his shoulder left right along with Renee, and he once again found himself staring at blank pieces of paper and the demise of his career.

He'd left a message at McCallum's office that morning, saying he'd be delayed a day or so, and just that slight intrusion of the real world had been enough to stop the creative process cold. Suddenly the fictional Margarita of his fantasies and the very real Meg he'd be working with at Lakeland House merged, and the real Meg was not about to be pushed around by Angelique Moreau. Not if she had anything to say about it.

He pushed his chair away from his desk and headed down the hall and into the gymnasium that overlooked the swimming pool. He'd tried meditation, free association, right-brain exercises and left-brain logic, and nothing had worked. So he yanked on a worn pair of boxing gloves and threw a quick left-right into the air. Maybe slamming his fists into the leather punching bag would somehow break the block that refused to budge for any more civilized approach.

At this point he'd try anything.

Eryk's long, sensitive fingers drew a line of fire across her shoulders and down the lush valley between her breasts. Isobel feared she would dissolve in heat if she didn't feel him pressed against her soon. With a swift, surprising movement, she slipped off the straps of her ivory lace chemise and stepped out of the confines of her petticoat. He pulled a tortoiseshell pin from her hair, and the coppery-gold tresses cascaded down her back, falling almost to her waist. Then Isobel undid the laces of the chemise and stood before him, naked and proud.

"Mon Dieu!" His eyes drank in her beauty and filled with emotion. "You are more lovely than I remembered."

She moved into the strong circle of his embrace and gasped at the first electrifying jolt of flesh against flesh. They fell together on the bed—for the rest of her life she would remember the feel of the cool silk bedspread on the fiery skin of her back as he slowly lowered his long, well-muscled body onto hers. She lifted her arms and—

It was the sound of a knock at her side door that forced Meg out of the nineteenth century and back to reality. For five hours Meg had been immersed in the saga of Isobel Carrington and her lover Eryk Depardieu. And for five hours she'd found herself thinking not as Meg Lindstrom but as Isobel Carrington, feeling what she felt, and—most of all—falling deeply in love with the magnetic Eryk, who now was irrevocably linked with Joe Alessio himself.

Again the quick tap-tap at the door and Elysse's voice calling, "Hurry up, Lindstrom. The soup's getting cold."

Meg put the book down and forced the image of herself and Joe Alessio in a highly compromising position from her mind. Damn Angelique Moreau and her passionate prose, anyway! She hid the paperback book beneath a black-and-gray sofa cushion and hurried to the side door.

"It's only a book," she repeated under her breath. "It's only a book." But just the thought of that gloriously graphic cover sent her fantasies spiraling shamelessly toward heights of pleasure she'd never believed possible.

"What took you so long?" Elysse, shivering in just a lightweight sweater and slacks, hurried into the kitchen carrying a bright red covered pot. "Did I wake you up?"

Meg, who was only now approaching reality, shook her head. "No," she said, lifting the cover and sniffing appreciatively of the delicious aroma of Elysse's special Irish minestrone soup. "I was reading."

"So that's it." Elysse took a clean bowl from the cabinet over the sink and ladled some steaming soup into it. "When you missed dinner tonight, I figured you were either catching up on your sleep or packing." She grinned and motioned for Meg to sit down at her own kitchen table. "I should have known better."

"Of course you should have known better," she said, choosing to misinterpret Elysse's words. "I always save my packing for the last possible minute."

Elysse sat down opposite her. "This *is* the last possible minute," she said, "and don't play dumb with me, Lindstrom. You know what I'm talking about." She propped her elbows on the table and her chin in her hands. "You were reading *Against All Odds*, weren't you?"

Meg took a spoonful of soup, then grinned. "You, too?" she asked.

Elysse's blue eyes widened, and she sighed, long and loud. "It's incredible. That man knows more about the inner workings of the female psyche than he has a right to." Meg got up to get the last half of a loaf of Italian bread from her countertop, and Elysse broke off a piece. "It must be done with mirrors."

"The way he described Isobel's feelings after making love with Eryk for the first time unnerved the hell out of me." Meg thought of the erotically charged passage. "You can't do that with mirrors. That's talent, pure and simple."

"No one understands a woman's thought processes better than another woman," Elysse continued, "but this Joe Alessio was right on target." She hesitated a moment. "Could he be gay?"

Meg almost choked on her soup. "I don't think so."

Elysse focused those therapist eyes of hers on Meg. "Are you sure? Sometimes they have this innate understanding of women that—"

Meg raised her hand to stop Elysse in mid-sentence. "Sorry, doctor, but your analysis is way off base. His hormones are just fine, thank you."

Elysse's eyebrows darted upward. "Firsthand knowledge?"

"No," Meg admitted. She thought of the look in his eyes as he traced the outline of her mouth on the coffee cup, thought of the feel of his hand in hers, the rugged and very male strength obvious in each movement he made. She may not have firsthand knowledge of his sexuality, but she didn't need to hear a weather report to see the sun shining. "Let's call it an educated guess."

Elysse chewed on a piece of bread for a moment, watching Meg very closely. "Men like that should be labeled 'Hazardous to a woman's health.' How are we going to maintain our feminine mystique with a Joe Alessio reading our minds?" Meg had no answer for that, which was just as well, because when Elysse was on a roll, no answer was necessary. "I think your carefully guarded heart is going to be in grave danger, my friend. Grave danger."

Meg finished her soup and put the bowl in the sink. "I've managed to get through twenty-six years with my heart intact, Elly. I think I can get through one more month."

"I don't think you'll get through the first week," Elysse said, brushing some breadcrumbs off the tablecloth into the palm of her hand, then into the garbage. "I've been to Lakeland House, too, Meg. The scent of pine, swirling snow, a roaring, crackling fire in the hearth..." She paused. "Just the two of you day after day, night after night."

Meg laughed in her friend's face. "You're wrong," she said. "We're going up there to work together, and that's it. I'm sure he's as anxious to complete this job as I am."

"Think about it, Lindstrom—a healthy man and a healthy woman all alone in a magical house. I bet you don't make it two weeks before the chemistry explodes."

"I'll bet you you're wrong, Dr. Lowell." Meg was teetering between a kind of reckless anticipation and downright annoyance of Elysse's certainty that she and Joe would become lovers. "Fifty dollars says Mr. Alessio and I will say goodbye as business partners and nothing more."

Elysse grinned. Her blue eyes danced in a way that made Meg want to hit her on the head with the rest of the Italian bread. "And I say you're protesting a bit too much, Ms Lindstrom. Fifty dollars says you and Angelique Moreau won't say goodbye at all."

They shook hands. Meg walked her friend to the back door. "I'll be very happy to prove you wrong, Elly," she said as Elysse started down the steps. "Sometimes you're too smug for your own good."

Elysse, quite smug indeed, chuckled. "Take a long look at pages 320 through 343, then tell me I'm wrong, Meg."

Meg watched as Elysse's small form dashed up the pathway to the main house, then slammed her door and raced back to the living room, where she'd stashed the romance novel.

Page 318, 319—there it was, page 320. She started to read.

And five minutes later Meg Lindstrom had a feeling she'd be out fifty dollars before the month was over.

"AND THAT IS EVERYTHING, Margarita." Patrick Mc-Callum leaned back in his swivel chair, his ready smile lighting up his basset-hound face. "Water, electricity, cleaning service. Everything has been taken care of by the foundation." He put his large feet up on top of his oak desk. "Would there be something I'm forgetting?"

Joe, Meg thought. *Where is he?* "Only one thing," she said instead. "The key."

McCallum laughed and pulled a brass ring from his pocket. "Keys," he corrected her, shaking the ring so that the four or five keys jingled merrily. "Anna believed in security."

"I can see that. I thought crime hadn't reached New Hampshire yet." She leaned over and took the heavy key ring from him and weighed it in the palm of her hand. "Should I worry?"

McCallum made a face. "Lock the doors and forget about it," he advised. "It's the isolation that worried Anna, not the crime. She was a city girl, born and bred. She never quite relaxed out here in the country."

Meg, a city girl herself, nodded. Miles and miles of emptiness did more to inspire dread in her heart than a subway platform at midnight.

"Well," she said, standing up. "I guess I'll be going now." Why didn't he say anything about Joe?

McCallum quickly rose to his feet and came around his desk to escort her to the door. "I'm going to drop in every now and then to make sure things are going well for you." He rested an arm on her shoulder for a second in a paternal gesture. "And don't be making yourself a stranger here. Come and see me when you're in town, Margarita."

She smiled at him. "That will be my pleasure, Patrick." She waited a beat, then said, "Whatever happened to Joe? Has he changed his mind about working on the history?"

McCallum clapped the heel of his hand against his forehead and groaned. "I'd be forgetting my head if it wasn't

attached to the rest of my body. Joseph called yesterday—
he'll be here tomorrow morning."

"Is he all right?"

McCallum shrugged. "I assume so. He said he had a
contractual obligation to meet."

They said goodbye, and Meg trotted across the parking
lot to where she'd left the limousine. So Joe had a contractual obligation to meet. She chuckled as she got into the car
and started the engine. Another Angelique Moreau novel,
no doubt. She thought about the four novels tucked into her
suitcase. Now that she knew he was still coming to Lakeland, she was able to relax and enjoy the fact that she'd have
an extra day to finish her crash course in the works of
Joseph Alessio.

She headed toward the highway, switching on her low
beams against the encroaching dusk. Although Joe wrote
from a woman's viewpoint, Meg was certain much more of
the real Joe Alessio was exposed in his novels than Angelique Moreau would care to admit.

She turned left off the main highway and began navigat-
ing the narrow, twisting road that led to Lakeland House.
That exposure of highly personal emotions was part of what
had attracted her to photography. Although she was dealing with concrete objects rather than created ones, the
viewpoint, literally the perspective, belonged solely to the
photographer. By tricks of lighting and angle, by choosing
to include one element of the whole or block it out, she had
been able to alter reality, glorify the beauty of the beast in
man as she saw fit. Even when she had tried to keep herself
out of her work, to concern herself only with form and line,
it had been impossible to obliterate her personal, creative
touch.

Her teachers at college had seen it. Her sister, Kay, had
noticed it, and Anna and the Kennedy Colony had re-
warded her for it. Indeed, a world of possibilities had been
opening up for her when Kay died and she put her own
dreams aside. But the desire to create hadn't left her. The

need to capture reality, to redefine life, had stayed with Meg—the creative urge as strong inside her as the need for food and air.

Meg rounded a hairpin curve, and instinctively her hand shot across the passenger's seat to keep her camera equipment from falling to the floor.

More than Joe Alessio and the delicious danger he represented, it was a different, more seductive danger Meg feared most. Lakeland House. There, surrounded by the ghosts of her younger self, it might be difficult to believe that she had chosen the right path and impossible to defend it—even to herself.

By the time Meg reached the gates to Lakeland House, it was fully dark. A stiff wind blew her coat open as she unlatched the gate, and when she crossed in front of the high beam of her headlights to get back into the limousine, she felt very alone. She didn't bother to close the gates behind her but started to make her way slowly up the rutted driveway. There was a garage behind the house, near the path leading to the ten cottages that were part of the Kennedy Colony. Patrick had advised her to keep the limousine there so it would be safe from the elements and from inquisitive forest creatures who might choose to hibernate beneath her hood.

The sky was darker in New Hampshire than she'd remembered, and Meg felt absorbed by the night. It seemed almost three-dimensional, enveloping everything it hovered over. On past trips, the lights on either side of the drive had always been lit to guide friends to Anna's house. The house itself had blazed with lamplight and candle glow and the friendly crackling fire from blazing hearths. Now the house seemed still, blank as an empty canvas, its windows dark and curtained against the night. Thick clouds obscured the moon and stars. The only illumination was the amber glow of the light over the front door, and that failed against the darkness.

As Meg locked her car in the cavernous garage and picked up her bags to make her way to the main house, she was tempted to give up on the whole idea and stay in a motel until Joe arrived. She, who had battled and beaten the New York City mass transit system for the first eighteen years of her life, found herself fearing the isolation of country life.

"You're acting like a fool," she said out loud as she crackled her way over fallen leaves that obliterated the path to the house. What was there to be afraid of? Raccoons? Field mice? The owls hooting softly somewhere in the towering trees overhead? There were no dangers lurking behind the evergreens, no perils waiting to befall her. Why, she was probably the only person for miles around.

While that fact didn't exactly send elation racing through Meg, it was comfort of a sort. She hurried down the path. About one hundred feet from the back door, she stopped. The canvas straps from her suitcases dug angry red grooves in her hands, and she paused to flex her fingers. Just as she was about to pick up her bags again, she felt an odd tingle at the back of her neck, the same feeling she used to get when someone approached her on a lonely city street.

She turned quickly and looked around her, trying to see into the darkness. Trees and bushes rustled in the wind. Nothing seemed out of the ordinary until she was at the door. She put her suitcases down on the top step and was sifting through her deep pocket for the keys Patrick had given her when she had the feeling she was being watched.

She turned around. The path to the house still seemed deserted; the only sounds were the wind and the owls. Yet the feeling of being watched persisted. She unlocked the door, then hesitated. Leaving the door open, she went back down the cement stairs to the edge of the path and looked around again. The cloud cover had shifted, and thin streams of moonlight illuminated some fat rhododendron bushes ten yards or so away.

A scream tore at her throat, and she fought it down. Two figures crouched in the semidarkness, partially hidden in the bushes. With no further preliminaries, Meg took the steps two at a time and slammed the door behind her, leaving her suitcases outside.

"That's it," she said out loud as she hurried to the telephone on the kitchen wall. After she called the police, she'd find herself a nice safe motel to stay in until Mr. Alessio showed up. She'd be damned if she'd stay out there in the middle of nowhere with two thugs lurking outside. She dialed information and waited, two rings, three, four—

"I need the police," she said to the operator when she finally got through.

The operator's voice was flat and bored. For a second Meg thought she was back in New York. "Where are you?"

"Gorham. No, wait a minute—I'm not sure. I'm on the north road, a little bit—"

"Are there any cross streets?" the operator broke in. "Any churches you can identify?"

"I'm at Lakeland House," Meg offered. "Anna Kennedy's—"

"Hold on."

Within seconds Meg was speaking to the town police, who assured her they would be there immediately.

"Thank God," Meg said as she hung up the phone and rested her head against the cool wall. She closed her eyes and was just beginning to recover her composure when she heard a noise in the hall.

She spun around. The tallest, skinniest man she had ever seen filled the doorway. He wore camouflage pants, a neon-yellow sweater and a battered fedora.

"You called the cops?" he asked in a lazy voice. A slightly manic grin broke across his craggy face as he adjusted the brim of his fedora. "Now I *really* wish you hadn't done that."

Chapter Five

The man took a step into the room. Meg picked up one of the heavy maple captain's chairs and held it overhead, thanking God and weight training for her strong arms. "I wouldn't come any closer," she said, riveting her dark eyes to his slightly glazed ones. "I won't think twice about decking you."

He looked amused and a trifle hurt. "What a thing to say to a fellow artist."

The chair lowered a fraction. "Fellow artist?"

He nodded. The overhead light caught and sparkled in the diamond stud in his right ear. For the life of her, Meg could never remember which ear signified what.

"Huntington Kendall," he said. He seemed to think that should mean something to her. "Huntington Kendall IV."

"I don't care if you're King Henry VIII." Meg tightened her grip on the chair and tried to ignore her screaming forearm muscles. "If you come one step further into this room, I won't be held responsible for anything I do."

He lowered his long-limbed body to the floor and took up a classic yoga position. "You have quite a temper, Margarita Lindstrom," he said, laughing. "I had no idea."

"How do you know my name?"

His brown eyes twinkled up at her almost as brightly as the diamond in his ear. She had the feeling he'd been imbibing—and not too long ago at that. "Patrick, of course."

"Of course," she muttered. She put the chair down but maintained her grip on it just in case. "Do you work here?" Perhaps he was one of the maintenance crew McCallum had told her about, or a New Wave gardener.

Huntington Kendall IV rolled his eyes. "First you don't recognize my illustrious name, and now you negate my art. You wound me, Margarita."

"If you don't answer my questions, Kendall, I just may do that."

"My life is an open book," he said, that manic grin still on his face. "Ask away."

"What in hell were you doing hiding in the bushes?"

"I wasn't hiding in the bushes."

"Don't lie, Kendall. I saw you and another guy in—"

Kendall threw his head back and laughed, his long light reddish hair bobbing around his shoulders. "I'm afraid not, dear Margarita. I've been in here all evening."

"Then can you tell me exactly who is out there lurking around?"

"Of course."

Meg waited for him to continue. He didn't, and she had to fight down the urge to hit him over the head just on general principles.

"That's my village out there," he said.

"Your what?"

"The citizens of my imaginary village."

Certifiable, she thought. The man was definitely certifiable. She heard the sound of the police cars snaking their way up the driveway. She looked down at the man; he was beginning to look more like an eccentric and less like a criminal every second. It was obvious she wasn't going to get a straight answer from him. "Just stay there," she said, opening the back door for the officers. "We'll let them straighten this out."

Huntington Kendall IV smiled up at her, closed his eyes and promptly fell over in a dead sleep.

"YOU CAN LET ME OUT HERE."

The cabdriver, rotund and garrulous, glanced at Joe through his rearview mirror. "That's one heck of a walk up that driveway," he said as he pulled over just outside the gates to Lakeland the next afternoon.

"That's okay," Joe said, handing him a twenty and waving off change. "I need the exercise." The truth was, the cabbie's nonstop monologue on why he left the wilds of Brooklyn for the wilds of the White Mountains was slowly driving Joe nuts.

The cabbie turned around in his seat. "Suit yourself. Wouldn't catch me walking if I could ride." By the look of his mountainous belly wedged behind the steering wheel, that was no lie.

Moments later Joe, suitcases in hand, watched the beat-up cab turn on to the main road and disappear from sight. The headache that had been gathering just behind his eyes disappeared, and he started up the driveway toward the main house. Most of the leaves had fallen from the white birch and sugar maple trees scattered amid the pines, and he crunched his way along the carpet of crimson, burnt orange and vivid yellow. It was a clear day and crisp, the kind of sharply beautiful autumn weather that New England was justly famous for.

Somehow he'd managed to crank out the outline Renee had demanded, and while it wasn't about to win a Pulitzer, it did contain the kernel of a terrific story if only that damned internal censor of his didn't keep stopping him cold. Once or twice that blinding panic had actually torn him from his seat before the typewriter and kept him from proceeding any further. But each time after he allowed his mind to run free and it unhesitatingly focused itself on Meg, both as he remembered her and as he imagined her, he was once more able to sink back into his fantasy.

When he reached the top of the steep driveway, he wasn't even breathing hard. Lakeland House sat a few hundred feet away, serene and beautiful, bathed in early afternoon sunlight. The curtains and drapes were open, and a thin curl of smoke drifted lazily from the chimney. McCallum had told him Meg was already there, and it seemed she had things in hand.

This time he knew there would be no Anna Kennedy to greet him, no loving friend to guide him, but he'd made his peace with that. It was enough to know he would be able to finish her work.

It was enough to know that Meg was waiting.

THE WARMTH FROM THE FIRE in the hearth and the three glasses of wine with lunch had combined to make Meg lazier and more mellow than she'd felt in ages. She was stretched across two pillows near the fireplace, letting her mind drift lazily around, while Huntington Kendall IV, sober now, worked on a series of sketches of her. Normally, she hated being scrutinized, despised being captured on film or canvas, but at that moment she was too content to care.

She covered her mouth and yawned, then started to stretch.

"Don't move," Hunt said. "I want to capture that line across your shoulders."

"Slave driver," she muttered, returning to her original pose.

They'd spent the entire morning inspecting Hunt's sculptures, which were scattered around Lakeland House property. It still amazed her, but those two figures she'd spotted crouched behind the bushes near the back door were life-size plaster-cast sculptures, just two of the fourteen that perched on the limbs of oak trees, sat behind the wheel of an abandoned Dodge and peeped into uncurtained windows. Hunt, unmarried and likely to remain so, had decided to populate an entire town with the children of his imagination, and these fourteen offspring were the beginning of the project. At Anna's request, Patrick had said Hunt could remain at Lakeland an additional two weeks to complete this segment of his work. His talent was quirky and brilliant, and despite their rather unconventional meeting, Meg found she liked the man as much as she admired the artist.

Now he wanted to add Meg to his "family," and she was too lazy and content at the moment to protest.

"You're moving again," he said, tearing a sheet of paper from his drawing pad and crumpling it up. "How can I capture the proportions if you keep moving?"

"Picasso found a way," she said, giving in this time to the urge to stretch her long arms skyward.

Hunt gave her one of his lopsided grins. "And you see the way his models ended up. Is that how you want to be immortalized?"

She grinned back at him. "Quite an ego you have there, Hunt. You're hardly Picasso yet."

He began sketching again. "And you're hardly the perfect artist's model. Now stay still, damn it."

Meg resumed her position, then winced.

"What's the matter now?"

Meg sat up and started kneading the back of her neck. "My muscles are all bunched up."

He put his sketch pad and piece of vine charcoal down and went to her side. "Lie on your stomach," he said, flipping Meg over before she could answer.

"What are you going to do?" Meg asked, trying to look back over her shoulder but stopped by the painfully contracted muscles.

"Not to worry. It's an old Hindu method I learned."

He knelt over her, one knee on either side of her hips, and began to pound and pull rhythmically at the muscles along her shoulders and neck. At first it was painful, and Meg wanted to push him off, but suddenly the pain gave way to relief; then relief quickly became pleasure.

"Oh, God, that's wonderful," she said, burying her face in the carpet, which was warmed by the fireplace a few feet away. "I've never felt so good."

Across the room a man cleared his throat. "I hate to interrupt this interesting scene. I tried knocking, but you both were—" he paused for dramatic effect "—otherwise occupied."

"Joe!" Meg bolted upright, knocking skinny Huntington on his derriere. "Hunt was just massaging away a muscle cramp for me."

Joe's dark brows were knotted in a borderline scowl. His gaze went from Meg to Huntington and back again. He obviously didn't believe a word she was saying. "I would have knocked again, but—"

"Don't be ridiculous." Huntington, who Meg could tell had already picked up the tension between herself and Joe, unfolded his lanky limbs and stood up. He towered over Joe, whose muscular body was more compact. "I'm Huntington Kendall IV."

Hunt extended a bony hand to Joe, and Meg watched Joe hesitate before shaking it.

"Joe Alessio," he said, tearing his gaze away from Meg. "You're the sculptor staying on an extra week or so?"

Huntington nodded.

"How did you know about that?" Meg asked, pulling her hair back off her face and quickly braiding it. "I was taken by surprise last night."

"So I heard," Joe drawled. "Let's just say having the police call Patrick about a burglary jogged his memory a bit." Joe took out a cigarette and sat down on the couch facing the fireplace.

"Too bad," Huntington replied, gathering up his sketch pad and the loose pieces of vine charcoal from the floor. "And here I was hoping my artistic reputation had preceded me."

Joe chuckled. It was obvious he was beginning to realize the situation had been exactly as Meg said, for she noticed his eyes drawn again and again to the blue eye shadow and matching jumpsuit and socks Hunt was sporting.

"It may have," Joe said more easily, "but I don't keep up on new artists the way I should."

"You should see some of the sculptures Hunt's done," Meg said, relieved the situation had lost its crackling tension. "They're so lifelike I called the police."

Hunt groaned and rolled his eyes toward the ceiling. "Dear girl, I wish you'd stop calling them sculptures. They're alternative citizens in an imaginary village."

Joe's eyebrows arched, and Meg shrugged her shoulders good-naturedly. "I'll have to remember that," she said.

"Please do." Hunt walked toward the front door. "I can tell I'm not going to finish the preliminary on you this afternoon, Margarita," he said, brushing some dust off the gilt frame of a tiny Renoir sketch near the piano, "but do let me borrow you for an hour tonight."

Meg nodded.

"And you—" Hunt continued, looking at Joe. "I'd love to do a few studies on you. I need a macho type for my civil-unrest tableau."

Joe looked amused but uninterested. "I'll think about it."

Hunt flashed them his loony smile, rapped his knuckles on the glossy molding around the door and disappeared down the hallway.

As soon as they heard the heavy front door swing shut, Joe let out a loud laugh. "Is he for real?" he asked, stubbing out his cigarette in an ashtray on the small end table near the sofa. "He reminds me of a cross between the Scarecrow in the *Wizard of Oz* and Cyndi Lauper."

"Don't be too quick to judge him, Alessio," she said. "His work is brilliant."

"An eccentric genius?"

"He just might be, if he ever gets the chance."

Joe reached for another cigarette, then hesitated. "Do you mind?"

"Does it matter?" He seemed to smoke the way other people breathed. "I doubt if you can do without."

"I could smoke in the bathroom," he said, that delightfully wicked grin she remembered flashing across his face.

She stood up and straightened her soft apricot sweater over her faded jeans. "You wouldn't want to do that, would you?"

He shrugged. "If it bothers you, I will. Besides, it might bring back some of the illicit pleasure that used to go with it."

"Far be it from me to deny you illicit pleasure," she said, relishing the words, "but since this is your house, too, I don't think I have any right to forbid you to smoke."

"Maybe what we need are some ground rules." Joe stood up and approached her. He was slightly taller than she remembered, but of course this time she was in bare feet, not heels. She couldn't help it, but her eyes lingered on the biceps that strained the sleeves of his black sweater and danced appreciatively over the way his jeans rode low on his hips. He carried himself with the same barely contained energy the men in his novels possessed, and Meg found herself suddenly mixing fantasy and reality.

"Ground rules," she said, yanking herself back to the subject at hand. "I think ground rules would be a wonderful idea."

"Okay, then. Shoot."

"If you could limit your cigarettes to one an hour when we're together, I could handle it."

He grinned. "But none in the limousine, right?"

"Right." She waited. "Your turn."

"I'd like to start work at nine and go until three."

"Without lunch?" Meg was horrified.

"That was the general idea."

"No way. If I don't eat, I'm a monster."

"Then how about a working lunch? I want the evenings free."

"Free for what?" she asked, unable to control herself. "You've only been in town half an hour. I doubt if you've found a date already." Even as she said the words, she knew they weren't true. She doubted Joe Alessio was ever at a loss for female companionship.

He let her remark pass without comment. She appreciated the fact that he didn't jump on every opportunity for innuendo and double entendre. "I work in the evenings," he said finally. But there was something in his eyes, a slight touch of fear, that belied his words.

"That's fine," she said. "I'm a morning person—I start to droop around nine P.M. I can always use that time to let Hunt do his preliminaries of me."

Joe's expression slid through a subtle series of changes that only someone well versed in catching nuance and mood could catch. She wished she had her camera to capture it—sometimes reality needed to be recorded before she could fully understand it.

"There's one more thing," he said.

"Another guideline?" she asked with a chuckle. "Shall we regulate kitchen privileges? Who makes morning coffee? Who files and who—"

"I don't want him to call you Margarita."

"What?" The word came out half laugh, half exclamation.

"I don't want Huntington Kendall the fifth—"

"The fourth."

"Whatever. I don't want Huntington Kendall to call you Margarita."

"It's my name," she said, trying to ignore the way pleasure was snaking through her body. "What's he supposed to call me?"

"What everyone else calls you." Joe wasn't smiling at all. In fact, his handsome face was solemn, almost stern. "Meg, Maggie, Margie—anything. Just not Margarita."

"Patrick calls me Margarita," she said, enjoying herself immensely. "Shall I stop him, as well?"

"Yes." Joe's voice was even and certain.

"You must admit this is a peculiar request, Joe." She paused, watching him closely. "Why should I ask that of them if it doesn't bother me?"

A muscle at the side of his neck twitched. "Because I asked you to."

"Sorry," she said, shaking her braid free until her hair spilled loose over her shoulders. "That's not good enough."

He stepped closer and rested his hands lightly on her shoulders, the palms covering her straight silky hair. He smelled slightly of cigarette smoke, which she didn't like, but it was overpowered by the clean, fresh smell of his skin, which she did like—very much, indeed. "Margarita is a beautiful name," he said. "I want to be the only one who calls you that."

Heat, sudden and powerful, rose from her feet to her scalp. "I don't know why I should agree," she said softly. "I've never been partial to the name myself."

He drew his fingers through her hair, almost but not quite grazing her cheek. "Foolish. The name suits you."

She was lost, and well she knew it. He exuded such incredible intensity, such strong sexual magnetism, that she nearly reached for the phone to call Elysse and tell her the fifty dollars was hers.

"Are you always this pushy?" she managed finally.

"When I see something I want, I go for it," he said. "If that's being pushy, I guess I am." She fell deeper under his spell. "I prefer to call it motivated."

"I don't like being pushed," she said. "It brings out the rebel in me."

"I'll remember that." His hands were still resting on her shoulders. The sensation, added to the wine she'd had at lunch, made it hard for her to think clearly. He zeroed back in on his target. "I want to be the only one to call you Margarita. Will you do that for me?"

"On one condition," she said.

He grinned at her. "Which is?"

"That I can call you Angelique." She wanted him to know she could push back when necessary.

Joe groaned, then began to laugh. "You drive a hard bargain, Margarita."

"As do you, Angelique."

He took her hand and started heading toward the kitchen. "When's lunch around here?"

"Whenever you want to make it," Meg shot back, enjoying the look of surprise on his face.

"Why do I get stuck with lunch detail?"

"Because I'm a morning person and I'll do breakfast." She sat down at one of the maple chairs that surrounded the enormous table. "Bacon, eggs, granola—you name it."

Joe winced. "How about black coffee and an extra hour's sleep." He narrowed his eyes at her. "I didn't know you were so organized. Artistic types aren't usually."

"I'm not an artistic type any longer," she said easily. "I've developed the more methodical side of my personality."

"Too bad," he said, opening the refrigerator and pulling out some ham and Swiss cheese the invisible housekeeper had provided. "I hate to see talent being wasted."

She looked up at him. "So do I," she said.

He hunted around in the refrigerator once more and found a loaf of fresh rye bread wrapped in plastic. "So why the limo?" he asked, sitting down opposite her and beginning to assemble some sandwiches.

Meg reached over and grabbed a piece of cheese off the top of the stack despite the fact she'd already had lunch. "Would you believe I have a talent for driving?" she asked dryly.

"Not after talking to Patrick, no."

"What's that supposed to mean?" Somehow all the delicious electricity between them had vanished, and Meg felt on the defensive. "No accidents, no moving violations, just one parking ticket that was totally unjustified—"

"I'm talking about the photography." He spread mustard on a piece of bread, slapped it down on top of a sandwich stack, then handed the whole thing to Meg. "Patrick told me you won the Institute of Photography's Rising Star Award two years running."

"Patrick has a big mouth," she mumbled, swallowing a bite of food, then reaching across the table for more mustard. "That's really not terribly important news."

Joe finished his sandwich and began assembling another. "Not in the scheme of world events, no," he said, "but it *is* important to the history we're going to be putting together."

Meg got up to get some milk. "A footnote, maybe," she said with ironic humor. "Not much more than that."

"You had a hell of a lot going for you, Margarita. Why'd you let it all slip away?"

"I didn't let it slip away." She sat back down at the table, forgetting the glass of milk on the counter. "I made a decision to stop. That's all."

"Why stop before you've even begun?" The open curiosity in his voice grated on her. "You win two contests, and you call it quits? Where's your drive, your ambition?"

"Listen, Joe, my best friend's a psychologist. I don't need any free-lance therapy, if you don't mind."

He didn't back off. "Maybe it was growing up in Staten Island," he continued. "I have a theory that the more you have as a child, the less you achieve as an adult."

"I don't think the Kennedy family would care for that analysis," she remarked. "They could almost be classed as overachievers."

"Not the new generation," he said, undaunted. "Maybe if you'd had it more difficult as a child—"

"Maybe you should mind your own business." Meg thought of the lonely days and nights as a child in her sister's shadow. A pleasant two-family home on a pleasant tree-lined street hadn't come close to making up for the love she craved. She bit into her sandwich and pretended it was

Joe's neck. "Where's your ambition, Angelique? Could there be some reason you hide behind a pseudonym?"

Bingo.

The second Meg's words came out, Joe knew she'd won the round, hands down. First he asked her if he could call her Margarita; then he tried unlicensed psychoanalysis. If he kept letting his curiosity—both personal and professional—get the better of him, this month would turn out a disaster.

He shut up and focused his intensity solely on his sandwich.

"If we keep up like this, it's never going to work." Meg's words startled him.

"I was thinking the same thing." He pushed his sandwich aside. They seemed to swing crazily between attraction and antagonism, and he was finding it impossible to keep his balance. "We're both being defensive, and there's no reason for it." She had been watching him closely, those hot and intense eyes of hers riveted to him, but now she looked away. "Our lives are an open book here." Her eyebrows shot skyward, and he laughed. "Our professional lives, I mean."

"That's better. You had me worried for a second."

He shot her his best lascivious grin. "No more worried than I. If you knew my sordid past, you'd never spend a night under the same roof with me."

"Don't worry about me," she shot back, raising her hands. "These are registered weapons. I can handle myself."

Her fingers were long and slender, the pale beige nails tapered into ovals. They were beautiful hands, the hands of an artist or musician, nothing he would think of as weapons. But she had such a look of independent strength about her that despite her slender body and fair-haired beauty, he had a feeling he was in much more danger than she. His days of fantasizing about her had left him feeling awkward in her presence, almost as if he'd been caught peeking through a keyhole into her mind. "Why don't you start?" he said.

She folded those lovely hands on top of the table, looked him straight in the eye and began, "I always wanted to be a photographer. I worked very hard to win those contests you mentioned, and I'm still very happy I did. For whatever reasons, when my sister died, I decided a photographic career was not for me. I traveled around for a year and finally ended up living in my friend Elysse's guest house and driving a limousine." Her voice was softer, almost as if she were speaking to herself. "That was a little over a year ago. The camera is my hobby now."

"Was it lack of money that made you stop?" Joe couldn't control his urge to know more. "Fear of failure?"

"Nothing like that," she said easily. "I was tired of changing time zones and packing suitcases. So Elysse and Jack 'adopted' me."

Telling nothing while telling all was an art, and she had it down cold. She had set the parameters of their relationship, and he would respect those parameters for now. He had to remind himself that a constant flow of words, of analysis, was his way and not hers.

"Your turn," she said. That wonderful mouth of hers, which had intrigued him from the first morning at the church, tipped in a smile that he felt deep in the pit of his stomach.

"I've written four books as Angelique Moreau, and I'm working on the fifth. I've traced Italian families and Jewish families and Polish families." He laughed. "I think I have the market cornered on descriptions of Ellis Island."

"Didn't you say you've written some Westerns?"

She had a good memory. "Thirteen Westerns as Bret Allen, thirteen *Star Trek* novels as Alex Dennison and more slick porn under more weird names than I care to tell you. I've never written one real piece of fiction under my own name." *Good going, Alessio,* he thought. *Spill your guts on the table.* "Don't ask me why," he went on, despite himself, "because I sure as hell don't know. Maybe it's Vietnam or—"

Meg raised her hand to stop him. "Just the facts, sir, just the facts."

He was glad she stopped him, because he'd probably be telling her next that the only barometer of success his family understood was money, that being a middle child meant never measuring up, that being verbal in a family who read just the *Daily News* and the *TV Guide* had kept him half in fantasy, half in torment throughout his adolescence. It was this ability to disappear into a fantasy world of his own imagination that got him through the very real horrors of Vietnam and cushioned his uneasy return to civilization. He created fictional families to make up for not creating a real one of his own. "Those are the facts," he said, turning his hands palms up. "I make all the best-seller lists, and no one knows my name."

She was leaning forward, elbows on the table, her chin in her hands. Her eyes were so dark against the delicate peach of her face that they seemed to draw him in as if to an inexhaustible source of warmth. A quick series of fire-and-flame metaphors popped up, and he prayed he'd remember them later when he got back to work. "Surely someone does?" she asked.

"My editors and my agent." He dragged his hand through his hair and wished he had his notebook with him. Ideas were beginning to hammer at him as he watched the way the sunlight from the kitchen window glittered in her flaxen hair. "Sometimes I feel like a journeyman," he said. "All things to all people."

"What are you to yourself?" Her eyes flickered across his face, searching with the relentless focus of the all-knowing camera. Her curiosity was evidently a match for his.

"I can't answer that." He shrugged. "Can you? How do *you* see yourself?"

"I don't. As I said before, analysis doesn't interest me."

The hell it didn't. She was electric with curiosity, her mind as vital and active as his, but for some reason she was trying to cloak her real personality behind a cool and calm exterior. But her eyes—those burning dark eyes—gave her away every time.

He stood up and stretched. His sweater rode up, exposing a few inches of lean muscle above his waistband. He wasn't an exhibitionist, but he caught her glance returning again and again to his body, and he took a swift, sharp pleasure in the fact that he pleased her.

She stood up to help him clear the table, and when she moved past him, he caught the sweet scent of her hair and felt the softness of a breast brush against his arm. The real Margarita was every bit as passionate as the Margarita in his fantasy who refused to be trapped by the limits of his imagination.

He couldn't wait to discover which woman he would conquer or be conquered by—fantasy or flesh. Somehow he didn't think he could lose either way.

Chapter Six

Joe seemed distant and preoccupied after lunch, and Meg found herself suddenly uneasy. This was one of those moments when she felt all arms and legs, painfully conscious of every movement she made and every word she uttered.

"I checked the library this morning," she said as they abandoned the kitchen for the drawing room at the front of the house. "There must be ten reams of material on writers alone."

Joe stopped near the doorway so she could precede him inside. "Is any of it organized yet?"

Meg sat down at the piano bench and ran her fingers quickly up and down the ivory keys simply for their cool satin feel beneath her hands. "Some," she said, trying to stop noticing the beautiful muscles of his shoulders and arms, the leanness of his belly. "From what I could see, Anna finished poets and almost finished playwrights and essayists. She'd only done preliminary work on journalists and novelists."

Joe sat down on the edge of the bench and idly picked out a simple version of the theme song from *Bonanza* with two fingers.

"I remember that," Meg said, laughing. "Ben Cartwright and Hoss and Little Joe and Adam—"

"You're too young to remember Adam." Joe broke in. "No one remembers Adam."

"Pernell Roberts." She grinned at him. "I saw him on the reruns."

He groaned. "That hurt, Margarita." He turned back to the piano and riffed through the theme songs from *Happy Days* and *Cheers.*

"You like television."

"Guilty. Old movies are my favorite, but I'll even watch reruns of *Gilligan's Island* in a pinch."

A kindred spirit. "I've never admitted this to a living soul," Meg said, "but when I was in college, I used to sneak back to my room on Tuesday nights and watch *Laverne and Shirley.*"

His thick black brows arched, and that sexy grin she was growing quite fond of slid across his face. "You should be ashamed of yourself, watching that kind of trash. How could you?" He paused a moment. "Now, *The Honeymooners—that* was a show."

He got up and did such a credible impression of Ralph Kramden sending Alice to the moon that Meg was helpless with laughter in seconds. She was also a *Honeymooners* fan, and she shot lines from the show to him, and he quickly shot back the next ones. Joe was successful and talented and sexier than he had a right to be, but he hadn't forgotten how to have fun, how to be silly, and that fact endeared him to her against her better judgment.

"Enough!" She leaned back against the edge of the piano and held her stomach. "I actually think I hurt myself."

Joe, who was standing right next to her, reached out and put the flat of his hand against her taut midriff. Her breath caught abruptly in her throat.

"You'll live," he said, the heat from his hand turning her skin to fire.

Want to bet on it? Gently, she placed her hand on top of his and removed it. "Don't," she whispered. "Please don't."

He stepped closer to her, his clear green eyes framed by thick dark lashes that made her gnash her teeth in envy. "I know what the problem is," he said, standing up and pinning her between the dangers of his hard body and the sharp angles of the piano behind her.

"What?" That one simple word was all she could manage, all she could think of.

"This." He dipped his head slightly, and without touching her anywhere else at all, his lips brushed her cheek, her jaw, then, inevitably, her mouth. He hadn't closed his eyes, and she found herself mesmerized by the sudden flare of desire she saw there.

He moved away a fraction; she could feel his breath warm against her skin. "That kiss has been between us since we met."

"Yes." She couldn't deny it. She just let the touch of him linger against her lips and the sight of him delight her eyes. It was a weakness, she knew, but she worshiped beauty in all its forms, and male beauty moved her more than was wise.

"I thought if we simply—" his sensuously mobile mouth hesitated around a smile "—got it over with, we'd be okay." His eyes slid over her face, and she had the sensation of being caressed. "We're not okay, are we?"

Meg shook her head. "No, we're not." She had to force herself to move away to the other side of the room so she could think. "We don't need complications, Joe." She looked at him. "I don't need complications."

"It wouldn't have to be complicated. I'm not asking for promises, Margarita."

He didn't understand.

"I don't want promises," she said, crossing her arms in front of her chest. "And I don't want complications. I'm a careful woman, Joe, and I don't want to start something I'm not sure about."

They stood on opposite sides of the room, and despite her well-chosen words, her mouth still felt warm and soft from his kiss, and her body yearned for the warmth she'd felt near him. But as she'd said, she was a careful woman, and careful women didn't begin affairs with men they barely knew even if they'd be living in the same house for a month or longer. It simply didn't make good sense. It simply couldn't work.

"I'm not sorry I did that."

"I'm not sorry you did, either." Meg had never mastered the art of the polite social lie.

"I'd like to do it again." He wasn't smiling, but there was a definite sparkle in his eyes.

"That's not a good idea." She sounded less certain than she had expected.

"I'm attracted to you, Margarita. I want to get to know you better."

"You'll know me quite well after we work together."

"But I won't know how you feel in my arms, will I?"

She had a quick vision of herself rising from a rumpled bed that was still warm from their bodies. "You're not playing fair," she said finally. "I don't think this is exactly what Anna had in mind when she asked us to be here."

He leaned against the windowsill a few feet away from her. "Are you sure? I'm beginning to suspect there might have been a lot more to this idea than meets the eye."

"Wishful thinking, Alessio," she said. "Anna never was one for playing matchmaker."

He nodded but said nothing. The idea that Anna may have hoped they would become romantic was absurd, totally and completely crazy. They couldn't be less suited to one another. Joe was verbal; Meg, visual. Meg was careful, while Joe was more impulsive. And, even more important, Joe seemed to almost vibrate with creative energy, while Meg had trained her own energy to stay at a slow simmer. It just wouldn't work.

"Our concern has to be the Lakeland history," she said, breaking the silence. "Our personal feelings have to come second."

"Are you admitting you have personal feelings about this?"

"I'm not dead, am I?" Her temper, unpredictable at best, heated up. "You know as well as I do that I enjoyed kissing you."

He shook his head and chuckled. "No, no, Margarita, you have it all wrong. You didn't kiss me—you *were kissed* by me. There's a slight but all-important difference there." His gaze lingered for a brief moment on her mouth. "I don't think it will always be that way."

She had no answer at all for that. She didn't know if it was simply Joe himself or the fact that she'd read so much of his wildly sexy best-seller, but he had to be the most sensual man she'd ever met. Even when he wasn't touching her—was actually a few feet away from her—Meg felt his presence like a physical caress. She'd met other writers before, and she knew it wasn't simply part of the package; none of them had ever seemed as blatantly physical as Joe Alessio. Most had come alive only on the pages of their books, as if whatever sensuality they possessed was drained into their work, leaving the man himself almost devoid of any passion for reality.

The silence between them was growing long and uncomfortable. Joe stifled a yawn with the back of his left hand and looked at his watch.

"No wonder I'm tired," he said casually, as if nothing else had gone on between them besides a pleasant lunch. "I've been up almost forty-eight hours."

"Forty-eight hours? What on earth for?" she asked.

He shrugged. "A deadline I'd forgotten about," he said. "I made the plane out of JFK with seconds to spare."

"A new book?" The idea perked her up considerably.

"Mmm." His answer was a vague mumble she took to be an assent. His eyes, normally direct and open, were averted a tiny bit to the left of hers.

"Care to divulge the title?" She was feeling more comfortable now away from the personal.

"Sorry. I always keep my working titles secret."

"Is that a private superstition?" She was fascinated by the quirks and eccentricities of the creative mind. Once, before her sister died, she'd done a photo-essay on Kay's unchanging routine before her nightly newscast that had been included in a posthumous tribute to Kay in *Ms.* magazine.

"A very private superstition." He looked extremely uncomfortable.

"I won't tell anyone." The balance of power had shifted in her direction now that they were out of the sexual battlefield. "Do you always wear blue socks when you write chapter one or a shower cap on your head or—"

The uncomfortable look on his face disappeared as he started to laugh. "If you think I'm going to bare my deepest secrets to you, Lindstrom, you're crazy." He stifled another yawn. "Listen, if you don't mind, I'm going to hit the sack for a while. I'm beat."

The thought of sitting down to finish the Angelique Moreau novel she'd been devouring sounded quite good to Meg. "How about we meet back in here around five and make a battle plan? I checked the freezer, and it's stocked with enough food to feed three armies, so we don't even have to worry about dinner."

Joe, looking terribly weary, nodded. "You're on." An odd expression she couldn't identify passed across his face, then disappeared. "We'll work well together, Meg. There won't be any problems."

He left the room. She listened to the sound of his running shoes squeaking over the polished wood floor in the hallway. He'd said they would work well together, and she believed him. He'd called her Meg, after all, not Margarita. The more intimate name had disappeared along with his apparent desire to get to know her better.

"You got exactly what you wanted," she said out loud, not caring that there was only a Boston fern and an extremely disreputable Swedish ivy there to hear her. She should feel relieved that she wouldn't have to fight her desire for him with one hand while working on the history of the Kennedy Creative Colony with the other. It was exactly what she'd asked of him.

Why, then, did she feel so damned disappointed?

JOE CURSED HIS WAY up the curving staircase to his room. From the second he'd arrived and found Meg and that scarecrow of an artist, Huntington Kendall the whatever, sprawled before the roaring fireplace, he'd been on the offensive. Seeing her long, slender body beneath the lanky artist's, her face flushed from the heat of the fire, had been enough to make Joe want to tear Kendall off her and fling him out one of the leaded windows without a second thought. It didn't matter that the situation was totally innocent or that Kendall was probably more interested in him than in Meg—Joe had felt the old macho instincts he'd spent the last decade sublimating take him over and make him push Meg much faster than he'd ever intended.

His room was at the end of the hall on the second floor of the old house, and he slammed the door shut behind him with his foot.

"Damn it!" he said out loud as he shoved his suitcase off the double bed and stretched out on the soft mattress.

"I want to be the only one to call you Margarita... That kiss has been between us... It doesn't have to be complicated..." If they gave prizes for stupid, asinine things to say to a woman you barely know, he would have managed to take first, second and third with some of the gems he'd pulled on Meg that afternoon. Even the worst of the 1940s B movies he was addicted to contained better dialogue than that.

Not that he'd been lying, though—everything he'd said to Meg was perfectly true. He felt drawn to her with an intensity that was disturbing despite the fact that his passions always ran deep. Spending the last few days creating his own fictional Margarita had blurred the edges of reality for him, making him feel more intimate with a woman who knew little more about him than his name—and even that was subject to change.

Being pushed into doing the outline for the next book had begun the process of crumbling the cement block that stood between Joe and his creativity. The fear that he'd tapped himself dry was receding into memory, and the urge to vanish into his work was rising strong within him. It began slowly like a buzzing somewhere inside his brain, building in intensity until the desire—no, the need—to write was so strong that it overrode his darkest fears and deepest inhibitions.

Margarita was his heroine; there was no changing that fact now, for she lived on paper as surely as she lived down there in that study just one floor away from where he lay. And there was no changing the fact that he found both of them endlessly exciting.

He groaned and put an arm across his eyes to block out the sunlight and the look on her face when he kissed her for what may have been the first—and last—time.

The palms of Eryk's hands were roughened from his work, but none of that mattered to Isobel as he drew them slowly up the ivory length of her inner thighs and drew closer to her heat.

Her breath grew quicker as her body arched toward him, eager to know the fulfillment that lay just moments away.

"You're ready," he said, pausing for one maddening instant. "My God, how warm and eager you are—"

It was no use!

Meg closed the copy of *Against All Odds* and tossed it down on the floor next to the sofa where she was curled up beneath the quilt Anna had made the year she broke her hip. Meg had thought she would be able to lose herself again in the delights of the nineteenth-century adventures of Isobel and her lover, Eryk, the piratical demon who plagued the Hawaiian Islands and helped Isobel found a twentieth-century dynasty.

Instead, she found herself unable to concentrate; those escapist delights were totally overpowered by the memory of Joe's simple kiss. In the two hours since he went upstairs, she'd replayed that moment over and over, shivering with pleasure at the remembered feeling of his lips on hers. She'd been kissed soundly by other men, but never had one elicited such a sensual response with that most basic of actions as Joe had. All of the ways in which their temperaments differed seemed not to matter when she thought of that wild surge of pure lust that rocketed through her when he drew near.

Reading about the lusty Eryk and the willing Isobel had done nothing to calm her down. Instead, she found herself feeling edgy and irritable and wishing she hadn't been quite so hasty before. The idea of giving into desire for its own sake was an intoxicating one—something she'd never had the time or the inclination to try before. She'd always approached her romantic life with caution bordering on the extreme, as if sharing herself with a man meant losing herself at the same time. She wasn't a woman who liked to lose.

Since she was a child and had her first camera placed in her hands, Meg had been afflicted with tunnel vision. The only things she understood as she grew up, the only things that mattered throughout her college years, were what could be perceived through the lens of a camera. She had been certain she was bound for success and had made sure she stayed firmly on track. It wasn't until her sister died and the underbelly of her own ambition presented itself that Meg put aside dreams of glory and settled for second best.

Joe Alessio said he wanted nothing of her—no commitment, no lifelong promises. He simply desired her, and God knew, she desired him, as well. But some instinct, some gut-level survival instinct she'd sharpened in the last few years told her nothing was as it seemed.

She thanked God and Patrick McCallum for letting Huntington Kendal IV stay an extra two weeks at Lakeland House to finish his collection. Maybe with a third party to keep things from getting too intense, she'd be able to skate by without falling through the ice.

Maybe after a few days of working closely together, the magic would disappear. But then she thought of Joe and the way his lips had felt against hers and pulled the quilt up over her head.

"And maybe pigs can fly," she muttered.

There was a rustle at the doorway, then, "I don't think they can, Margarita."

She pulled the quilt down and saw Huntington Kendall, still in his bright blue jumpsuit, stroll into the room.

"I believe you need a refresher course in barnyard lore," he continued as he sat down on the other end of the couch.

"I didn't hear you come in." Meg tossed the quilt aside and sat up, straightening her sweater and smoothing her hair off her face.

"Evidently not." Hunt leaned forward and plucked the copy of *Against All Odds* from the polished oak floor and inspected the cover. "Divine-looking couple," he said, flipping the book over to read the blurb on the back. Then he stopped abruptly and looked at Meg. "How interesting. Doesn't he look a lot like our very own Mr. Alessio?"

"Not a bit." Meg stood up.

"You have no eye, darling." Hunt took a closer look at the cover. "Look at those biceps, that chest. Our Mr. Alessio could have been the model."

Meg shook her head. "Sorry, Hunt," she said, pausing for a second. "He's not the model—he's the author." She folded the quilt neatly and placed it over the arm of the sofa where she'd found it.

"There's no need to get waspish, Margarita." Hunt looked genuinely wounded. "I promise not to intrude on your territory."

Meg took a deep breath. "He's not my territory," she said calmly, "and you wouldn't be intruding. Besides—" she took the book from him and placed it on the piano bench "—I'm telling you the truth. Joe Alessio is really Angelique Moreau."

"Well, well, well." Hunt seemed quite enchanted with that bit of news. His eyes, which matched both the blue of his jumpsuit and his eye shadow, twinkled. "How fascinating."

"Don't go getting any ideas, Hunt," Meg warned, for Hunt had spent the morning telling her about his love life. "He may write under a female name, but that's as far as it goes."

Hunt let his lanky body droop in a parody of profound disappointment. "You're a hard woman, Margarita. I think you enjoy breaking my heart."

She gave him a playful sock in the arm. "You have no heart to break," she said with a grin. "You're wedded to your work, and you know it."

Hunt couldn't deny it. "I'm in the mood for a stroll through my plaster-cast paradise," he said, plunging his bony hands into the pockets of his jumpsuit and looking out the window at the sculptures populating the backyard. "You said you wanted the complete tour."

Meg glanced at the clock on the mantel; there was at least an hour until Joe would come down to start working on the annotated history of the KCC. Hunt had shown her some of his works in progress earlier that morning, and the taste had only whetted her appetite for more.

"Can I take some pictures?" She was already deciding on lenses and filters and shutter speed.

"For publication?"

She shook her head, and Hunt's long face seemed to stretch even longer. "Just for me," she said. "It's my way of keeping a journal.'' In the last year she'd shot literally hundreds of rolls of film in her effort to record life in all its forms and had done nothing with any of it save making prints to stash away in a dark closet.

"You're not Samuel Pepys, my dear," Hunt said archly, referring to the famous diarist. "We creative types do have to earn a living, you know. Or had you forgotten?"

"Why do you think I drive a limo, Hunt?"

Meg escaped to the hall closet where she'd stashed her camera equipment the night before. Not once since she'd put aside her ambitions for a career in photographic art had she felt guilty about her decision. Now, less than twenty-four hours after arriving at Lakeland House, she found herself feeling defensive, apologetic and totally unworthy of her place in Anna's heart.

The beautiful old house nearly crackled with creative energy. Hunt's unbridled genius, Joe's intense concentration and her own sharp need to define life in visual terms made the air sizzle with dreams. Danger was all around her, in her strong attraction to Joe and in the restlessness that was building inside of her.

She slipped into an old brown leather jacket she'd brought with her, slung her camera over her shoulder and fled to the relative safety of the backyard where Huntington Kendall IV and his imaginary village awaited immortality on film.

JOE GAVE UP TRYING to sleep around four-thirty. He'd tossed and turned and done everything short of self-hypnosis to trick himself into sleeping, but his mind refused to let his body drift away. Scraps of dialogue for Margarita and her pirate lover, pieces of description from remembered trips to Riviera hideaways and visions of Meg all vied for his attention until he gave up all pretense of rest and got up.

He took a cold shower, dressed in a clean pair of jeans and a fisherman's sweater and went downstairs to find Meg.

She wasn't in the library where he'd expected to find her or in the study where he'd left her. A copy of *Against All*

Odds was facedown on the piano bench, and he couldn't resist the urge to see what point in the amorous adventures of Eryk and Isobel she was up to. Millions of people read and enjoyed his novels, and that fact had never given him the slightest pause. He'd been hailed a brilliant storyteller, lambasted as a soft-core porn artist; he had received mountains of mail from fans and foes alike and managed to take it all in his stride. He probed deeply into a woman's heart and exposed the hidden layers of a man's psyche. Although his sensuously detailed descriptions of lovemaking were rooted firmly in his own experiences, the dangers of revealing himself took a distant second to creating a believable, moving book.

However, knowing that this one woman was reveling in his public fantasies and private dreams threw him off balance and made him vulnerable in a way he'd never before allowed.

He put the book back down on the piano bench and was about to leave the room when a flash of bright blue outside the window caught his eye. Darkness was gathering and the backyard was bathed in that lovely half-light the French called *l'heure bleu*. Huntington Kendall IV, looking like a Boy George clone, was cradled in the arms of his robust *Earth Mother* statue that stood near the cluster of white birch trees. His arms were wrapped around her indecently generous bosom, and he looked like a slightly wacky cherub.

Huntington was flinging his white silk scarf off his face and fluttering his Bette Davis eyes, while Meg slithered along the leaf-littered ground snapping pictures like a woman possessed. She rested her head on the *Earth Mother*'s bare foot and took a shot of Huntington feigning sleep. Joe watched while she crawled under one chubby plaster leg and angled upward for a topsy-turvy shot of the creator. He fully enjoyed the view when she moved a few yards away and bent over to take a shot from a child's eyes view. Her battered leather jacket rode up a bit, while her unbelted jeans rode down and the expanse of smooth skin revealed seemed as delectable as a ripe peach.

He opened the French doors and stepped out into the yard. Huntington noticed him right away—Joe could tell by the way the man's bushy red eyebrows raised—but Meg was so engrossed in her work that he doubted a nuclear blast would have penetrated the creative fog she was in. She kept up a running stream of commands, low voiced and urgent, that Huntington followed with amused resignation while Joe stood in the shadows and took it all in.

Only a hobby now? He watched the total concentration she brought to the process, noted the way her body and the camera seemed to work as one complete unit and shook his head. Whether Margarita Lindstrom knew it or not, photography was much more important to her than simply a hobby.

She stopped to change the film, and Joe stepped out of the shadows. "Isn't it getting a little dark to take pictures?"

Meg jumped as the sound of his voice broke the early-evening stillness. "Is it five o'clock already?"

Joe walked toward her, enjoying the slightly unfocused look in her dark eyes as she came slowly back to reality. "Ten after," he said, nodding to Huntington, who observed them from his perch on the *Earth Mother*'s shoulders.

She fumbled with a tiny metal canister and popped an exposed roll of film inside. "Sorry. If you just give me a minute, I'll be ready to go in."

"No rush," he said, putting out his hand to take some of her paraphernalia. "We're not on a timetable, are we?"

If possible, her eyes seemed darker, more unfathomable, than ever. "I guess we're not."

She handed Joe the canister and bent over to load a new roll into her Hasselblad. Her hair was parted down the middle and drawn smoothly back from her face into one intricate French braid that swung between her shoulder blades. Rather than a uniformly pale color, her hair was actually a mixture of flax and wheat, with shimmers of moonlight and sunshine that made it glimmer.

"Well," she said, slinging her camera back over her shoulder and looking up at Huntington, "I guess that's it for now. We're going to get to work."

"And here I thought you were already working, Meggie."

Joe's attention was riveted suddenly to Huntington. Meggie? Hunt leaped down from the statue's ample lap and met Joe's eyes.

"Meg is just doing this for fun, you know," Hunt said, watching Joe's face carefully.

Joe nodded. "I know." A ridiculous feeling of pleasure blossomed. His absurd request had been granted. "She told me."

Next to Joe, Meg shifted uncomfortably. "I don't know about you two, but I'm freezing." She glanced briefly at Hunt, then to Joe. "I'll start the coffee, and we can get to work."

Hunt, who had an appointment in town for dinner with an artist's model named Ivan, ambled toward the garage where he kept his ancient van stashed. Joe followed Meg inside the house.

"Thank you," Joe said when they reached the kitchen.

"For what?" Meg turned on the water to boil and took a coffee filter out of the drawer. Her expression was bland, unreadable.

"For granting me my stupid request."

"My pleasure." Her incredible mouth tilted in a half smile. "Besides, I'm not that fond of the name Margarita." She took the tin of coffee from the refrigerator and put it down on the counter. "The fewer people who use it, the better."

He began to tell her about the heroine of his work in progress, then thought better of it. The muse was too newly with him to risk frightening it away. Instead, he gathered up some spoons, mugs and a chocolate cake some divine providence had thoughtfully left in the refrigerator.

"Where will we be working?" he asked as he picked up the tray they had arranged. "The library?"

Meg nodded and grabbed some paper napkins from the kitchen table. "Anna had all the papers in the safe in her room," she said, leading the way up the short, narrow staircase that went to the library. "I found the information on essayists this morning and set it up in there for us."

She pushed open the heavy door to the library, and Joe preceded her inside. Both Anna's desk and the main table were littered with enormous stacks of papers and photographs, so he deposited the tray on a small pine side table near the bar. "You're very organized," he observed, gesturing toward the sharpened pencils and fresh new notepads stacked at the edge of the desk.

She nodded. "Disgusting, isn't it?"

"Unusual for a creative type," Joe said, pouring them each some coffee.

Meg took a mug from him and cupped her hands around it. "I think we've been over this territory before," she said, stopping his words cold. "How about we get down to work, Alessio?"

Alessio knew when he was up against a brick wall. "Good idea," he said. He could wait. Even a brick wall could tumble in a month.

"HE WEARS BLUE EYE SHADOW?"

Meg shifted the telephone from her right ear to her left and smiled at the unconcealed note of surprise in Elysse's voice. "Sometimes mauve," she said. "Depends on what he's wearing."

"I must say, this isn't at all what I'd expected to hear." Elysse had managed to wait six days before she succumbed to her curiosity that Sunday afternoon and called for a day-by-day report of Meg's first week at Lakeland House with Joe Alessio.

"I know what you expected to hear, Lowell. All you can think of is the fifty dollars you think you're going to win."

"I've already spent it," Elysse admitted. "I thought the firelight and scent of pine would have worked their magic by now."

If it weren't for Huntington's presence at Lakeland House, Meg had little doubt their magic would have worked, but she refrained from saying that to Elysse. The woman was too perceptive, and Meg was feeling too private to share such an intimate thought.

"What can I tell you, Elysse? There's been no magic and no romance."

"Are you certain?"

"Positive."

On the other end, Elysse sighed. "There's still three more weeks. I haven't given up hope."

"The eternal optimist."

Elysse laughed. "Just don't spend that fifty-dollar bill, Lindstrom. I may be vindicated yet."

They said goodbye, and Meg laughed at the thought of her eminently practical and logical best friend whose Ph.D. hid the soul of a true romantic. Elysse had wanted to know all the details of the first week at Lakeland House, and as Meg filled her in, she realized just how beautifully she and Joe worked together.

She picked up a stack of résumés on musicians but found it impossible to concentrate. Elysse's phone call had broken her momentum, taken her from reality to fantasy in just five minutes. Despite the fact she functioned best before eight A.M. and he only came alive after noon, and despite the fact she believed in orderliness and he thrived on chaos, the detailed job of fleshing out the history of the Kennedy Creative Colony was proving to be much easier—and more delightful—than she'd ever dreamed.

In just two days they had cataloged seventeen essayists who had been associated with the colony and developed full biographies, complete with quotes, for the five most important ones. By yesterday morning, they had already moved into tracking down all the novelists, Joe included, who had been part of Lakeland House.

Their days acquired a lovely rhythm that began with the breakfast Meg fixed each morning and flowed through hours of work right up until the dinners that had become Joe's specialty. Patrick had popped over twice for drinks, and Hunt had taken to spending a good deal of his free time with the two of them, talking with them sometimes and silently drawing at others, and in a way Meg was glad, because his presence forestalled any more of those probing, intensely personal questions Joe was prone to asking. She was already falling beneath the spell of creative seduction that Lakeland House had always cast over her—the number of rolls of film she'd shot in just seven days were a testament to that. Using the darkroom in the basement had thrilled her as much as a trip to Paris would thrill someone else. A part of herself she'd long denied was asserting itself again, and it excited her as much as it terrified her. If Joe were to add his own potent charm to it—well, she wasn't fool enough to think she'd last more than five minutes before she fell into his arms.

Now it was Sunday. They were well ahead of schedule and had decided to treat themselves to a morning of work and an afternoon of play. Lakeland House was quiet. The housekeeping service that had disrupted everything the day before was gone now, and even Huntington Kendall wasn't around. He was holed up in his studio, finishing the third in a planned series of four sculptures depicting laborers at work. He hoped to at least have the fourth sculpture in the beginning stages before he left the colony the following Saturday.

"How's it going?" Joe appeared in the doorway, carrying a huge sheaf of papers on essayists and journalists.

"This is a bit like playing God," Meg said, tossing one résumé and an eight-by-ten glossy of a woman harpist down on the reject pile. "I could get to like this feeling of power."

"Don't get too fond of it, Lindstrom," he said. The afternoon sun was slanting across the room, and it all seemed gathered in his beautiful green eyes. "You may not be so happy when we start working on the photographers."

Meg put her pen down and stretched. "Don't worry," she said, aware of the way her topaz sweater slid across her breasts as she moved. "I have no illusions about myself." She reached back and unbraided her hair, letting it go free over her shoulders. "I know I'm a footnote, nothing more."

Joe sprawled out on the Turkish carpet near her chair and slipped on the glasses she'd gotten used to seeing him in when he was doing detailed work. They were dark-rimmed and very masculine, and she rather liked the oddly intellectual look they gave to his decidedly nonintellectual body. He reached for a folder that rested under a pile of books scattered next to him. "The Institute of Photography's Rising Star Award, two years running; a photo spread in *Ms.* magazine; credits with *Lifestyles* magazine; an invitation to exhibit at the VonWageman Gallery in Los Angeles." He took off his glasses and gestured toward her. "Hardly a footnote, Margarita."

"And hardly Pulitzer Prize material." She stood up and leaned over, massaging the small of her back. "It's history, Joe. It's from another time of my life."

Joe propped himself up on one elbow and reached for the camera on top of the table to his right. "This isn't history," he said, cupping the intricate piece of machinery in the palm of his hand. "It's practically an extension of your arm."

"Some people meditate; some people take pictures. It's for relaxation, nothing more."

"Come on, Lindstrom, who are you kidding?" He gestured toward the papers scattered around. "I have it here in black-and-white."

"Ancient history, Joe."

She grabbed her camera away from him and put it on one of the bookshelves near the desk. Damn Lakeland House and the creative energies that sizzled through the halls and into her subconscious. She leaned over Joe and took a look at his watch. "Quitting time," she said. "We are now officially off duty!"

Joe gave her an "I know you're trying to change the subject" look but let it pass. "Any special plans for your afternoon off?"

Meg, who had assumed they'd spend their time together, hesitated. "Well, I . . ."

He grinned and removed his glasses. "Since your dance card doesn't seem to be filled, why don't you spend it with me?"

A most annoying sensation of relief washed over her, but she refused to acknowledge it. "I've always wanted to take the Cog Railway up Mount Washington," she said. "Unless, of course, you don't have the nerve."

"The hell I don't, but it'll never run in this weather."

Meg looked out the window at the heavy curtain of rain that almost obliterated the yard from view. "Antiquing?" she asked. "Sightseeing?"

He shook his head. "Not in the rain." He thought for a moment, then said, "Let's go into town."

"For what?" she asked. "All they have is a supermarket and an apothecary. Hardly enough to amuse us for a whole afternoon."

"Ah, Margarita. How unobservant you are." He put his arm around her and began leading her out of the library and into the hall. "There's a wonderful little shop right near the delicatessan that has the answer to all our problems."

"The butcher shop? A steak isn't going to amuse us for an afternoon," she said as he took their jackets out of the hall closet and tossed her the car keys. "Besides, I refuse to cook."

He put her jacket over her shoulders and hustled her out the door despite her loud protests. "Trust me, Margarita," he said with a laugh. "Trust me."

Chapter Seven

It ended the way it always ended—with honor overriding the petty concerns of individual people, with Humphrey Bogart looking deeply into Ingrid Bergman's eyes before she boarded that plane and went out of his life forever.

And, as always, it wiped Joe out.

The wonderful store Joe had taken Meg to in town was Video King, a place stocked with enough movie tapes to satisfy even an avowed videophile like him. Meg's eyes had widened at the selection of old movies, and he'd been horrified that she'd never experienced the pleasure of *Casablanca* or the charm of *Indiscreet* or the sexy thrill of *Charade*. Fully intending to rectify the alarming gaps in her movie knowledge, he'd piled up a stack of vintage films, then hustled her back to Lakeland House. There they poured some Cointreau, stretched out before the fire in the study and returned to a place he knew so well.

Beside him, Meg cleared her throat. "Hand me a Kleenex." Her voice was hoarse with tears. She was curled up on the floor next to him with her back leaning against his right side. She'd been there for the last two hours, and despite the fact *Casablanca* was his all-time favorite movie, he'd been hard put to follow the star-crossed romance of Rick and Ilsa while the warmth of Meg's body and the scent of her perfume mesmerized him.

"Here." He pulled a clump of Kleenex from the box on the arm of the sofa and handed it to Meg.

"Thanks," she muttered, wiping her red and swollen eyes. "Now I understand what all the commotion has been about." She blew her nose.

"It still holds up pretty damned well, doesn't it?" he asked, noting just how well she held up despite her tears.

She looked at him, fixing him with those dark eyes. "Thank you for making me watch it," she said. "I had no idea what I'd been missing."

He handed her another tissue, which she took with a grateful smile. "My pleasure. You realize, of course, that you'll never forget this afternoon." He paused, enjoying the look of curiosity on her face. "The first time you see *Casablanca* is like the first time you make love—you never forget who you were with."

"I hate to interrupt you two—" Huntington Kendall's reedy voice surprised both of them "—but pass the Kleenex over here." His skinny body was drooped over his sketch pad, and his great mournful eyes were wet with tears.

Joe chuckled and tossed him the box. "When did you get in here?" He'd been so swept away by the nearness of Meg and the intensity of *Casablanca* that he hadn't even noticed the other man's presence.

Hunt caught the box of tissues and dabbed at his eyes. "I came in when Bergman says to Bogey, 'Was that cannon fire, or is it my heart pounding?'"

Next to him, Meg began to cry again, and Joe gently stroked her hair off her face. "Don't cry, sweetheart," he said in an imitation of Bogart so bad that it made her laugh. "We'll always have Paris."

"No," she said. "Not for us. This—" she gestured toward Lakeland House around her "—is our Paris."

Joe knew she meant all the recipients of Anna's generosity when she said "our Paris" but for him Meg's statement went much, much deeper. Lakeland House was where he'd changed, but not in the way she meant. The vague yearnings for commitment, for a fulfillment that went beyond his work, beyond the boundaries of his imagination, had coalesced in the past few days. He'd fallen head over heels for the real-life Meg Lindstrom much as he'd already fallen for the fictional Margarita who haunted him each night when he worked. A look from her in the morning over coffee, the feel of her body against his while they watched the movie—anything at all was enough to send his emotions skittering around like billiard balls on a tilted table. The thought of starting his own family saga was a wonderful one indeed.

"Don't move!" Hunt moved closer to them and was quickly sketching both him and Meg while she rested her head against his shoulder, sniffling quietly.

"What are you up to?" Meg asked, starting to sit up.

"Don't move!" Hunt repeated, louder this time. "The light from the fire is hitting you both on the left side—" He paused. Quick scratching movements of charcoal on paper. "Ah! That's it. Perfect."

"Are we being immortalized?" Joe asked.

Hunt laughed, made a few more quick strokes, then handed the large sheet of paper to them. "Here," he said. "I call it—*Casablanca—Sunday Afternoon*."

Joe looked over Meg's shoulder at the sketch. *He's nailed you*, he thought, looking at the spare but evocative drawing. In a couple of deft strokes with a vine of charcoal, Huntington Kendall IV had pinned Joe's heart down on that white piece of paper and laid it bare for Meg's inspection. Love—or at least the beginning of love—was written all over his face.

Meg laughed, and he felt his face flame. "Hunt!" she said, pulling the sketch closer for inspection. "I'm surprised at you. You made Joe's chin much too long."

Hunt's painfully thin body seemed to puff up with outrage. "I'm not a literalist like you, Lindstrom," he said testily. "I interpret life—I don't simply copy it."

Joe grabbed the sketch from her and inspected it himself. Was it possible that she was blind to what Huntington saw only too well? "Well, you caught Meg just fine," he said honestly. "Especially her mouth."

"How could I miss?" Hunt said. "With Bergman staring at me on the screen and this beautiful replica in front of me, I'd deserve to have my artistic license revoked if I screwed up."

Hunt had said he wasn't a literalist, but Joe didn't believe it. Every angle and shadow on Meg's face was perfectly reproduced in the black-and-white sketch. The high, lovely roundness of her cheekbones, the way the shadows deepened the hollows below, the tempting sensuality of her full lips, which made it hard for him to keep from taking her in his arms and kissing her, were all there. However, those dark, intense eyes of hers were masked, the expression in them guarded—precious little of the inner Meg Lindstrom was going to be captured, not even by a pro like Huntington. At least not if she could help it.

Meg was busy sifting through the pile of videocassette tapes they had yet to watch. Joe handed the sketch back to Huntington, and the other man's eyes met his over the piece of paper. "I know," Hunt's look said. "She doesn't, but it's just a matter of time."

Joe stood up and stretched; his nerves were suddenly so tightly strung he thought he'd explode. "I'm starved," he announced to no one in particular. "Why don't we grab something to eat before the second part of our triple feature?"

Meg looked up from the videotapes. "There's beef bourguignonne, chicken curry and four-alarm chili in the freezer," she said, then grinned at him. "Unless, of course, you're going to treat us to your gourmet cooking."

"Spare us, Meggie." Hunt flipped to a fresh sheet of drawing paper and crouched down in front of Meg. "His gourmet frankfurters last night are still haunting me."

"If you two will let me break in for a moment," Joe said, "I was going to suggest we bring in pizza."

"Terrific," Meg said, her dark eyes laughing up at him. "Make it pepperoni."

Hunt threw a vine of charcoal at her. "Sausage, with extra cheese."

"I was thinking more like mushroom." Joe laughed as the other two yelled their protests. "All right," he said finally. "How about one regular and one pepperoni with extra cheese. That way everyone's happy."

"You're not," Meg said. "What about your mushrooms?"

"I'll live. Not having to cook tonight will compensate for it." He patted the pockets of his jeans, then remembered he had no car keys because he had no car with him. "Can we take the limo, Meg?"

She nodded and started to get up, but Hunt shook his head and pushed her back down with a hand on her shoulder. "I'll go," he said, putting his sketchbook down on the rosewood table near the window. "I haven't used the van in a few days—it probably needs a run."

Joe took out his wallet and pulled out a twenty-dollar bill. He handed it to Huntington, for despite the number after his name and Fortune 500 family background, he was forever broke. "It's on me," Joe said, meeting the other man's eyes. "It's the least I can do."

Hunt's wide mouth split into a smile as he looked from Joe to Meg, then back again. "That it is," he said softly. "Margarita's something quite special. Don't forget it."

"Don't worry," Joe said. "There's no chance of that."

Meg watched the sotto voce exchange between the two men with a great deal of curiosity. She hadn't been able to make out more than a few of the words spoken, but the knowing look on Hunt's face and the oddly vulnerable look on Joe's told her there was definitely something going on that she was not privy to. Ever since *Casablanca* ended, she'd had the distinct feeling that something had changed—some balance had been tilted.

The afternoon had been singularly splendid. How much did it take, really, to make a person happy? A wonderful movie, some Cointreau, a roaring fireplace—she stopped.

And Joe.

The rest of the accoutrements were fine indeed, but the component that turned a nice afternoon into a golden one was Joe Alessio. She liked the insightful way he saw beneath the surface of Rick and Ilsa to the deeper ramifications of love; she liked the way he knew when silence was better than speech; and damn it, she loved the way he smelled of brandy and after-shave and the way his body felt strong and solid when she leaned against him as they enjoyed the movie. At times it had been difficult to follow the story line, for her concentration was riveted on the way she could feel his heart beating against her back, the way its accelerated rhythm matched her own.

"What was that all about?" she asked as Hunt loped out of the room. "Some clandestine plans for the pizzas?"

"Nothing so interesting." Joe put out his hand. She took it, and he helped her to her feet. "I was just thanking him for venturing out into the darkness so we can eat tonight."

She laughed, achingly aware that they were standing just inches apart from one another and that her hand was still in his. "Where are my shoes?" she asked, looking down at her feet in their red-and-white striped socks. "I thought I put them by the piano."

"They're in the hall," he said. "With mine." That dazzling grin broke out. "I like you better without them."

"I'm still taller than you are, Alessio," she managed weakly.

With shoes on, Meg clearly had the advantage in height. With Meg shoeless, Joe's eyes were almost level with hers, and her advantage was not as great.

His thumb was stroking the inside of her wrist and that, combined with who knew how many glasses of Cointreau, was making it very hard for her to think.

"How tall are you?" he asked.

"Tall enough." Memories of high school dances spent holding up the wall threatened to surface.

Joe, however, seemed amused and not threatened in the slightest. "No matter," he said cheerfully. "I'll cut you down to size in no time."

"Didn't Spencer Tracy say that to Katharine Hepburn when they first met?"

"I have no idea," Joe said. "I thought I made it up."

"Better be careful," Meg warned. "You can get sued for stealing lines."

"Don't worry, Margarita," he said softly, the sound of her name on his lips turning her blood to warm honey. "The important lines are all original."

"You wanted Hunt to leave us alone, didn't you?" Her words surprised even herself. This was dangerous, uncharted territory, and well she knew it, but the fever was in her blood, and she couldn't stop.

"Smart lady, Margarita," Joe said, pulling her even closer to him so that her breasts grazed the front of his black sweater. "I didn't think I was being that obvious."

"You weren't," she said softly. "It was what I wanted, too."

He let go of her hand and drew her up against his body so that she could feel every muscle, every degree of heat desire was generating. Her arms were pinned at her sides, and there was no escaping the way he grew hard against her hipbone. Her breasts flattened against his chest, and a shiver ripped through her. An answering tremor rocketed through his body, and she smiled, resting her soft cheek against his roughened one so that he couldn't see the look in her eyes. She chuckled low. Obviously, Joseph Alessio had taught Angelique Moreau everything she knew.

He turned her toward him with his left hand, his fingers gentle against her chin and jawbone. "Private joke?"

Oh, God, she thought, looking at the open and vulnerable expression in his eyes. *Do I look like that when I look at him?* The thought of such naked emotion so fearlessly displayed was almost enough to make her turn tail and run. But this time she didn't want to run at all.

"Margarita?" His eyes never left her face; they devoured her.

She was going to make light of it, tell him how she'd been thinking about his alter ego, how she understood now where the sensuality so prevalent in his work came from, but desire burned inside her with a heat so quick and intense that she feared she'd go up in flames.

"Ahh, Joe." Her hands slid up his wide and muscular chest, across his shoulders, and plunged into his thick, shiny black hair. His hair was fine and silky beneath her suddenly sensitized fingertips except for the random white strands whose coarseness provided a tactile counterpoint. She was a visual person, but she closed her eyes as she brought her lips to his. Her life was so entangled with what she could see and how she could capture it for others that sometimes the visual was her only reality. Now the feel of him, the scent of him, the sound of his ragged breathing—these things were enough.

His hands were sliding up her hips, fingers splayed out against the bare flesh beneath her sweater, destroying her sanity inch by marvelous inch. She slid the tip of her tongue across his bottom lip—teasing, taunting—until he suddenly pulled her closer than she'd imagined possible and opened his mouth over hers to stake his claim.

She had started out the aggressor and now found herself fighting to keep her balance in a world that was defying the laws of gravity. His tongue was sliding over her teeth, exploring the moist and dark recesses of her mouth, making her hips arch toward him in a movement as fluid and natural as breathing.

He found her breasts, which were free beneath the loose confines of her sweater, and the sensation of his warm hands on her delicate skin made her moan softly into his mouth. Without hesitation, she slid her own hands beneath his sweater and quickly drew it up over his chest so his skin was bared and she could revel in the sensation of her own flesh moving against his. It was probably the first truly dangerous thing she'd ever done in her life.

Joe broke the kiss. Meg opened her eyes and gasped softly at the look of unbridled passion on his face. She didn't dare think about what she looked like to him. Her sweater was pulled up high above her waist, just exposing the lower slope of her breasts. She fought the instinctive urge to cover herself as his hot eyes seared their way across her body. He had that right, for she was finding it impossible to ignore the taut planes of his stomach, the incredible musculature of his chest. Joe drew his right hand through his tousled hair and fixed her with a look so filled with desire that her heart seemed to be pushing its way through her breastbone.

"He'll be back soon," Joe said, referring to Hunt.

Meg nodded. "I know." She reached out and gently ran a finger across his abdomen, relishing the tremor her touch set off.

Again that lopsided grin that took her breath away. "I couldn't wait for him to leave."

"I wish we'd ordered a seven-course meal," Meg said. Actually, she wished they'd ordered Italian food from Rome or Chinese from Beijing—anything to give them more time to explore the miracle they'd just discovered.

Joe laughed. "This isn't the first time we've done this, you know."

"I don't know what you mean."

His sweater had slipped back down to its normal position, covering the beauty of his body. She suddenly felt terribly exposed and vulnerable, and as if he could read her mind, he gently pulled her sweater back down over her hips, the edges of his fingers leaving fire where they slid across her skin.

"I've been making love to you, Margarita, every night since we met."

"Oh, Joe, please—"

He put two fingers over her mouth to silence her. She touched his slightly salty flesh with her tongue, savoring the taste of him.

"Just listen," he said, his voice smoky with urgency. "Unfortunately, we don't have time enough now for more than words...."

But what words they were.

He told her how he'd imagined her naked across his body, her long fine hair like strands of moonlight against the skin of his stomach. He told her how her eyes would widen when he entered her, how she would move beneath him as she welcomed him deeper inside. Her legs began to fold and she leaned against the back of the couch for support.

"Do you remember Friday night when I found you in the study hours after we said good-night?"

Meg nodded. They'd worked long and hard on the index of musicians and had retired to their individual rooms early. Meg had heard the intermittent sound of his typewriter until around midnight, when it stopped.

"I thought you'd fallen asleep," she said. "I went down to do a little more work."

"I heard you," he said, not coming closer but drawing nearer to her just the same. "That's why I came downstairs. I watched you before you even knew I was there."

She'd been sitting on the rug near the fire, the pale gold caftan she'd purchased in Morocco draped lightly over her body. A stack of typewritten notes was spread on the floor in front of her, and as she bent forward to examine them, the V of the caftan's neckline dipped, exposing the rounded top of her breasts. She'd felt Joe's presence before she saw him, and she delayed acknowledging him—the feel of his eyes roaming her body was too exquisite to give up.

"I knew you were there," she said with a smile. "I knew all along."

"Do you know what I was thinking?"

She shook her head. *Tell me,* she thought. *Tell me all.*

"In the firelight, your skin was the color of a ripe peach. I could see the tops of your breasts, and I wondered if you were the same color all over."

The thought of being naked before those incredible green eyes excited her more than she'd imagined mere thought could.

"I knew you were watching me," she whispered, wondering if she could survive the burning heat that threatened to sear her mind. "I wanted you to watch me."

In the fireplace a log shifted, and the sudden leap of flame was reflected in Joe's eyes. "I wanted more than to watch you. I wanted to push aside that caftan and let your breasts rest warm and smooth in my hands."

"You should have." Meg's voice was rough with desire. "I wanted to know how your skin would feel against mine."

Joe's laugh was husky. "Beautiful Margarita, you have no idea how near you came to knowing. If our eccentric friend hadn't suddenly come in—" He broke off his sentence and shook his head.

Meg's body tingled; vivid, detailed fantasies of Joe's body beneath her hands were making breathing difficult. "Hunt keeps the most bizarre hours," she said instead. "I hear him walking the halls some nights till three or four."

Joe chuckled. "He showers at midnight. I can hear him bellowing his version of *Pagliacci* until I feel like washing his mouth out with soap."

"You never know where he'll turn up."

"Or when." Joe moved closer to her, so close that she could feel the heat of desire rising around the two of them. "He won't always be here," he whispered, touching her ear with his lips.

Meg's breath caught at his touch, then slipped out in a soft exhalation. "I know," she said. "He leaves on Saturday night."

Joe cupped her face with his large, warm hands. "Should we give him an extension?"

"Not on your life."

"It won't be easy to wait." His hands slid down her neck until his thumbs rested in the pulse at the base of her throat. "I want to make love to you, Margarita."

"No," she said, thinking of his words on kissing and being kissed. "That's not enough." She slipped her hands beneath his sweater once again and ran her palms up the rippling muscles of his back. "I want to find out how it feels when I—"

"Doesn't anyone around here answer a doorbell?" They both jumped at Huntington Kendall IV's reedy voice from the doorway.

It was probably the closest Joe had ever come to contemplating murder. When Huntington popped up in the doorway, his skinny arms wrapped around two white pizza boxes, the thought of wringing Hunt's scrawny neck was uppermost in Joe's mind.

"Well, don't just look at me, you two," Hunt said petulantly. "Give me a hand! These damned things are hot as blazes."

Next to him, Meg immediately shifted into gear. She hurried over to the temperamental artist, took the two steaming boxes from him, then laid them down on top of the worktable on a bed of newspapers.

Joe was still suspended somewhere between desire and frustration.

"We could use some glasses for the wine," Meg murmured as she brushed past him, trying to snap him out of his daze before Hunt noticed what had been—or *almost* been—going on. Her dark eyes were still dreamy, and the way her mouth tilted in a secret smile told him he hadn't imagined the whole interlude.

IT WAS NEAR ELEVEN O'CLOCK when the final frame of Jimmy Stewart's classic *It's a Wonderful Life* faded from the TV screen. Although it was considered a Christmas movie and they were still two months away from the Yuletide season, its corny but powerful depiction of one person's value to his family and community was painfully on target.

"I wish it were that simple," Joe said, pushing the rewind button on the remote control and removing his glasses. "Family happiness isn't that easy to come by."

Hunt, who had been sketching Meg and Joe during the movie, said, "Tell me about it. My family cut me off without a cent when I decided to ditch law school and become an artist."

Meg, curled up in a corner of the couch, took a sip of brandy. "My family doesn't even know I'm an artist." She shook her head. "Can you imagine? They never even noticed when I won my first award."

Joe, who had been stretched out on the couch next to her, his shaggy head resting on her hip, sat up. That sparkle in the eye peculiar to writers was present, and she wondered what she'd said to cause it.

"Well, well, Lindstrom," he said with a grin. "So you finally admit you're an artist at heart and not a cabdriver?"

Her face burned with embarrassment. Damn the Cointreau, anyway! "I'm not a cabdriver," she protested. "I'm a chauffeur. There's a difference."

"Not much of one," Joe persisted, glancing quickly at Hunt, who was crouched down in front of them madly sketching.

"You should see my W-2 forms," she shot back. "There's one hell of a difference."

"You're evading the issue, Margarita," he said, more softly this time.

"That's my right."

He shook his head. "When you make a provocative statement, you owe it to your listeners to explain it."

She started to laugh despite her embarrassment and need to cover up. "Robert's *Rules of Order* again?"

"Maybe." He rested a hand on her knee. "Bare your soul. It will do you good."

"Wait just a minute, Alessio." Meg put the brandy down on a side table and sat up straight. "I haven't heard you volunteering any provocative statements."

He shrugged, those powerful shoulders of his pulling at the seams of his black sweater. "Writer's block," he said. "How's that for an excuse."

"Sorry." For a moment Meg wondered if he might not be telling the truth. That could explain the prolonged silence at his typewriter some nights. "Writer's block covers only creation—we're just asking for family facts."

He leaned forward, his elbows resting on his thighs, head hanging down. His profile was sharply delineated, the proud lines of his forehead and nose reminding her of statues she'd seen in Rome. No wonder Hunt loved to sketch him.

Hunt, however, had put his sketch pad down and was sprawled out on the floor at their feet. "I love family secrets," he said, his long and skinny frame stretching almost from one end of the Oriental rug to the other. "Can you believe I'm the black sheep in the Kendall closet?"

Meg and Joe looked at one another and burst out laughing. Hunt seemed more amused than annoyed. "Evidently you believe it," he observed. "No Kendall had ever ventured into any profession save law and medicine. I am a consummate disgrace to a long line of ambulance chasers and quacks." His narrow face was righteous with anger. "My dears, can you imagine this—they wouldn't even let me wear my turquoise jumpsuit to my sister Eleanor's wedding?"

"I'm astounded," Meg said, giggling. "I'll bet they even wanted you to take off your earring."

"I'm no fool, Meggie," he said. "Even I know you wear a matched pair to a wedding."

He went on to tell them how his family had cut him out of the inheritance that he had been due on his twenty-first birthday, a year ago. He went from heir to a fortune to being heir to a truckload of bills. A career in the art world could be heartbreaking at best. Trying to pay for the supplies he rather elaborate sculptures demanded was backbreaking, as well.

"How do you manage?" Joe asked. "How in hell do you manage to keep body and soul together?"

Hunt made a face and gestured at his bony frame. "The body's tough," he said. "Friends in the arts help keep the soul alive."

Meg was quiet. His words had reached a part of her heart she'd been trying to shield. Where she had liked Hunt before and been amused by his sardonic wit and bizarre sense of style, now she admired him for pursuing his dream. Joe apparently felt the same, for she saw a softening in his eyes as he looked at the younger man at his feet.

"And you want to show them, don't you, Kendall?" The intensity Meg had come to recognize as being part of his creative process gave his words more impact than they usually would. "You want to be the best damned success you can just to prove they were wrong."

Hunt threw his head back and laughed. "So right, but it's not as simple as that."

"It's never simple," Joe said. "Family dynamics seem to shape us all our lives."

"How about you?" Meg loosened her French braid and let her hair tumble over her shoulders in waves. Joe seemed spellbound by her movements, something she noted and enjoyed. "What about your own family dynamics?" Her own curiosity was almost a rival to his.

"Complicated," he said, pushing a lock of straight black hair off his forehead with the back of his right hand. "Complicated and classic. I'm the middle of seven kids; three sisters before me, two after—"

"Oh, God," Meg broke in. "The only son! Your cradle must have been lined with gold."

"Better check your math, Margarita," he said. "That only comes to six kids." He stood up, stepping over Hunt, and walked over near the fireplace. "We're forgetting the jewel in the family crown." He picked up an andiron and prodded the dying fire. Embers sputtered, and a tongue of flame shot up with a hissing, sizzling sound. "My brother Marco was born when I was five."

"With five sisters, I'm sure you weren't starving for attention," she said.

"In a normal family, maybe not. But Marco was the baby—and their last. He became the sun, and the rest of us revolved around him."

Meg, who understood all too well what he was saying, nodded. "What's he like?"

"Handsome, charming, talented—" Joe stopped and shook his head. "He's only twenty-eight, and he already has his doctorate in physics from Cornell."

Hunt had slid over to a spot about ten feet away from Meg and was furiously sketching her while she watched Joe.

"Surely you're not jealous," Meg said, getting up and walking over to where Joe stood near the hearth. She ignored Hunt's mumbled protests about changing his perspective. "My God, you have twenty-six books to your credit—you're an enormous success in your field. Your family must be so proud of you."

Joe arched a thick eyebrow at her. "Guess again, Lindstrom. It was bad enough when I was writing sexy Westerns and *Star Trek* novels—family sagas under a woman's name are completely beyond their comprehension."

She thought of what he'd told her a few days ago about his working-class family and their distrust of artists in general and writers in particular. According to Joe, the Alessio family respected those who worked with their hands and proved it by working up a good sweat in the process. Cerebral activities were highly suspect.

"I wouldn't think a Ph.D. would be high on their list, either." This time it was she who forced him to meet her eyes. "That was hardly physical labor."

"No, it wasn't," he admitted. "But it's respectable."

"Respectable?" Meg's voice went high with indignation. "What you do isn't?"

"Not to them," Joe said. "I don't get dressed each morning and go out to a regular nine-to-five job. I don't get regular paychecks from a fancy university. And most of all, I don't appear on television with Johnny Carson to talk about Halley's Comet. I'm just the one who buys them houses and bails them out of trouble."

"Your brother was on Carson?" Hunt sounded quite impressed despite his counterculture tendencies.

"Twice," Joe said. "Once with Carl Sagan and once alone."

"Well, what about you?" Meg persisted. "You must have been on TV, too. I mean, all those books! You must have done plenty of—"

Joe shook his head. "You're forgetting one very important fact, Lindstrom. I write under a woman's name." He leaned over and picked up a cigarette from the top of an end table and lit it. "When they ask to interview Angelique Moreau, they hardly want a jock with five o'clock shadow showing up in their studio."

"That's terrible," Meg said. "To write all these books—to even get on *The New York Times*'s best-seller list, no less!—and not even see your name on the cover." She shook her head in amazement. "I don't think my ego could cope with it. I'd want to see my name somewhere."

Joe stubbed his barely smoked cigarette out in one of the many crystal ashtrays scattered throughout the house. "I got my own back on this last one," he said.

"On *Against All Odds*?" she asked.

He nodded. "You may not see my name on that cover, but you see just about everything else of me."

A vivid picture of that highly erotic cover popped into her mind. She could remember every angle and plane of that gloriously dark, deliciously virile man on the cover who looked so much like Joe—

"My God!" she breathed. "You?"

"Me."

"You posed for the cover?"

"That's right."

"But that man was practically naked!"

"Not 'practically,'" Joe said. "Completely." His grin was wicked.

"Wasn't that a little bit...difficult?" All she could think about was the lushness of the heroine's body and the way his hands had been poised just above her ripe and welcoming flesh.

His grin widened. "Extremely."

"You look like you enjoyed it."

"I did." His eyes twinkled as he looked at her. "Immensely."

The alarm on Hunt's watch sounded. "Speaking of posing, it's time for me to go." He gathered up his sketch pad and pencils. "I have a model coming over in half an hour."

Joe glanced at his watch. "It's almost midnight, Kendall. Why not tomorrow morning?"

Hunt glanced at Meg and gave her an exaggerated wink. "There's a full moon tonight," he said, heading toward the hallway. "Ivan only poses on the night of the full moon. He—"

Meg laughed and put her hands in the air. "Spare us the details, Hunt, please! Have fun."

"I fully intend to, darling." He waved at them, but just before he went upstairs to get the keys to the studio across the yard, he turned to Meg and mouthed the words "I told you so."

"What was that all about?" Joe waited until Hunt disappeared upstairs before he spoke.

"He's gloating," she said. "He told me last week that you were the model on *Against All Odds*. I told him he was crazy."

"You didn't see a resemblance?"

Meg's visual memory was superb; again the cover in all its full-blown eroticism filled her mind. "Oh, I did," she said finally. "It just never occurred to me that it could be you."

He made a face. "I'll admit it's a flattering picture," he said, "but I'd think you would know it's me."

"Of course I would." She couldn't tell him that the reason she didn't dwell on the possibility he'd been the model was because although his jeans and T-shirts hinted at a splendid body, the thought of living closely with that much male pulchritude was a bit overwhelming. She'd always loved beauty in all forms, and she knew it could easily be her downfall.

"Now that I think of it," he said, "it looks more like Marco than me."

"Marco, the wonder boy?"

Joe's laugh was bittersweet. "One and the same."

"Not to me," she said. "I can't imagine anyone but you on that cover."

"You haven't seen Marco. Maybe then you'd feel differently."

"I don't want to see Marco. I'm satisfied with the original."

His smile was minus the sadness of a few moments ago. "I appreciate the kind words, ma'am. When I'm in my dotage, I'll look back upon them and be mighty grateful."

"Watch it, Angelique," she said with a laugh. "You're slipping back into your Western mode."

"Don't worry," he said. "The only time we're in trouble is when I fall back into my *Star Trek* days and start muttering, 'Beam me aboard, Scotty.'"

Meg got up and poured them each a bit more Cointreau. She handed Joe his glass, then curled back up on the couch. She watched as he took a long sip.

He sighed in appreciation. "Anna knew her liquor, didn't she?"

Meg took a sip of her own drink. "That she did. It's a wonder anyone accomplished anything here with a bar like she had."

"Don't be fooled by the mighty accomplishments we've been cataloging," Joe said, sitting down next to her on the couch. "For every artist or writer who made the grade, there must have been ten who ended up selling suitcases in Macy's."

Meg toyed with the rim of her glass. "Or driving limousines."

He nodded. "Or driving limousines." There was a long pause. "Why, Margarita?" She wondered how he made his deep voice sound so sweetly seductive. "What made you give it up?"

She put her near-empty glass down on the end table and sighed. "I lost it," she said quietly. "One day I was filled with burning ambition, and the next—" She snapped her fingers. "Gone."

He reached over and took her right hand, lacing his fingers loosely through hers and resting them together on his knee. "It's never that simple, Margarita."

"Of course it's not." She took a deep breath, marshaling her thoughts, trying to put complex and irrational emotions into a simple and rational form. "I suppose it's a case of family dynamics again. For you, there's Marco; for me, it was Kay."

"Your sister?"

Meg nodded. "Kay gave me a little Instamatic camera when I was about ten years old that started the whole thing. No matter how busy she was with her career, she was always there for me, always pushing me forward, always opening doors for me." She shook her head. "She was even responsible for my discovering the colony. When she died—well, success suddenly didn't seem so important anymore."

Joe squeezed her hand for an instant. "You were afraid you'd fail without her guidance?"

Meg looked at him, a half smile on her face. "Maybe I was afraid I'd succeed."

"I don't understand."

"Neither do I," she said. "Not really. All I can tell you is when I won my second award two months after Kay died,

I withdrew from professional organizations, stopped submitting my work and started traveling.''

"Maybe you were burned out," he said. "It happens."

"I was only twenty-three years old, Joe. I hadn't had time to even catch fire yet, much less burn out. It went deeper than that." It seemed paradoxical that the less gifted daughter would survive the brilliant star. The look of betrayal on her parents' faces had reinforced any vague feelings of injustice and guilt that Meg had been feeling at the time.

"You said we were talking about family dynamics. So far you've only mentioned your sister. What part do your parents play in this?"

"Very little now." She took her hand away from Joe's and wrapped her arms around her chest. The fire had dwindled, and she was suddenly chilled. "We were a classic example of how not to handle a tragedy. When Kay died, we fell apart—each of us in his or her own way."

"Where are they?"

"They retired to Arizona. I don't see them much."

"I'm sorry."

"I would be, too," she said, "if things had been different. Kay's death, though, only confirmed something I'd always known—they really had just one child, and that child was Kay. When she died, they lost everything."

How strange, she thought. How strange it was to be able to say those words and not feel her heart break. She'd always imagined she would shatter in a million pieces if she admitted the way things had always been—would always be—with her parents, but there she was, still breathing, still whole, sitting there on the overstuffed sofa in Anna's study, sharing the secret of her heart with a man who watched her with beautiful green eyes that absorbed her sadness and helped take away the hurt.

He moved closer to her, his hand resting gently on her shoulder, fingers moving against the back of her neck with long, soothing strokes.

"They still had you," he said, a tinge of anger coloring his words. "Why couldn't they see that?"

"There was never any contest," Meg said, and there wasn't. Kay had been a child of wonder and light, while Meg was a child of uncertainty and shadow. "Kay was everything I wasn't. She was courageous and confident, while I was solitary and insecure. For God's sake, she even died a heroine." She sighed. "All in all, I think my parents thought she was the better deal."

Joe's fingers were toying with a lock of her silky hair. Every now and then he would brush against her cheek with the back of his hand, and a tremor would rock her body. "How did she die?" he asked. "That is, if you don't mind talking about it."

Her pale eyebrows arched. "I've told you everything else," she said. "Why not this." She cleared her throat; despite her words, it was still hard to think of Kay's death. "Kay was working in Manhattan for the independent news station as their anchorwoman. A man whose daughter died during a simple appendectomy was holding hostages at the University Hospital. The SWAT teams couldn't get through to him. He said he'd release the hostages if Kay would come and interview him on camera."

Across the room the grandfather clock chimed midnight, and they could hear Hunt racing around upstairs, humming a tune that was indecipherable.

"Of course, the police were completely against it, but Kay was an idealist," Meg continued. "She didn't care that much about the story—she wasn't a street reporter any longer, and she had nothing to prove. But she did care about the hostages. She went."

"Did he release the hostages?"

Meg closed her eyes against the vivid images that had been forever captured on tape. "Yes. Kay was inside the administration office with him when he did. Everything would have been perfect except one of the SWAT team members decided to play hero. He rushed the gunman. The cops swarmed in, and there were shots—'' There was nothing more to say. Kay Lindstrom was the feature story that night on the six o'clock news.

Joe was quiet for a moment. "I think I remember that," he said. "But didn't she go under another name?"

Meg nodded. "Kay DeMartino," she said. "She used my mother's maiden name. They already had Pia Lindstrom on Channel Four, and I guess they didn't want to be outnumbered by the Swedish contingent."

"Your sister was good."

"I know." She forced a smile but knew it wasn't one of her best. "Tough act to follow, wouldn't you say?"

"Definitely," he answered. "But well worth the effort, if you're not afraid to stumble a few times before you can run."

How did you explain to someone as goal-oriented as Joe that sometimes stumbling is the least of your worries? Meg didn't believe in false modesty; from the very beginning she had known she was blessed with a particular vision and the talent to express that vision through fine-art photography. She had fully believed she would one day be as successful as Kay, and the pleasure she'd get in proving to her parents that their second daughter was a force to be reckoned with had fueled her ambition. Given her competitive nature, it was miraculous that she hadn't hated Kay, resented her every success, but she hadn't. Kay had pushed and prodded her, opened doors for Meg, then pushed her through. Meg had loved Kay, and when she was murdered, her powerful ambition was dwarfed by a grief so intense that she knew her heart had broken as surely as she'd heard her parents' hearts break.

The front doorbell sounded. The eight tones of the Westminster chimes rang out in the silent house, and they listened as Hunt galloped down the stairs, making more of a racket than such a skinny man had any right to. Through the half-closed door to the study, she and Joe were able to make out Hunt and another tall, skinny, almost identically bizarre man walk down the hall toward the kitchen.

"I guess they're not going out to the studio yet," Meg observed. She was glad their game of Truth had been interrupted.

"I guess not."

Joe's hand was wrapped around a lock of her hair, tangled in the waves left by the French braid she'd worn all day.

"I'm glad we rented those movies."

"Any excuse to see *Casablanca* again," he said.

"I suppose I should be going upstairs."

"I suppose so."

She looked at him, willing her dark eyes to let him see how much he was beginning to mean to her. "It felt good to talk about it," she offered. "I didn't think it would."

"You know I'd like to give you a lecture on achieving your full potential, don't you?"

"I had a feeling." His hand was resting against her cheek, and she closed her eyes briefly. "You're a pushy man, Alessio."

"So I've heard. I'd like to tell you to not be afraid to try again."

"You won't, though, will you?"

"Not if you don't want me to." His eyes told her it was against his better judgment.

She thought of the backward progress of their intimacy—from almost sharing their bodies earlier to sharing their souls tonight. "Sometimes just having someone listen is enough."

With one smooth movement he moved closer, enveloping her in an embrace that managed to be both terribly erotic and extraordinarily tender. It was Meg's undoing.

Her arms slid around his waist and slipped once again beneath his sweater. She needed to feel his warmth beneath her hands, feel the glide of his skin as she traced patterns on the strong muscles of his back. Desire loomed large, but it had become just one reason why he was becoming so important to her.

"I could stay here forever," she murmured, surprising herself with her words.

"Let's." He stretched full-length on the enormous sofa and pulled Meg alongside him, her body half resting on his. His mouth covered hers for a long, luxurious kiss.

The total body contact with him was shattering. There wasn't a part of her that wasn't in touch with a part of him. Her breasts flattened against his chest as they embraced; her hips seemed to curve around his to accommodate the desire she felt burning against her thigh; even their legs were entwined, feet resting on top of one another's.

They heard laughter from the kitchen and the muted sound of a radio playing. Meg made a move to extricate herself from this alarming tangle of limbs.

"I should go upstairs," she said weakly. "I meant to do a little darkroom work before I went to sleep."

"Don't go."

"You must have some work to do," she persisted. "I thought you like to work after dinner."

"We declared this a day off." His lips brushed against the side of her face. "Or don't you remember?"

"It's after midnight."

"I can't tell time."

She said nothing, just let herself glory in the feel of his body against hers. The truth was she could barely remember her own name at that moment. Her body was tingling with excitement that was just this side of torture. Beneath his sweater, she slid her hands up his abdomen and ran them over his thick mat of chest hair, enjoying the feel of his flat but taut nipples beneath her palms. "We said we weren't going to make love until Hunt left Lakeland."

His fingers had slipped inside the waistband of her jeans and were pressed against the curve of her derriere through her silky panties. "We're not," he said. His voice sounded raw with desire. "But if you keep doing that . . ."

She stopped the sensual attack and smoothed his sweater back down over his chest and stomach. Instead, she cradled his face in her hands and let each of his features imprint themselves forever in her mind. "I should go upstairs," she said at last. "I would hate for Hunt to find us in a compromising position."

Her jeans hadn't afforded him much room to explore. Now his hands held her by the waist, his large tanned fingers almost spanning it. "I don't think it would bother Hunt very much."

She listened to the laughter and music coming from the kitchen. "Probably not," she admitted. "But it would bother me."

Joe nodded. "Not in the best Lakeland tradition?"

"It's not that exactly. I just don't want the work we're doing here to be criticized because of our relationship. I want more for Anna." She stopped, trying to read the expression in his eyes. "Am I making any sense at all?"

He sat up and helped her straighten her sweater and smoothed down her hair. "Very good sense, Margarita. We can wait."

The fire had died out, and the only light came from the hurricane lamp across the room. Joe snuffed the candle, and as the light flared before it died, he seemed sultry and mysterious, the sharply angled cheekbones and jaw jutting out against the soft darkness. He was beautiful to her, and she longed to tell him.

"It won't be easy," she said instead as he took her hand to leave the room. "I want you very much, Joe."

He placed her hand where she could best understand how much he wanted her. His heat and power surged through her body and fired her imagination.

"Can you feel how much I want you, Margarita?" He was watching her with those incredible eyes that made her insides ache with longing. She nodded. "When we're together, there will be no holding back. I promise you that."

They went upstairs and retired to their separate rooms, hoping work could help sublimate desire.

That night the lights at Lakeland House were on till nearly dawn.

Chapter Eight

Despite the fact that he hadn't fallen asleep until nearly dawn, Joe was awake by 8:00 A.M. He was too charged up with energy, both sexual and creative, to be able to lie there in his narrow bed and sleep.

So he got up and took a quick cold shower, dressed and went downstairs. He doubted if Meg was up—no sane person would be after such a late night—and the idea of surprising her with a luxurious breakfast rather appealed to him.

Meg, however, had beaten him to the punch.

"Good morning," she said, turning from the stove where bacon sizzled on the grill. "You've ruined my surprise." She gestured toward the butcher-block table where a wicker tray, set with the best china and garnished with a red rose in a crystal bud vase, rested. "I was going to serve you breakfast in bed."

"What happened to our daily dose of cornflakes?"

"I thought we needed a change."

"Some change," he said. "I'm impressed."

She brushed a strand of hair off her face with the back of her hand and smiled at him. Joe felt that smile in every cell of his body. To him it was more brilliant than the sunshine that seemed netted in her hair as she turned back to the stove. She was wearing a pair of khaki pants and a red Shaker knit sweater with the sleeves pushed up past her elbows. Her feet, as always, were shoeless. Instead of her favorite red-and-white-striped socks, today she wore a pair in a shade of neon yellow that made him wince.

"Have you been taking fashion lessons from Hunt?" he asked, motioning toward her Day-Glo socks.

Meg laughed. "It looks that way, doesn't it?" She put a strip of bacon on a mat of paper towels to drain. "Actually, I'm not much of a shopper, but I saw these in Macy's before I left and couldn't resist. They're really something, aren't they?"

Joe put his hand up as if to shield his eyes from the glare. "You could say that."

"You don't know what it's like to dress in a sober black suit every working day," she said as she broke three eggs in a bowl and beat them with a whisk. "When I'm on my own time, I tend to go a little color mad."

It doesn't have to be that way. He thought of her photography and all she'd given up. He wanted to tell her she was crazy to waste herself behind the wheel of a limousine, but at this point it was still none of his business. He bit back his words.

Meg was fussing with the eggs and mumbling beneath her breath about it all being harder than it looked, and it wasn't difficult to see that her concentration was elsewhere. Joe took the plates and silverware off the tray and set things up on the table, arranging the rose smack in the center. He stashed the tray behind the kitchen door.

"Sit down," she said, grabbing the toast from the toaster oven and pulling a stick of butter from the refrigerator. "Everything will be ready in a second."

Joe did as he was told. He settled himself down on one of the maple kitchen chairs and watched her as she turned the heat off under the eggs, scraped butter across the cooling toast and cursed softly as she brushed against the plate that held the draining bacon.

"Plates," she said. "Where are the plates?"

"Here." He handed her the two china dinner plates.

When they worked together, she was the essence of efficiency; she kept detailed lists, set a work schedule for them and made sure they stuck to it. She even flew through the tedious task of indexing material, finishing list after list while he was still trying to remember if P came before R. However, this Meg—the queen of chaos—was more to his liking. He thoroughly enjoyed watching her disorganized way of preparing a simple breakfast, listening to her mutter curses at the bacon as her dark eyes flashed in counterpoint to her cool blond beauty.

So it wasn't at all difficult for his mind to leap ahead a few steps and conjure up a more permanent, but just as wonderful, scene. They were married—or maybe living together, but his domestic fantasy had always included marriage—and Joe was just finishing his work on the Vietnam book that was going to make his name, his *real* name. Meg had, of course, given up the limousine driving and was riding on a wave of success that culminated in a story in *Time* magazine. Lakeland House had become their permanent home, and it was just a matter of time until—

"Joe!"

He jumped. Meg was sitting in the chair opposite him, her fair brows knotted in a scowl.

"I don't think the meal looks *that* bad."

He blinked, reluctant to let his daydream slip away. A plate of scrambled eggs, a bit brown around the edges, sat in front of him. Two pieces of bacon, slightly underdone, framed the right side, and triangles of toast, mangled from too-cold butter, framed the left. A balanced composition, yes, but appetizing? That was another matter.

"Sorry." He smiled and picked up his fork. "I was just thinking about a story I'd like to work on." No lie there.

"I think I know where I went wrong," she said, watching him as he put a forkful of scrambled eggs in his mouth. "I shouldn't have waited for everything to be finished before I served."

"Care to run that by me again?" Joe unobtrusively maneuvered a piece of eggshell to one side of his mouth to be disposed of when Meg wasn't watching him quite so closely.

Meg pushed her own breakfast plate away from her and leaned her elbows on the table, resting her chin in her hands. "My problem was my timing," she said. "I should have served the breakfast in three courses—bacon, eggs, then the toast." She grinned at him. "Sort of appetizer, entree and dessert."

"What about after-dinner coffee?"

She closed her eyes and groaned, and he quickly hid the eggshell in his napkin. "Damn it all!" She jumped up and turned the kettle on to boil. "I'm beginning to think you have to be a time-and-motion expert to get breakfast on the table."

He took a bite of toast. "Back to cornflakes tomorrow?"

She rolled her eyes. "Back to cornflakes."

He took another bite of egg. "What's on the work schedule for today?"

She brightened up. "We're attacking that stack of novelists, Joe. I can't wait to see all your credits in black-and-white."

He thought of some of the sleazier publications he'd written for earlier in his career. "You may not like some of them," he cautioned her. "Six stories sold to *Hot Stuff* magazine and three to *Cheap Love* are not exactly a credit to the Kennedy Colony."

"We'll be selective," she promised. "We'll only mention the finest literary quarterlies," she said, then paused. "And *Star Trek*, of course."

He shook his head. "You're a cruel woman, Lindstrom. I didn't know you had it in you."

"Stick around a little longer, Alessio," she said, getting up to pour the boiling water into the coffee maker. "There's a lot you don't know about me."

Tell me everything, he thought. *There's nothing about you I don't want to know.*

"Did you work last night?" he asked. "I thought I heard you in the hallway."

She glanced at him, dark eyes twinkling. "I heard your typewriter."

He grinned. "Trouble sleeping?"

Those limitless eyes swept over him. "You could say that."

Last night, the night of magic and promises, vibrated in the air between them.

"I printed up scores of photos," she continued, getting up to pour the coffee. "You should see the series I have on Hunt."

"You have to show me."

"I made up a copy of the set for each of us. They'll be dry in a couple of hours."

"Where *is* our resident genius? I didn't hear him come back up to bed last night."

She put a mug of coffee down next to his plate, then took her seat again. "He came in about an hour ago." Her mouth curved in a smile. "I think he and Ivan had a falling-out. Hunt's sketch pad was in tatters. I'd hate to see his studio." She gestured upstairs. "He's probably sound asleep right now."

Joe swallowed some cold toast, then pointed at Meg's own untouched plate. "Eat up. We have a lot of work to do today."

She looked at the food and made a face. "You must be kidding. I don't have to worry about hurting my own feelings." She patted his hand. "It's all right, Joe. I know I'm a rotten cook."

He sighed in relief and put his fork back down. "I wouldn't go that far," he said, trying to be kind.

"Then how come you're turning a little green around the edges?"

He was trying to think of a diplomatic answer when the hall phone rang. "Saved by the bell!" He pushed his chair away from the table. "Pour me another cup of coffee while I get the phone, okay?"

"If it's Patrick, tell him dinner is still on for Friday night," she called after him.

He picked it up on the fourth ring.

"I was about to give up, Joseph."

Joe glanced at his watch—8:15. "A little early for a social call, isn't it, Renee?" He had just spoken to her the other day on business, and things seemed under control.

"For a social call, it would be," she answered, not zinging him with one of the one-liners she was justly famous for. "This is business."

Immediately he thought of the five-page outline he'd submitted before leaving for Lakeland. "Audrey hates the story. I have to come up with another outline." Please, God, not another outline. He'd been lucky enough to come up with the one he did.

Renee laughed. Some of his apprehension lessened. "Ever the optimist, Joseph. As a matter of fact, I have good news for you." She paused. "Audrey is thrilled with *Fire's Lady*. She wants more."

Joe leaned against the wall, breathing for the first time since Renee began to talk. "She'll get it," he said. "Things are really starting to roll." Meg—watching her, listening to her—seemed to trigger his creativity in a way it hadn't been triggered in months. "I should have six chapters to show you when I get back."

Renee paused, then said, "Well, that's terrific, Joseph, but I'm afraid Audrey needs something right now."

"Right now, as in when I get back home?"

"Right now, as in tomorrow afternoon."

He was quiet for a few moments, thinking of the chapters he'd worked on and the varying stages of completion they were in. None of them were as polished or as professional as they would be when he finished the manuscript, but neither were they an embarrassment.

"How much does Audrey need? I have four, maybe five chapters I could send you."

"Make it five."

A reprieve. "Terrific," he said. "I'll pack them up and send it Express Mail. You'll have it before noon tomorrow."

Renee laughed. "Great idea, Joseph. Now if you'll just send yourself to me Express Mail, we have it made."

A few pungent curses nearly popped out. "What in hell do you need me there for? We both know Audrey's only interested in my work."

"Remember that clause we fought so hard for in your last contract, the one that gave you the right to approve the ad campaign?" Renee's voice had the tone a parent would use on a recalcitrant child. "Well, the ad campaign for September is gearing up already. Audrey needs your okay on a storyboard."

"That's almost a year away. Can't it wait until I'm finished up here?" *I don't want to leave her,* he thought. *Not now.*

"Sorry, friend. I put them off as long as I could. The big guys are getting restless." Renee quickly explained that it would be just a twenty-four-hour swing through town; he could be back in New Hampshire by dinner the next night.

There was no point in arguing. "Okay, okay," he said finally. "I'll make a few calls to the airlines and let you know when I'm coming in."

"No need," Renee said. "I've already done it. You're flying out at five o'clock this evening."

"Pretty sure of me, weren't you?" He wasn't sure whether to be amused or annoyed.

"You're a professional, Joe. You know when to fight and when to acquiesce."

"A professional," he said ruefully when he hung up the phone. Sometimes he wished he were less professional and more concerned with the other parts of his life that were lying fallow, barren of any new growth. He would go down to New York as Renee asked, but he'd damned well be back in New Hampshire before Meg had a chance to break free of the spell that had woven itself around them both last night.

That was something he owed to Joe Alessio, not Angelique Moreau.

NOTHING IN LIFE lasts forever—not even a perfect day. As soon as the phone rang, Meg knew deep down in the pit of her stomach that this blissful idyll she and Joe had been enjoying was about to come to an end. The real world beckoned once again, and now she was standing in the hallway, watching for the taxi that would whisk Joe off to the airport.

Meg hated the fact Joe was leaving with a ferocity that took her totally by surprise. Working quietly in the library after breakfast, they had both tried to pretend it was an ordinary morning, but she was sure he felt the tension in the air the same as she did.

Last night they had come so close to one another—and not just in the physical sense—that having Joe called back to town was akin to tearing out a piece of her heart. She found it hard to believe she was the same woman who had boasted to Elysse that she managed to keep her heart intact for twenty-six years and was sure—oh, so sure!—she'd manage for another month.

Famous last words. In two short weeks, Joe had managed to come closer to knowing the real Meg than anyone else ever had. The day-to-day intimacy created by their work on Anna's history of the Kennedy Colony, coupled with her own memories and dreams, was a potent addition to Joe's keen intellect and physical beauty. The combination left Meg vulnerable—just how vulnerable she had discovered the previous night. Knowing they were going to make love when Huntington left Lakeland House had added an edge to their friendship, forging a sizzling sexual bond that was a perfect complement to their finely tuned working relationship.

All in all, it was a dangerous combination for a woman who had never given a thought to falling in love.

A horn beeped in the driveway. Meg's heart dropped to her feet.

"Cab's here!" she called up the stairs just as Joe appeared with his overnight bag, stuffed with manuscript pages and a change of clothing.

"I wish you'd let me drive you to the airport," she said when he came downstairs. "We could have had more time together."

He leaned over and kissed her forehead, her eyes, her lips. "We'll have all the time we need, Margarita," he said. "It's pretty deserted around here. I didn't want you on the roads late."

She laughed. "You forget something, Joe. Being on the road is my job."

He started to say something, then obviously stopped himself, a fact for which she was grateful.

"Do you have everything?"

"I think so. Manuscript, toothbrush—" He looked at her. "What about those pictures you took?"

"The ones of the three of us?"

He nodded.

"I put them in my room."

The taxi outside honked its horn again.

"Get them," Joe said. "I'll stall the taxi."

"Why should I get them? They'll still be here when you get back."

He touched the side of her cheek with his hand. "It's a long plane ride," he said, smiling.

"It's not. It's no more than an hour and a—"

"Humor me." He opened the front door and hollered down to the taxi to hold on a second. "Hotel rooms are barren. Give me something nice to look at."

She hurried up the stairs to her room. Thank God she'd already separated the photos into three complete sets. Quickly, she slid one set into a brown envelope and rushed back downstairs.

"Here," she said, handing the envelope to Joe. "Enjoy your trip."

"I won't. I'll be miserable as all hell."

"Good." She smiled and kissed him briefly on the lips. "That's as it should be."

"I'll miss you."

"I should hope so." The taxi's horn blared, one impossibly long blast. "You'd better go," she said. "Otherwise I think he's going to drive right up here and mow us down."

"I'll see you tomorrow night," Joe said, heading out the door and down the pathway. "I'll be here by six o'clock."

Meg shivered in the cold late October wind. "I'm counting on that."

She stood in the doorway and watched as the taxi headed down the driveway toward the gates at the bottom of the hill. For the last two years, she'd picked up and moved when and where she liked, been serenely independent—it was always Meg who left, Meg who had the plane to catch, Meg waving good-bye as someone else stood in the doorway.

And now here she was waving good-bye to a man she'd known for less than a month and feeling as if her heart were following him, leaving nothing but an aching void in her chest where it once had been.

BY EARLY AFTERNOON Meg had indexed all of the poets and essayists and drawn up bio sheets on the top three in each category. It was the kind of detailed work she enjoyed— mechanical, relentlessly logical and certain to drive someone like Joe crazy. At around three o'clock she stopped working, bleary-eyed and starving, and headed into the kitchen. The refrigerator yielded no surprises—tuna salad, hard-boiled eggs and bologna, none of which appealed to her. Hunt, fighting the aftereffects of an obviously difficult night, had slept until nearly two, then gone out in search of Ivan.

The thought of eating hard-boiled eggs alone was depressing—almost as depressing as the empty way the house felt without Joe's presence. Impulsively, she grabbed her car keys from the countertop, raced through the hall to snatch her battered leather jacket from the closet and headed into town to see Patrick McCallum and invite herself to lunch.

Patrick, of course, was the soul of tact and charm. If he'd been at all surprised to see a blue-jeaned blonde in a jacket that had seen better years pop up in his office, he never let on.

"I'm glad you're feeling so chipper, Margarita," he said as he led her to a booth near the window in a charming coffee shop a few yards away from his office on the main street in town. "Our New Hampshire weather seems to be agreeing with you." Indeed it did. Less than two weeks before, Meg had seemed the same serious, beautiful woman he had met the day of Anna's funeral. However, today she seemed to be blooming with good health and good cheer; her exotically dark eyes twinkled with a thousand stars. It made him feel good just to look at her.

"Your New Hampshire weather is superb," she said, glancing out the window at the brilliant sunshine that bathed the woods across the road. "You should have it patented."

A gingham-clad waitress handed them each a menu, and Patrick's basset-hound face lit up in one of his quite extraordinary smiles, a smile that had more to do with Margarita's happiness than the navy bean soup that was the lunchtime special.

"How is the project progressing?" he asked after they placed their orders and the waitress bustled away.

"Beautifully. I'd say we're about two-thirds of the way finished."

"With the whole project?"

She nodded. "Once we caught on to the way Anna had been evaluating the material, we really started to fly."

His blue eyes watched her intently while the waitress deposited Meg's tomato juice in front of her. "So it would seem." She took a sip of juice, and his gaze never wavered. "And how would you and Joseph be getting on?"

He could see that his question surprised her. "Quite well," she said. "I'm good at cutting through the hyperbole and getting to the heart of the material. Joe knows how to take the facts I'm left with and turn out a brilliant essay."

"Sounds like you two are well suited." The waitress placed a cup of coffee and a Danish in front of him and a cheeseburger and fries in front of Meg.

"Well, we haven't come to blows yet," Meg said with a laugh, "if that's what you mean."

Of course, that wasn't what Patrick meant at all, but as soon as he saw the lovely young woman direct her full and undivided attention to the enormous cheeseburger, he knew the answer just the same, and it didn't surprise him at all.

"Where is our Joseph today?" he asked, adding some cream to his coffee. "Would he be under the weather?"

Meg shook her head and dabbed at her lips with the edge of her paper napkin. "He's fine. He was called down to Manhattan on business. He'll be back tomorrow evening."

Patrick noted the way her cheeks reddened slightly as she spoke. "Good, good," he said between sips of coffee. "I wouldn't want him to be missing our farewell dinner Friday night."

"Oh, he'll be there." Meg said, twirling the straw around in her glass of Tab. "He gave me his word." Her lips curved around the straw in a secretive half smile, and for a brief instant Patrick found himself wishing he could call up Anna Kennedy and tell her that her matchmaking was working.

He looked down at his coffee cup, hoping the twinkle in his eye wasn't as bright as he feared. Oh, yes, he was *quite* sure Anna's matchmaking was working.

NEW YORK SEEMED DIRTY, dismal and terribly depressing to Joe as his cab snaked its way from the outskirts of the borough of Queens to midtown Manhattan.

Usually he welcomed the sight of Manhattan after an absence, just as he welcomed the sight of the ground below his window on a plane flight. However, this time the sadness he felt as the glorious countryside of northern New Hampshire tilted and dropped beneath his plane as it took off had stayed with him, and even the sight of the UN building or the twin towers of the World Trade Center couldn't cheer him up.

He'd told Meg he didn't want her to take him to the airport because he worried about her on the deserted roads. That had only been a half-truth; actually, he'd feared if she had been there at the airport when it came time for him to board his plane, he'd rip up his boarding pass, grab her hand and race back to Lakeland House and the tranquillity he'd found there.

"Damn stupid SOBs." The cabdriver, a skinny man with a red Afro that grazed the roof of the car, leaned on the horn. He met Joe's eyes through his rearview mirror. "Where in hell are the cops when you need them? Can you answer me that, pal?"

Joe, of course, had no answer, and from the look of the traffic surrounding them, neither did anyone else. Gridlock, the urban commuter's nightmare, had them trapped near the entrance of the Midtown Tunnel, which wound beneath the East River and joined the boroughs of Queens and Manhattan.

He was already an hour late for his dinner meeting with Renee and destined to be a lot later. The cabbie spread a copy of the *New York Post* across his steering wheel and was engrossed in the sports section. He obviously wasn't sweating the situation, and with a shrug, Joe decided to give up and wait it out with as much good grace as he could muster.

He opened his briefcase and took out the series of thirty pictures Meg had given him before he left Lakeland. He'd been too hyper on the plane to be able to get beyond his appreciation of the clarity and wit apparent at even the most casual glance. Now, however, he had all the time in the world to enjoy them.

He glanced out the window and saw two uniformed cops clambering over the hoods of a line of taxis, fighting their way to the center of the confusion. He slipped on his glasses and flipped to the photo where Margarita was looking full into the camera, her dark eyes reflecting the sun and shadows of that late October day. His memory leaped at the thought of how she'd felt in his arms not twenty-four hours ago.

All the time in the world wouldn't be time enough for all he wanted for them both.

OLD MOVIES WERE NO FUN to watch alone, so Meg retired to her room around eleven o'clock. She was just about to drift off to sleep when the phone at her bedside rang.

"Did I wake you, Margarita?"

"No." She cleared her throat, grinning into the darkness. "I'd just turned out the light."

"A little early, isn't it?"

"Depends on your point of view," she said. "A little late to call, isn't it?"

His low chuckle sent shivers radiating outward from the center of her body. "I thought you and Hunt would stay up late tonight and watch *Gone with the Wind*."

"I tried, but it was just no fun alone."

"Where's our young friend?"

She turned over on her right side and twisted open the blinds so she could gaze out at the moon-swept yard below her window. "Would you believe Ivan came back to pose for him tonight?"

"I thought he only worked on the night of the full moon."

"He made an exception." She laughed softly. "I guess the night after the night of the full moon is acceptable, too."

"Artists!" Joe said with mock exasperation. "Crazy, eccentric—"

"Moody, arrogant—"

"Beautiful, sensual—"

"And wonderful liars."

They laughed, and she closed her eyes, conjuring him up in the darkness of her room. *Hurry back. I want to feel your arms around me.* "How did your meeting with your agent go tonight?"

"What meeting?" He sounded exasperated in earnest now. "My plane was late, I got stuck in gridlock on both sides of the tunnel, and the hotel couldn't find my reservation. By the time I got to the restaurant, Renee had left." He groaned. "Cars should be banned from the island of Manhattan."

"Tell me about it," she said. "I spend half my workweek driving through Manhattan. It takes a will of iron to get out of there without committing homicide."

"Either a will of iron or a tank."

She was aware they were talking all around the real purpose of the phone call. His need to connect with her again was as real, as intense, as hers.

"The house is very empty without you," she said, keeping her voice light and breezy. "I missed your lunchtime conversation so much that I inflicted myself on Patrick this afternoon."

She told him a bit about their pleasant hour together and the plans Patrick had made for Hunt's farewell dinner.

"I'm looking forward to Friday night," he said quietly.

"So am I."

"I looked at the photos you gave me."

She wished she could see his face; she was unable to tell anything from his tone of voice. "And?"

"I don't know a hell of a lot about photography, but they're sensational, Margarita."

"Damning with faint praise?" Despite her words, she knew instinctively Joe said little he didn't mean.

"Listen, I don't know f-stops from bus stops, but I do know art when I see it."

Her body grew so warm from his praise that she threw the blankets aside and sat up. "Do you like the ones of you?" She was particularly fond of a shot of Joe with his arm around one of Hunt's alternative citizens, which was perched way up in an old oak tree in the backyard.

"I like the one of us."

"I didn't mean to give that one to you." *Cover up, Lindstrom!* Most people saw only themselves in photos. Just because she thought she looked like a love-struck teenager in it didn't mean Joe would notice. "I hate the way I photograph."

"I don't. At least not in this one."

He'd noticed. Meg's temperature went up another few degrees. She got out of bed, and balancing the phone between her ear and shoulder, opened the window wide. She'd welcome a blast of Canadian air to cool her blood down to a more reasonable level.

He was talking, but it took a couple of seconds before she zeroed in on what he was saying. "... So I should get there by dinner tomorrow night."

"Should I make us dinner?" She thought of her calamitous scrambled eggs and laughed out loud.

"I'll eat on the plane."

"Airplane food is notoriously bad, Joseph." She was smiling broadly. "Are you sure?"

"I'll take my chances with it."

"It's late," she said. "You'd better get some rest."

"Promise me you won't meet me at the airport tomorrow. I already have a cab reserved."

"I promise."

"Sleep well, Margarita."

She wrapped her arms around her waist and shivered. The sound of his voice was enough to curl her toes.

After they hung up, she stood at the window and looked down over the tops of the trees and the bright lights of Hunt's studio across the yard. There were other, more urgent promises they had made to one another on the night of the full moon. Promises she was eager to keep.

THE SEAT-BELT SIGN flashed off, but Joe was no fool. He wasn't about to loosen his only ties with safety until that ridiculously little commuter plane he was in landed in New Hampshire.

Beneath the smog and the gathering dusk, New York lay dark and dangerous, and he was glad to be leaving it far behind. More and more, the guerrilla tactics necessary to urban survival were reminding him of his time in the jungles of Vietnam where you couldn't tell friend from foe. What a pleasure it was to leave granite and glass behind. New Hampshire's mountains and lakes had never seemed more alluring than they did now that Margarita Lindstrom waited for him there.

After their long and elliptical conversation last night, he'd been too keyed up to sleep but too tired to work. Instead, he spread the photos she'd given him out on the pale beige bedspread and marveled at her sense of line, the way she played tricks with perspective and contrast until her black-and-white pictures of Hunt and his imaginary village turned into what Joe imagined Alice would find through a twentieth-century looking glass.

He couldn't help but concentrate most of his attention on the photos she was in; the beautiful structure of her face and shimmering hair drew his eye back again and again. So when he showed Renee the photos over breakfast that morning, he was surprised when her eye was immediately drawn to the sequence that depicted Hunt completing work on a sculpture showing three little girls in 1950s party clothes sitting on a park bench.

"Joe!" Renee's voice had been incredulous when she picked up the final print. "Where have you been hiding this woman? She's phenomenal!"

He leaned over to see which photo had garnered such a reaction from his normally coolly discerning agent. "Bizarre, isn't it?" he asked, taking a bite of a bagel. "It seems like something from the Mad Hatter's tea party."

Renee chuckled. "Or a hallucinogenic dream." She sifted through some of the other photos, stacking some near the Alice in Wonderland marvel she was holding. "How on earth did she get this effect?"

"Don't ask me," Joe said, laughing. "Remember, I'm the guy who bought a talking Minolta that told him to get his money back."

"Well, no one is going to tell this Lindstrom to get her money back," Renee said, bringing the photo nearer for close inspection. "She's fantastic."

Joe pushed his chair closer to Renee so he could take another look at the picture. He'd been so mesmerized by the photos of Meg and him that this quite extraordinary montage shot had been overlooked. Somehow Meg had taken a photo of the girls-on-the-bench sculpture from the back so that just the park bench and their small heads, bedecked in elaborate Easter bonnets, showed. Hunt had positioned the sculpture in the center of a path that wound around the rear of Lakeland House, and from Meg's angle it looked as if the little girls were sitting at the start of the Yellow Brick Road. Large, nearly leafless oak trees flanked the edges of the path, angling closer and closer to one another as the path extended farther from Meg's camera. Right at the artistic vanishing point, Meg had somehow superimposed a head shot of Hunt, its creator, with the midday sun backlighting his thick head of hair so that it resembled a halo.

It was an extraordinary picture, the mechanics of which Joe stood no chance in hell of comprehending. If Meg had told him she had just photographed what was there, he would have believed her implicitly, for there seemed to be no other rational explanation for the photo.

So when Renee asked to borrow a few of the pictures, Joe had been more than happy to say yes. Back in the days when he was just starting out, many a terrific career break had come about because another writer or friend had helped him in just such a networking opportunity. So today he'd been thrilled that Renee, a woman whose opinion he respected, had liked Meg's work, and he hadn't hesitated at all when she asked to borrow some of the prints.

However, now that he was on his way back to New Hampshire in this rickety airplane, he was certain that he'd acted too hastily. He had no doubt that Meg was a photographer—and a damned fine one—through to her bones; hadn't he seen her wedded to her Hasselblad ever since they arrived at Lakeland House? But on Sunday night, the night of magic and dreams, she'd let him peer inside that solitary heart of hers, and he'd seen more than a glimpse of the fears that had guided her, especially since her sister's death.

What he'd done amounted to nothing, really, no transgression or slight. But on some unspoken level he knew that she wouldn't take it that way, that his eagerness to have her appreciated would be seen as meddling, that his love would be construed as control.

So let Renee keep the pictures for now, he decided. As soon as he returned from this sojourn at Lakeland House, he'd ask her to return them, and that would be the end of that. If by some chance Meg asked for them back before then—well, he'd deal with that when, and if, it happened.

A flight attendant stopped near his seat with a cart of beverages. "Would you care for anything, sir?"

Joe scanned the assortment. "Cutty Sark," he said. "On the rocks."

Moments later he settled back in his seat. The sky was growing quickly dark as they flew north; the more urban areas were spreading out into the rugged and wooded New England landscape. He sipped his drink, letting its warmth take the edge off the apprehensions that gnawed at him. He shuffled through the photos on his lap until he came to the one of Margarita with her head resting dreamily on his shoulder, both of them cradled on the lap of Hunt's *Earth Mother*.

His worries about giving the photos to Renee, his fear of flying that usually tilted his stomach sideways—everything else disappeared as he looked into those dark and mysterious eyes of hers and let himself sink once again into the world of fantasy.

He looked at his watch and smiled to himself. Fantasy that in two short hours would be reality. He settled down to wait.

Chapter Nine

"Pass me the index on sculptors, would you, Margarita?"
Joe was lying on his back on the floor near the fireplace,
reading the list of accomplishments Hunt had submitted for
consideration. It was Friday afternoon, three days after Joe
returned from his trip to New York.

Meg sifted through a few of the dozens of papers scattered on the floor around her, then tapped him on the head
with a sheaf of five stapled pages. "Here you go."

He mumbled his thanks, and she smiled, once again noting the way he threw himself into each part of the project.
His love for Anna was evident in the way he tackled even the
most boring and routine of jobs necessary to compiling information for the history of the Kennedy Colony. He was a
man of deep conviction and strong loyalties, and Meg found
herself respecting him more with every day.

The one-day disruption of their working schedule hadn't
affected them at all, except for the loneliness that had been
her companion while he was in New York. Despite the differences in their temperaments, they were able to blend their
strengths in a way that propped up their individual weak-
nesses and produced some very fine work, if she did say so
herself.

Besides, it was such a pleasure to be able to look across
the room and see Joe, dressed in faded jeans and Jets T-shirt
and looking for all the world like a football player in the off-

season, peering over his glasses at a list of sculptors. She wondered how many people had judged him strictly on appearances and missed who and what he really was. His rugged good looks and tough New York accent hid one of the sweetest souls she'd ever encountered. His innate goodness was evident even in his work. She'd zoomed through the complete works of Angelique Moreau and was delving into the Alex Dennison *Star Trek* series, and she saw Joe in the way his characters met adversity and embraced good fortune. A certain sense of ethics and a fine sense of humanity colored every action of every major character, and Meg was sure that in this case the creation manifested all that was good and true about its creator.

Joe leaned up on one elbow. "You realize Hunt has ten times the talent of any of these guys, don't you?"

She glanced at some of the photos scattered around her. No doubt about it, the artwork was second-rate when compared to Huntington's imaginary village. "You're right," she said. "It would take a blind man not to see it."

Joe sat up, glasses slipping toward the end of his nose, hair ruffled over his forehead. "Then why can't we include him in the compendium? He deserves it."

It was old territory. "Come on now, Joe," she said with a sigh. "You remember what Patrick said. Only participants registered before July 1984 are eligible."

"That's the most damned ridiculous thing I've ever heard. Of all the arbitrary, asinine—"

"Whoa! Whoa!" When roused, he had the temper of a righteous angel. "I want to include Hunt as much as you do, but we have to have some rules, don't we?"

Joe jumped to his feet, and now he stood near the fireplace, the heat of his anger surpassing the fire in the grate. "Talent is the first rule, Margarita. Talent makes its own rules."

"Maybe talent should make its own rules," she answered, "but in the real world that's not the case. We each

have someone standing over us, defining our boundaries for
us, don't we?''

Joe said nothing, but it was clear from the look on his
face that he disagreed.

"Your editor makes boundaries, doesn't she?"

"And I keep butting my head against them," he said.
"But we're not talking about boundaries on creation.
There's no question that they're detrimental. I'm talking
about an arbitrary rule that will keep Hunt from getting a
little publicity. I can't buy that."

"You saw the guidelines Patrick drew up with Anna,
didn't you? We can't circumvent them, Joe, no matter how
badly we want to.''

He frowned, grew quiet for a moment, then exploded
with another burst of energy. "Why don't we present Patrick with the idea of adding a list of artists to watch out for
in the coming year? We could update it every fall—make it
a guide to stars of the future.''

"I don't know how you do it," she said, shaking her head
in disbelief. "You work yourself up into an emotional
storm, then manage to come up with a solution so logical it
defeats all arguments." She shook her head. "You're
amazing, Joe.''

"Not amazing," he explained. "Obsessed is more like it.''

He had a point. Meg knew that if the bomb dropped
smack on Lakeland House right now, Joe's last thoughts
would be of getting Huntington Kendall IV listed in the history of the Kennedy Creative Colony. It was passion in its
purest form—a passion for life. She watched him as he
crossed to the window, memorizing the strength and beauty
of his body, the beauty of his soul.

How easy it would be to fall in love with a man who cared
that deeply.

JOE WIPED AWAY some condensation on the window and
looked down at the yard. Since early morning, Hunt and
Ivan had been covering the sculptures in bright red blan-

kets and systematically loading them in Hunt's beat-up van in preparation for Hunt's departure the next morning. The yard, which had once been peopled by Hunt's fertile imagination, seemed desolate, a ghost town. The yard reminded Joe of his life before Lakeland House, of his life before meeting Margarita. It was no wonder his creativity had been so badly blocked. His life had grown so narrow, so arid, that his ideas had no chance to take root and grow. The daily contact with Meg, the constant dual stimulation of her fine mind and equally fine beauty, seemed to break through whatever barriers his subconscious had created, and he found himself unable to stem the flow of ideas.

Even without turning around, Joe could feel her watching him with those dark, intense eyes of hers. His entire body seemed sensitized, vibrating with awareness as her gaze lingered upon him. He knew when her eyes swept across his shoulders, knew when they slid along the muscles of his back and buttocks. It sounded bizarre, especially from a man who'd been celibate for the past six months, but the sensation of simply being watched by a woman like Margarita did more for his libido than having another woman in his bed.

Behind him he heard Meg leap to her feet. "My God!" she said as he turned around. "It's after four already. I'd better start dressing for dinner."

He laughed and walked toward her, shaking his head. "We don't meet Patrick until seven," he said. "Unless you're planning a total make-over, you have plenty of time."

"What time I have is barely enough." She bent from the waist and picked up the scattered papers. "I have to wash my hair, do my nails—" She glanced down at her tan cords and baggy blue sweater and grimaced. "Believe me, Joe, I need every minute I can get."

He was just about to dispute her statement when she riffled through a stack of photos on the desk, then looked up at him. "I almost forgot to ask you. Do you still have the pictures I gave you when you went to New York?"

A vivid image of himself handing Renee a sampling of Meg's work rose before his eyes. He felt as if his clothes had suddenly grown too tight. "I—" He stopped and cleared his throat. "Up in my room. I haven't unpacked completely and—"

"Well, don't bother to unpack them," she said, pulling her sweater down around her narrow hips. "I meant to tell you before that they're just contact prints. I've finished a set for each of us on some Multigrade paper—the contrast and detail show up so much better. You can just toss the others out."

He felt as if he'd been granted a full pardon from the governor. Giving the photos to Renee was no big deal—at least he hadn't thought so when he did it—but the last thing he wanted to do on this special night was anything that could alter the closeness between them.

"Fine," he said. "I'll do that."

She smiled at him. "Well, time to perform a few minor miracles."

Joe, who would find Meg beautifully dressed in castoffs or haute couture, smiled back at her. "Go," he said. "All I have to do later is shower and shave." He gestured toward himself. "There aren't many miracles I can perform."

Meg touched his forearm for a second, and spirals of warmth whizzed through his body. "You don't need miracles, Joe," she said. "You're perfect as you are."

She hurried out of the room, leaving behind her the faint scent of her perfume and a feeling of delight that stayed with him the rest of the afternoon.

THE RESTAURANT was tucked away on a side road off Route 6, south of town, hidden behind a grove of trees and an old, abandoned post office building. While so many of the finer dining establishments closed between the summer season and the ski season, Mario's stayed open, and Patrick

McCallum had long ago discovered it was well worth the search.

It was the front part of an old brick house, and its main dining room was centered around an enormous stone fireplace. Candles flickered in sconces on the wall, and the faint, unmistakable scent of mountains and pine seemed to fill the air. He'd reserved a lovely round table near the fireplace, and as he gazed at the three young people seated with him, he felt such a sense of well-being and joy that tears, sudden and unexpected, sprang to his eyes.

His eyes lingered on each one of them in turn. In just two weeks at Lakeland House, the years seemed to have slipped away from Joseph. The worry lines that had been so deeply etched in his forehead when he arrived for Anna's funeral had eased, and in his dark suit and tie he seemed boyishly handsome. Patrick had the feeling that Joe had made peace with some inner turmoil, and he felt glad.

Huntington Kendall had forsaken his occasional bouts with eye makeup and had chosen what, for him, was quite a conservative outfit. His tall skinny frame was clothed in baggy black trousers with two-inch cuffs, a pale pink satin shirt and red suspenders that delighted Patrick's sense of whimsy. A white carnation was pinned to his shirt pocket.

Although Joe and Hunt seemed as dissimilar as any two men could be, Patrick detected a real affection between them in the way the younger man deferred to Joe in conversation and in the way Joe seemed almost paternal in his concern for Kendall's artistic future.

But it was Margarita in her shimmering black dress who captured and held every eye in the restaurant. Being a widower, Patrick had forgotten the mysterious things a woman can do to turn herself into a creature of magic. With her blond hair tumbling in waves over her shoulders, as pale as moonlight against the silky black dress, Margarita seemed to be a wild thing tamed for one night to delight the beholder. And if he wasn't missing the mark entirely, that beholder was Joe.

Patrick poured the champagne with a flourish. "To life,"
he said as he handed a glass first to Meg and then to Joe and
Huntington. "To wherever life takes you. May the journey
be its own reward."

They clicked glasses, the silvery sound of crystal against
crystal, the sound of celebration and circumstance. Without a drop of champagne in him yet, Patrick already felt
intoxicated on simple high spirits.

How wonderful it was to be surrounded by people at the
beginning of things, people young enough to feel life was
still a series of choices to be made, roads to be explored. No
wonder Anna's life had been so long, so happy—it was a
privilege indeed to be part of a system that helped artists
such as these three to develop their full potential.

And oh, how sweet it would be to watch the progress of
Margarita and Joseph. It wasn't often a man got to witness
a miracle in the making.

"Drink up, my friends," he said, beaming at them across
the table. "This is definitely our night to celebrate!"

MEG WENT EASY on the champagne, delicious as it was, because she was driving that night. Besides, she was feeling so
giddy with excitement and pleasure that champagne was
superfluous. She had attributed her high coloring to the
proximity of the fireplace, but she—and probably everyone else in the room—knew that was a lie. Sitting next to
Joe, knowing that the next day would find her in his arms,
was enough to send her blood bubbling through her veins.

From appetizer to entree to dessert, she'd been hard
pressed to keep her mind on the conversation around her.
Being as visual a creature as she was, Meg found herself
mesmerized by the candlelight. Its soft glow surrounded all
of them, and she relished the sight of Patrick gazing fondly
at all three of them and the way Hunt's face seemed somehow young and vulnerable.

But it was upon Joe that her eyes feasted. Half of his
beautifully molded face was in shadow; the other half was

lit with a golden glow from the candles on the table. Now and then a flicker of flame was reflected in his dark green eyes, and she found her pulse quickening in response to the promise she saw there.

"There's just one thing missing from Mario's," she said as she finished her cheesecake and put her fork down. "Music." She caught Joe's eye and smiled. "There should be music and dancing here."

"Ah, but there used to be such dancing here," Patrick said, pouring Hunt his third cup of demitasse. "They had a band that was the talk of five counties. My wife, Pegeen, and I used to come here every Saturday night and fox trot to our heart's content."

Hunt's bushy eyebrows lifted. "Fox trot?"

"An ancient courtship rite," Joe said dryly. "Performed as a mating ritual by twentieth-century men and women to the accompaniment of Big Band music."

Everyone chuckled, and beneath the table Meg quickly patted Hunt's hand. For the last day or so, he'd been seeming terribly young, and her heart went out to him. His veneer of sophistication, his counter cultural, sarcastic wit, had disappeared with the last remnant of Indian summer's warmth, and he seemed no more than a young artist about to conquer the world with only his talent to shield him from heartbreak.

"They're a cruel bunch, Meggie," Hunt said as he gulped down his third demitasse. "Only you understand the soul of an artist." He glared at both Joe and Patrick, but Meg could see the sparkle in his blue eyes. "You Philistines will eat your words when I return to Lakeland a hero."

Patrick raised his cup of coffee to Hunt in salute. "I'll plan a parade for you, Huntington," he said with a smile. "We'll have a marching band heading down Main Street in your honor."

"I'll design a float," Meg said, catching the spirit from Patrick. "We'll have scads of balloons all attached to a papier-mâché replica of the *Earth Mother*." She looked to Joe.

"You will come back a hero, Kendall." Joe's voice was serious, and that took her by surprise. "You have it in you to break through any barriers you choose."

Meg's eyes unexpectedly flooded with tears. With two short sentences, Joe had given the young man the greatest gift of all—confidence. From one artist to another, it was the most generous act imaginable. Her admiration for Joe Alessio tripled on the spot.

For a second the mood at the table changed as the future, held at bay during most of dinner, intruded upon the four of them. But this was to be a celebration as well as a farewell, and sentiment, however lovely, was out of place.

She was about to start a conversation about the days when Joe worked on *Star Trek* novels when a sudden burst of taped music filled the dining room. It was an old Cole Porter tune, not at all her normal taste in music but something she loved nonetheless.

"Come on, Meggie," Hunt said, unfolding his long frame from the hardback chair and extending his hand to her. "Why don't you teach me one of those fox trots you were talking about?"

"I was the one who mentioned fox trot," Joe said with a good-natured scowl. "I should be the one dancing."

Hunt's long face lit up with a wicked smile, his cosmopolitan veneer slipping back into place. "Don't worry, darling," he said over his shoulder as he led Meg to the dance floor. "I promise I'll save you a spot on my dance card."

Meg proved to be quite inept as a dancing instructor, and before she had a chance to attempt a fox trot with either Patrick or Joseph, the music ended, replaced with some bland, easy-listening music that made for hard dancing.

They lingered over coffee as Patrick and Joe tried to top one another with tall tales, and it wasn't until the maître d' approached them to say the restaurant was about to close that any one of the four of them made a move to end the evening.

Patrick lived only fifteen minutes away from Mario's. Meg steered the limousine up the circular driveway and rolled to a stop at his front door.

Patrick shook Hunt's hand heartily. "I want full reports from you, Kendall," he said. Meg could see the emotion by the way his blue eyes shimmered with unshed tears. "It's not often that I can say, 'I knew you when...'" Hunt mumbled his thanks, turning suddenly shy. Patrick got out of the limo and closed the door, then leaned in to say good-night to Meg and Joe. "Remember, we have a progress meeting at my office on Tuesday."

"Another progress meeting like the last one?" Meg asked with a laugh.

"A three-hour lunch and a half-hour chat," Joe said. "Definitely my idea of the perfect business meeting."

Patrick moved away from the car, his house keys dangling from his fingers. "It's not my fault you two are being so efficient," he said as Meg shifted back into drive. "I've never been paid so much for doing so little in my life."

He waved at them, and Meg slowly moved down the driveway toward the road to Lakeland House. Hunt was quiet in the back seat, and they respected his need for privacy. Joe put a Beatles tape into the stereo, and they both sang along, blissfully off-key, as she drove. At one point Joe reached over and gently stroked the back of her neck, and a potent mixture of sexuality and tenderness flooded her senses, making her drive a half mile past the gates to the Kennedy Colony before she even realized her mistake.

Ah, Lindstrom, she thought as she made a U-turn and retraced her path, *what on earth are you getting yourself into?*

SOMEWHERE BETWEEN Mario's and Lakeland House, Huntington Kendall IV decided to leave for New York that very night. Meg was trying to convince him to stay until morning, but Joe could tell from the set of the younger man's jaw that it was a losing battle.

"There's no point, Margarita," Joe said to her as she paced up and down the length of the study, her short black dress riding high on her thigh with each stride. "He's got the van packed up; he's wide awake and stone-cold sober. There's no good reason for him to stay here another night."

She stopped and put her hands on her slender hips. "It's after midnight," she said sternly. "The roads are unlighted, and he has a sense of direction like yours. I think those are three pretty good reasons for him to stay."

Hunt, the object of this conversation, was leaning against the mantelpiece. Joe could almost feel the adrenaline zinging through Hunt's veins. The creative juices were flowing, and Hunt had to get to his next destination before the need left him high and dry. It was something Joe could well understand.

He turned to Hunt, noting the way even his red hair seemed bushier than usual. "It's the *Earth Mother*'s influence," he said with a grin. "It has our Meg here wanting to mother everyone in sight."

Meg glared at Joe, and he laughed.

"Speaking of the *Earth Mother*," Hunt said, his voice minus its customary note of irony, "Ivan gave up before we finished packing up the trailer I rented." He hesitated a second, his big, sad eyes fastened to Joe. "I need a hand getting her in."

"No problem," Joe said easily, noting Hunt's sigh of relief. "Between the three of us, we should be able to manage in no time."

Meg kicked off her dangerously high sandals and slipped into her worn running shoes, which looked out of place, yet somehow appealing, with her sexy black dress. They followed Hunt out the back door and into the yard. Strips of silvery moonlight filtered through the trees that towered overhead, and he watched Margarita move in and out of the magical light as if in a dream. A sudden ferocious gust of wind, presaging the winter ahead, whistled past them, and

Joe shrugged out of his suit jacket and placed it around her narrow shoulders.

The *Earth Mother*, swaddled to her shoulders in one of the protective red blankets, looked surreal and comical alone in the bare backyard.

"I think she grew," Meg said, circling the statue and shaking her head. "I don't know how you'll ever get it into your trailer."

"Neither do I," Hunt said, looking over at Joe. "I was hoping one of you would have an idea."

The *Earth Mother* was as wide as she was tall, and there was absolutely no way Joe could see that anyone could get a grip on her and lift her into the rented vehicle. Twice he tried to grab the statue around the waist, its narrowest part, but his grip slipped each time, and he ended up with a handful of plaster-cast bosom and a very red face.

Meg and Hunt were trying to keep a straight face, but the third time his hands roamed *Earth Mother*'s matronly bosom, Meg burst out laughing.

"Why don't you try it, Lindstrom?" Joe said, unable to resist the urge to laugh at himself. "There's absolutely no other place to grab the damned thing."

Meg was laughing too hard to answer him.

Hunt, on the other hand, was looking more miserable by the minute. "I wanted to get on the road before dawn," he said sadly, with a long look at his creation. "I should have put wheels on the damned sculpture."

"Or built it inside your van." Joe put an arm around the younger man for a second. "Don't worry about it," he said reassuringly. "We'll find a way yet."

It was part Joe's affection for Hunt and a greater part his desire to be alone with Margarita that fueled his ingenuity, but one hour and four glasses of Asti Cinzano later, Meg and Joe had rigged up a ramp made of sturdy pine boards they'd found in the basement, and with a mighty and concerted effort, the three of them managed to push the great lady up the ramp and into the safety of the U-Haul trailer that was attached to Hunt's van.

Hunt, whose adrenaline had been heightened by the pot of coffee he'd consumed, collapsed dramatically on the cold ground, his red suspenders drooping off his bony shoulders. "That's it," he groaned. "In my next reincarnation I'm coming back as a miniaturist."

"The hell with that," Joe said, leaning against the edge of the truck, breathing heavily. "Come back as a chiropractor—we could keep you in business." He rubbed his right thigh where the *Earth Mother*'s sharp left foot had dug in.

Meg, looking absurdly sexy in her dress and his oversized suit jacket, was sitting next to him, her feet resting on the ramp they had improvised. The long elegant line of her legs from ankle to knee glimmered in the moonlight, drawing his eye up, toward the delights still hidden. He saw her proudly astride a white stallion as she raced across the black night, her angel's hair flowing down her naked back.

It took him a long moment to surface from his fantasy and realize he was being spoken to.

"I thought lack of oxygen to the brain had done you in." Meg's voice, low and laughing, teased his ears. "I convinced Hunt to stay for one last cup of coffee. Are you game?"

Joe stood up and helped her to her feet. "If our coffee's Cinzano," he said. Acting on impulse, he draped one arm around Meg's waist and another across Hunt's shoulders. For a moment, brief and sweet, he wished he could stop time and preserve that instant where he felt poised on the edge of something he couldn't quite define. The last time he'd felt that sense of benevolent destiny, he was seventeen years old and had yet to go to war. He'd almost forgotten how it felt to be young and hopeful. It was nice to be reminded that life could still hold some wonderful surprises.

But he'd learned that the place where Hunt was standing shifted more swiftly than quicksand beneath a young man's feet. He wanted to give Hunt a few more moments of Lakeland's protection before the artist left, even if it meant delaying the moment he and Meg had been anticipating.

"Come on," he said, leading them toward the kitchen. "Let's have one more for the road."

Chapter Ten

"Call me when you get back to New York." Hunt, his voice sounding uncharacteristically shaky, embraced Meg in a hug so strong she feared her ribs would crack. "Do you have my number?"

Meg patted the pocket of Joe's jacket, which still lay across her shoulders. "Right here," she said. "I'll put it in the Rolodex as soon as I go back inside."

"I could do it for you." Hunt, who had been in such a hurry to hit the road, now seemed reluctant to leave the safety and isolation of Lakeland House. "Just take a minute."

Joe stepped forward, and Meg watched as he extended his hand to the younger man to shake. "No more delaying, man," he said, not unkindly. "You've had four cups of coffee and three goodbye scenes. It's time to make your exit."

Hunt took Joe's solid hand in his own large and bony one. Solemnly, they shook hands, and Meg watched Hunt's ever-present control falter and fail as his brown eyes filled with tears. Joe patted him awkwardly on the shoulder and said something that Meg couldn't quite make out. Hunt nodded, and even though his Adam's apple was contorting with emotion, she could see that he was reassured. Despite the chill wind that was blowing steadily across the driveway, making the trees overhead moan softly with movement, Meg felt warmed from within, filled to overflowing with love and hope in a way she hadn't been warmed in many years.

"Let us know what happens with that gallery owner," Joe said, plunging his hands into the pockets of his trousers. "We'll be thinking about you on Monday."

Hunt rolled his eyes dramatically in an attempt to regain his old insouciance. "You?" he asked. "I'm the one who has to sidle up to those bourgeois types and get them to open their minds to me."

"They will," Meg said, thinking about the scope and brilliance of this young man's work. "And then they'll open their galleries."

Hunt snapped his suspenders with his thumbs and opened the door to his van. "I'm off," he said. *"Andy Hardy Conquers the Big Apple."*

Joe laughed. "You will conquer it, Andy. Keep the faith."

Joe put his arm around Meg, and she moved closer to him. Hunt climbed into the van and closed the door. He looked young and thin, and it was painfully obvious that his sophisticated veneer shattered before real emotion. Meg's heart went out to him, for he reminded her of herself not too many years earlier.

The engine roared to life, and the headlights flashed on, their glare blinding her for a moment. Gears clunked as Hunt shifted into reverse.

"Drive carefully!" she called out, shielding her eyes from the bright white lights.

Hunt saluted them with a beep of the van's horn and began to ease slowly down the driveway, disappearing around the first curving turn.

Next to Meg, Joe cleared his throat. "Can you tell me why I feel like a parent?" he asked, his voice noticeably husky.

Meg chuckled. "I'm the wrong one to ask. I feel like I'm sending my firstborn off to war."

A strong gust of wind rocked them on their feet. "Come on," Joe said. "Let's go inside."

The house seemed very still after the night noises outside. It wasn't an unpleasant stillness; rather, it reminded Meg of just how alone she and Joe really were now that Hunt had left to seek his fortune. She followed Joe into the study where he offered her the last of the champagne.

"I'll split it with you," she said, slipping off her running shoes, then curling up barefoot on the sofa.

Joe handed her a half glass of the golden wine, then sat next to her on the sofa. Her bare feet were pressed against his thigh. Meg flexed her toes for a second and felt a tremor run through him. She hid her smile with the glass of champagne.

She was feeling pleasantly high, decidedly mellow and more sensually alive than at any time in her life. Somehow her universe had been compressed into this moment, this split second in time, and she longed to hold it in the palm of her hand. Joe was watching her, those wonderful eyes of his skimming over her face as if he were trying to capture her heart.

She took another sip of champagne. "What are you thinking about?"

His mouth tilted in a smile. "How it felt to be Hunt's age, standing right at the edge of a cliff and not being afraid to fall." She watched his chest rise and fall as he drew in a long breath. "Somewhere along the way you lose that feeling."

"Maybe you have to lose it," Meg answered slowly. "Maybe that's what helps you cope with reality. Life could be very painful if you kept on tilting at windmills."

Joe chuckled and put his empty champagne glass down on the end table near him. "And maybe I'd rather keep tilting at windmills."

"My sister was like that," she said, the champagne taking the edge off sorrow. "Always running after her dreams."

"That's the only way you can make them come true," he said, touching her hair with his strong, tanned fingers. "She made them come true, didn't she?"

"Maybe if she'd settled for less, she'd still be alive today," Meg answered softly. "Maybe she shouldn't have wanted so much."

"The wanting is what keeps us alive, Margarita. When you lose that feeling, that's when you're really dead."

But it scared Meg to think about chasing after her dreams, and she let the champagne and the honeyed sound of his voice lull her. He got up and crossed the room, switching on the FM radio nestled on the shelves between the *Encyclopaedia Britannica* and the *Oxford English Dictionary*. Lush, soft music wrapped itself around her heart.

As he walked back toward her, he slipped a finger into the knot of his tie and drew it down, then deftly unbuttoned the neck of his white shirt. Simple, spare movements performing a quite basic male procedure. Nevertheless, the way he captured and held her gaze while he released himself from that most civilized garment made Meg's pulses quicken with pleasure. She took another sip of champagne.

He held out his hand for her empty glass, then put it on the end table with his own. Then he drew her swiftly to her feet.

"You owe me a dance." His breath was sweet, intoxicating with champagne and desire.

"A fox trot, to be precise." She could barely keep the tremor from her voice.

"A fox trot, a waltz, anything that will bring you into my arms." He placed one hand at the base of her spine, his fingers lightly splaying out over the sweet hollow there. As if on cue, the radio switched into a song so poignant that she felt tears threaten. She placed her left hand on his shoulder, and he took her right hand in his. "Enchantment requires music," he murmured in her ear, beginning to move to the melody surrounding them. "I know your scent, Margarita, the way your lips taste like the ripest fruit. I know how you look in sunshine and in candlelight. The sound of your voice lingers in my ears after we say good-night.''

She was drowning in the flood of sensation his words opened up in her. She ducked her head slightly and rested her forehead against the side of his neck. That masterful hand at the base of her spine pulled her closer until the line of her body rested firmly and fully against the line of his. Stabbing pinpoints of pleasure—so exquisite that they bordered on pain—radiated out from her core. She was pure sensation.

"Now I want to know how you'll feel beneath me, Margarita." He kissed behind her ear, the curve of her jaw, the vulnerable spot at the base of her throat. "I want to slide my hands under your skirt and feel the softness of your thighs against my fingers. I want to find that you want me as much as I want you."

She moaned. Instinctively, her body pressed against his, and the feel of him, hard and demanding, against her thigh set her heart on fire. She took his hand and placed it just under the hem of her dress. His strong fingers shook as they hungrily savored the slither of silk stockings over firm flesh. His obvious pleasure intensified her own.

"I don't want any barriers between us, Margarita," he said, his fingers sliding over the tops of her stockings and touching bare flesh. "Not tonight."

She met his eyes and smiled. "No barriers," she said, unbuttoning his shirt and sliding it over his incredible shoulders.

"I want all of you." His gentle, powerful fingers played with the lace trim on her panties. "Your mind, your heart—" His fingers slipped inside the elastic band, and her body went molten with longing. "Everything."

His chest was bare. She leaned slightly forward and put her mouth over one of his flat nipples, flicking her tongue lightly across its surface, taking blatant pleasure from the way his heart pounded beneath her lips. The thick curling hair of his chest was soft against her skin as she kissed a trail down his flat abdomen, her fingertips playing just beneath the waistband of his pants in a way that caused his body to tremble.

His hands slid up her hips and grasped her by the waist, pushing her away from him until she found herself looking deeply into his eyes.

"I've waited all my life to find you, Margarita." Beautiful words. Words she believed.

"I know," she said, touching his mouth briefly with her index finger. "I never believed I would find you." She felt as if she'd been released from a state of suspended animation, as if all of her life that went before had been nothing more than preparation for the bursts of pure emotion that rocketed through her now.

Reaching behind her, she unzipped her dress and let it fall off her shoulders, exposing her breasts to his eyes. She moved away from his touch and let the dress fall the rest of the way to the floor. Then, never taking her eyes from him, she shed hose and garter belt, then panties. She'd ridden white waters and traveled places where law was nothing more than a word, but she knew this offering of her heart and body was the first truly dangerous thing she had ever done in her life.

IN HIS LIFE, Joe had found beauty in words, in paintings, in many women. But when Meg Lindstrom, his Margarita, stood before him, naked and proud, he felt as if he were looking through the gates of heaven. She shimmered in the fire glow; her pale hair drifted across her shoulders, one long wave curling across her left breast. Her dark eyes never left his face.

"You're beautiful," he said, small tribute to the womanly splendor that made him ache inside. "Even more beautiful than I'd imagined."

She smiled, and he saw a blush rise from her breasts to her throat. "You've been thinking about me?" she asked gently.

"Every day," he said, moving closer to her. "Every hour." He pulled her into his arms, shuddering at the deep pleasure of her flesh against his as her high, firm breasts flattened against his chest. "Every minute since I met you."

"Joe," she whispered against his lips. She pressed warm kisses along the sides of his jaw, then worked her way back to his lips again. "Love me, Joe."

Desire rose up inside him like a gathering storm. A flood of words pounded in his brain, words he'd committed to paper a thousand times, placed in the mouths of a thousand different characters, yet never fully understood. Now they echoed inside his heart, their rightness making him believe in magic again.

Quickly, he rid himself of the remainder of his clothing; then, despite the fact they were nearly the same height, he easily swept Margarita into his arms and carried her to the sofa that fronted the blazing fireplace. He placed her gently down, her long slender body in sharp relief against the dark blue cushions that shifted to accommodate her sweet curves. Kneeling on the floor next to her, he kissed her eyes, her cheeks, her incredible mouth, then began the slow, teasing journey down the column of her throat to the soft contours of her breasts and the proud curve of her rib cage.

As his mouth moved lower, his tongue circled her navel, and she arched closer to him. He could hear the small sounds of pleasure that came from deep in her throat—his name, whispered endearments, moans of delight that inflamed him further. The silky blond triangle of hair at the apex of her thighs slid softly across his face as his lips and tongue tantalized the edges of her feminine delta. Her scent—musky sweet, intensely female—filled his head and brought him dangerously close to exploding.

He moved his head away and instead cupped her with one hand, delighting in the feel of her passion-drenched flesh against his palm. Its heat made him feel invincible, a feeling he'd often imagined but never known.

"Joe?" Meg was leaning up on one elbow, her face flushed with desire, those deep eyes of hers heavy lidded and glittering in the firelight. One hand rested on top of his head encouraging him to continue. He knew she was balanced on the edge of madness just as he was. "Don't stop," she whispered. "Don't stop."

"Stop?" He chuckled, low and deep. She trembled at the feel of his breath against her thigh. "Sweet, sweet lady, I haven't even begun."

He moved between her thighs, one of her legs flung over his shoulder to accommodate the awkward position on the sofa. He parted her gently with his hand and tore his gaze away from her lush femininity to meet her eyes, to tell her, if only with a look, that what he wanted to give her—what he wanted to be given—went far beyond the boundaries of the physical delights a man and woman can share.

She smiled—the little half smile of both the conqueror and the conquered—and he bent down to savor all that was offered him, all that he needed to live.

SHE KNEW SHE HAD DIED and gone to some paradise, for surely bliss such as Joe's mouth pressed against her body could never exist in the ordinary mortal world. His warm mouth, his magical hands, combined to transport her somewhere out of her own existence, beyond anything she'd ever dreamed possible.

His mouth was hot and eager against her most sensitive flesh; he drew from her wave after wave of shimmering, undulating pleasure until she cried out in her delight, certain he had reached all the way to her heart. She opened beneath his lips and tongue like a night-blooming flower, rare and visible only to one who knew the value of its blossom.

She who had kept herself securely apart from the risk of intimacy of all kinds, safely barricaded behind her shield of reserve, was captured in the most intimate embrace possible with a man for whom she would lasso the stars and lay them at his feet. She shuddered as those stars exploded in her head, showering hot glowing fragments of dreams across her body, branding her for all time as belonging to this one man.

He gently moved her leg from his shoulder, kissing her behind the knee, then slid along the length of her trembling, pulsating body until he lay fully against her. And that part of his body that still burned with life urged against her, still seeking its haven, its home. She reached down and stroked him, her fingers gliding effortlessly across his own dampness, then just barely surrounding him, bringing him nearer her own fire.

"Now, Joe," she said, her lips brushing his. "Now."

His face, hot and dark and sweet with the scent of her, was so close that he seemed blurred, slightly out of focus. She wanted him inside her, to be a part of her body the way he had surely become a part of her heart, for the physical need was only part of the way she felt about him. He parted her thighs with one knee; she rested one of her feet on the floor in an attempt to compensate for the confining narrowness of the couch.

Suddenly, Joe grasped her tightly about the waist, then eased them down onto the floor so her back rested against the soft rug near the fireplace. She started to say something, some silly exclamation of surprise, but he pressed his lips against hers and murmured, "No words, Margarita. Just feelings."

It was an unnecessary statement, for the second his hands cupped her breasts, his rough palms making her nipples tighten with pleasure, rational thought left her, as if she were no longer capable of human speech but reduced, instead, to an existence defined by what she could taste and smell and feel burning beneath her hand. Fears that her own inexperience would somehow be her undoing faded as she let her long-dormant sensuality rise to the surface and command her body. She nipped at his lower lip, then slid her tongue along his strong teeth, gasping when his mouth opened to her and his tongue met hers and drew it into a battle where each was victor and vanquished, if only with desire. His tongue entered the hidden recesses of her mouth, tasting and touching the soft inner flesh, the strangely erotic spot on the roof of her mouth. She had become so sensitized to him and, apparently, he so attuned to her that the only limits on erotic play were those of the imagination.

Then he raised himself up, the finely sculpted muscles of his arms and chest thrown into relief against the firelight. Her eyes were drawn and held by the part of him that burned, large and dangerous, so near to her own flames. And then she raised her eyes to meet his and watched as, inch by incredible, demanding inch, he began the descent to total possession.

For Joe, it was as close to heaven as any mortal experience could possibly be. The sound of her voice as she whispered his name, the way her eyes, so dark, so luminous, never left his face, the softness of her thighs as he parted them—all these things combined to bring him near a kind of ecstasy he'd never found with anyone before. Only in his work, where his imagination had held the reins and guided his characters toward storybook bliss, had he encountered the kind of lovemaking—for that was what it was—that he was experiencing with Margarita.

He'd held off for so long, making certain she had scaled the highest peaks of pleasure, before he was even able to think of his own. But now, as his body was waiting, past reason, past anything but the primitive desire to find himself entrapped in her waiting warmth.

And God, but she was warm, so warm as he slowly eased himself into her body, feeling the power and wetness surround him, drawing him deeper inside. The urgency of his need for her had almost robbed him of his mind until he suddenly, unexpectedly, hit a tender, trembling barrier of flesh. He hesitated, his eyes meeting hers. She nodded. Her hands, which had gently gripped his buttocks, tightened their hold, pulling him past her body's resistance until they both gasped as he filled her totally.

She seemed hesitant at first, waiting for him to give her some clue as to what happened next. He was so overwhelmed by his discovery, so excited by the scent and feel of her beneath him, that he found it difficult to slow his movements down. He forced himself to begin, easily sliding in and out of her body with a lazy rhythm until she raised her hips to meet his, her body catching his fever and raising his temperature even higher.

Her movements were silky, fluid, as she instinctively cradled him inside her with all the feminine power at her command. He was rising higher and higher, his mind focused only on pleasure, on the way his whole being centered on the part of his body that seemed to grow stronger and more demanding with each contraction of her body around his.

And when he felt the next step was surely a leap into madness, his body grew unbearably taut; then he called out in wonder as the explosion of pleasure shattered him.

Joe didn't know if it took seconds or hours or several lifetimes to descend back to reality; his absorption in their mutual pleasures had been so intense, so demanding, that he was almost surprised to find himself still in that same study, with the same fire crackling in the hearth, just as if he hadn't been to paradise and back again. But then he became aware that his full weight was resting on Meg's slender form, and he held her close and rolled onto his side, bringing her with him.

Meg glanced down to the place where they were joined, and his eyes followed hers, noting the crimson stain that marked both his thighs and hers.

"Did I hurt you?" he asked, kissing her neck and chin, gently, quickly. "I never wanted to hurt you."

She cradled his face in her hands for an instant. He felt as if he were being devoured by those dark eyes of hers. "For a moment," she said, her full lips curving in a smile. "But it made what came after all the sweeter."

"I didn't know." He hardly knew how to phrase the statement. He felt awkward, almost foolish with his words. "I never guessed."

"There's no reason you should have guessed," she said, her breath soft against his neck. "It's hardly what you'd expect from a twenty-six-year-old woman these days, is it?"

"No, it's not what you'd expect," he said honestly. "Why?"

"Why haven't I been with a man before?"

He took a deep breath. His question was more complicated; his heart hung in the balance. "Why now?" *Why me?*

"Because you touched my heart the way no one else ever has."

The words "I love you" rose in his throat, and he pushed them back down. Too fast, he thought. Too easy for her to believe it was something said in the aftermath of passion to ease a woman's fears, something to be forgotten in the light of day. He wanted there to be no doubt in her mind when he told her all he felt, had always felt, for her.

"Ah, Margarita," he murmured, bending his head to capture one taut nipple in his mouth. She laughed softly, and desire began to build within him again.

"You're amazing," she whispered against his ear. "I thought it took men longer to—"

"It usually does," he conceded, cupping her breasts in his hands where they filled his palms with warmth and life. "You happen to bring out the best in me." You make me feel young, he thought. *You make me feel that the best part of life is yet to be.*

"I don't want to hurt you," he said.

She covered his mouth with the palm of her hand to cut off his words, and the scent of their lovemaking filled his head.

"You won't hurt me," she said, then rolled him onto his back and straddled him. "You could never hurt me."

She bent over him, her long hair trailing over his face and chest. She was every fantasy, every creature of starlight and magic, he'd ever imagined, ever wished existed but never believed he'd find.

When she lowered herself onto him and he watched his power slowly disappear into her warm and willing body, he knew that she possessed him, body and soul, and always would.

There was no turning back from it.

HOW AMAZING.

That feeling of security, that wonderful feeling of being cradled in a lover's arms, didn't disappear when Meg's eyes opened the next morning. She'd hovered at the outer edges of consciousness for hours, unwilling to relinquish the extraordinary delights she and Joe had been exploring in her dream. A feeling of warmth, laced with excitement, flooded her, making her loath to face daylight.

So when she finally opened her eyes and found that it wasn't a dream, that Joe was indeed curled against her back, an arm wrapped around her middle, one of his legs companionably draped over one of hers, Meg was certain that it must be Christmas morning, because a gift such as this was certainly possible only once a year.

They were cuddled in her soft and wide bed, buried beneath a puffy patchwork quilt Meg had found two years ago in West Virginia and known Anna would love. The air in the room was cool, almost cold, as an early November wind— filled with the threat of a harsh New England winter—buffeted the big house. However, beneath the covers, Meg was warmed by the feel of Joe's body snuggled spoon fashion around the curve of her own.

Lazily, she wondered what the proper etiquette of the situation was. Should she get up and brush her teeth before he awakened? Put on some makeup before he got the surprise of his life when he saw her *au naturel* for the first time? The least she should do was brush her hair.

Ah, but it was so wonderful simply to lie there in that warm bed with nothing on earth to do but revel in the sight and scent and touch of this man who had taken possession of her body last night long after he'd already taken possession of her heart. All the restless dissatisfactions with her life, all the feelings of insecurity, of never quite measuring up, had vanished as if cast away by a magician's hand.

He had thrilled her beyond description last night. The doors he had opened for her had led into places she'd never imagined existed. And rather than feeling shy, feeling afraid, love had freed her imagination, and she was able to use her body in a way that told him all that was in her heart.

She thought of Elysse and the funny, tender looks Meg sometimes caught her giving her husband, Jack, looks that up until now Meg had been unable to understand. Now she knew those looks were made up of nights of love and longing, of mornings curled in each other's arms, of words whispered and secrets shared in the soft darkness.

Joe sighed against her neck, and a shiver of love and desire rippled through her body. He moved closer to her until his body pressed against the high curve of her derriere. She gave up all thoughts of hair and makeup and the mundane details of earthly existence.

Only a very foolish woman would willingly leave paradise a second before she had to.

Listening to his even breathing, she drifted back to sleep.

IT WAS SATURDAY AFTERNOON, one week after they had become lovers. Joe and Meg were working in the study on the final stages of the history of the Kennedy Creative Colony while the housecleaning crew began setting up their equipment in the living room across the hall. Meg was busy indexing all visual artists according to discipline. Her blond head was bent over a long list of names and accomplishments, and he watched, with the fascination of one bordering on lovesickness, as she scribbled notes on a pad of yellow paper next to her.

For the past two hours she'd been working silently and efficiently, pausing only now and then to refill her coffee mug or flash him one of her incredible smiles that he felt clear down to the soles of his feet. Joe watched the elegant line of Meg's body as she leaned forward to retrieve a photo of some minor poet and shook his head.

She glanced at him, her dark eyes puzzled. "Is something wrong?"

"Not a thing," he answered, smiling. "I was just thinking it's a testament to Anna that we've managed to get anything done this past week." He got up from his seat and crossed behind her, nuzzling his face beneath her silky mane of pale blond hair. "The fact that I can manage to construct a simple declarative sentence while you're in the room with me is remarkable."

She chuckled. "I'm hardly that major a distraction, Alessio," she said with that slightly sharp, self-mocking wit he enjoyed so much. "I would think you could manage even an occasional complex sentence—" She paused, leaning into his embrace. The increased tempo of her heartbeat fluttered beneath his palms.

"What were you saying, Lindstrom?" His thumbs traced lazy circles on her nipples through the silky fabric of her shirt.

She sighed and pushed away the index she was alphabetizing on away from her. "I don't have any idea at all." Her incredibly sensual mouth curved in a smile. "When you do that, I can't remember if A comes before B, much less anything more complicated."

"Good." Her eyebrows darted up in question, and he laughed. "I don't want to be the only one at a disadvantage here."

She glanced down toward the area below his waistband where his rising excitement was becoming visible. "Hardly a disadvantage, I'd say." Her night-dark eyes sparkled up at him. "In fact, I would say the opposite."

He pulled her to her feet, pinning her arms to her sides with his embrace. He tilted his head toward the desks, piled high with paperwork. "Why don't we forget all of this, shut the door and do wonderful things to each other?"

The sound of the vacuum cleaner manned by the Fitzpatrick Housekeeping Service grew ominously near. Meg laughed and rested her forehead against his. "It depends on how you'd feel about having Mrs. Fitzpatrick finding you in the altogether on her spotless carpet."

He pulled her even closer, letting her feel the fullness of his excitement. "If Mrs. Fitzpatrick wouldn't mind vacuuming around us, I'm game." He grinned, thinking of the wiry sixty-five-year-old woman whose tightly curled hair wouldn't budge in a nor'easter. "I'll bet she wouldn't even bat an eye."

The vacuum's roar was just a few feet away from the door to the study. Meg slipped out of his embrace and stepped away just as a young man with the Fitzpatrick trademark red hair smiled at them and began to clean his way into the room.

Meg and Joe beat a hasty retreat but found there was no place in the house where they could talk, work or do anything else with any degree of privacy. An army of workers, it seemed to Joe, were swarming all over the old house, waxing and polishing and buffing anything that didn't move and even a few that did.

Joe grabbed their coats from the hall closet. "Let's go." He tossed Meg her worn leather jacket. "I'm afraid I'll end up being lemon-oiled to death if we hang around."

He slipped into his own leather jacket. "Come on, Lindstrom. Don't tell me you have a yen for lemon furniture polish?"

"The callbacks, Joe."

He stared at her, knowing he must look as blank as he felt.

"We're supposed to hear from two pianists and one fiber artist this afternoon."

A blue-uniformed woman wielding a floor-waxing machine the size of a small jeep hurried by. Joe, whose interest in the mechanics of good housekeeping was minimal, edged closer to the door. "Let them call back a second time," he said, reaching for Meg's hand. He flung open the front door, letting the crisp air and pale sunshine of early November flood the vestibule. "Freedom, Margarita." He took a deep breath and grinned. "Come on; make a break for it."

He could see that she wanted to, but in the end duty won out. "I can't," she said finally. "Our deadline's next week, and this might be our only chance to speak with these people."

With a melodramatic sigh, Joe closed the door and began to take off his jacket. "Far be it from me to shirk responsibility," he said, letting his shoulders droop comically.

Meg, however, stopped him before he could remove his jacket. "You go," she said, fishing her car keys out of her jacket pocket and tossing them to Joe. "No sense in both of us being prisoners."

"You trust me in the limousine?"

She nodded, grinning. "I've heard the myth about male drivers is highly exaggerated. You're not nearly as bad as insurance tables would lead us to think."

"Thanks a lot," he said, pleased, however, that she'd trust him with the expensive car that was her main support. "What will you do while I'm gone?"

"Wait for the phone to ring, I suppose." She paused for a moment. "Maybe make a few calls to some of the other alumni to verify names and dates. I'll be fine."

"I feel guilty leaving you here alone with all this racket."

She made a face, her eyes twinkling. "Guilty enough to stay behind and risk the lemon oil?"

He shook his head. "Not that guilty."

However, they decided that since he was going into town, it wasn't a bad idea if he took the enormous sheaf of papers they'd accumulated and photocopied the whole mess at the printer's shop on Main Street. And since he'd be on Main Street anyway, he could always stop at the market for some milk and cheddar cheese, and wouldn't it be nice if they had some wine to go with dinner, and of course a pound of those incredible chocolate-chip cookies with pecans that Gordon's Bakery made on Saturday mornings would be fantastic...

"I'll be lucky if I get back before dark," he said, standing in the doorway, his arms piled high with papers and lists and dry cleaning to be dropped off. "You're damned good at delegating authority."

He knew he must be looking pretty disgruntled, because she laughed at him and ruffled his hair.

"One of my many talents," she said, leaning over the parcels in his arms and kissing his mouth. "Now, off with you."

He headed off down the flagstone path, pausing once to turn around and savor the sight of her standing in the doorway to Lakeland House—their house—her arms wrapped around her slender form against the chill wind. Sunlight seemed to pool at her feet, giving her a mystical look. Even without his glasses on, he knew that the look in her dark eyes was soft, and a stab of emotion, pure and strong, tore at his heart from the inside out.

She waved at him, then slipped back inside the warmth of the house, closing the door behind her. A quick intense fantasy of a life where the door never closed on him, a life that he and Meg Lindstrom could share permanently, rose before him, more vivid than his actual surroundings.

Somewhere along the way he had discovered that the woman he'd created to found his fictional family had been eclipsed by the woman with whom he worked and ate and now slept beside each night. He'd loved Isobel and Mireille and Abigail, all the women who peopled his imaginary landscapes. They had always been more real, more dependable, than the women with whom he'd shared a night's pleasure.

Meg was a miracle, a woman who managed to be everything he'd ever fantasized about but one who still surprised him over and over again. She was a rare woman of intelligence and kindness and a beauty that moved him deeply. She inspired within him not only the creative intensity he needed in order to work but the desire to do more, to become more, if only in her eyes. She was a woman he could imagine spending a lifetime getting to know, a lifetime building a home.

"I love you," he said out loud, his words swept away from him by the stiff breeze that rustled the trees. "I love you, Margarita Lindstrom."

And even he who knew the power of words was awed by the wonder of that simple phrase, by the magic such words still held for a man who'd doubted magic would ever be his.

Chapter Eleven

After a two-hour bout on the telephone with hard-to-reach artists and authors, domestic ambition overtook Meg and sent her down to the newly sparkling kitchen to try her hand at cooking Chinese style, with a little help from her friend.

"Okay, Lowell, I finished chopping the scallions," she said, the telephone wedged between her right ear and right shoulder. "Now what?"

"Mix the cornstarch with the rest of the ingredients." Elysse's voice was patient despite the fact Meg had had her on the telephone for half an hour, guiding her through the intricacies of Szechuan shrimp.

Meg opened the kitchen cabinet over the sink and rummaged through the contents. "Flour, arrowroot, baking soda..." There was no sign of cornstarch anywhere. She was beginning to wonder if another one of their high-tech dinners, courtesy of freezer and microwave, might not be in order. "Are you sure I couldn't use flour in the sauce?"

"Flour!" Elysse sounded as if Meg had single-handedly defamed the long history of Chinese cuisine. "Would you put cornstarch in a layer cake?"

"You're asking the wrong person that question, Elly," she said, climbing up on a chair so she could examine the upper shelf. "I'm the one who can't boil water." A yellow box, half hidden behind a container of pancake mix, caught her eye. "Okay, I've got the cornstarch." She climbed down from the chair. "Now what?"

"A few answers," Elysse said. "What's with these sudden domestic yearnings? Can't you two artistic types call out for Chinese?"

Meg laughed and tried to duck Elysse's question. "Not around here we can't. Now what happens with the cornstarch?"

"You mix it with the liquid ingredients. And don't change the subject."

"I didn't. The subject was Szechuan shrimp, if I remember right."

"Oh, you remember right, Lindstrom. I can hear you're just as evasive as ever."

Meg measured two tablespoons of cornstarch into a metal bowl. "I've only been gone three weeks, Elly. You can hardly expect a total personality change, can you?"

Elysse's laugh floated across the wires. "Love can do strange things, Meg."

A flush rose from Meg's shoulders, staining her cheeks deep red. "I don't recall mentioning that word." Damn! One of the major problems with having a psychotherapist as a best friend was the disconcerting habit Elysse had of reading Meg's mind. "Joe and I are friends, Elysse. Good friends." That much, at least, was true. The incredible sexual chemistry between them was wondrous to behold, but the fact that it was rooted securely in mutual friendship gave Meg a freedom to express her sexuality in a way she never could have without it.

Elysse, however, still sounded unconvinced. "We'll see," she said. "If Mr. Alessio is one half the hunk he seemed on that cover—well, I just hope you put fifty dollars aside to pay me when you get back. A bet *is* a bet, you know."

"I hear you." Meg poured a quarter cup of Kikkoman into the metal bowl and stirred it into the cornstarch, sugar and sherry. Little did Elysse know, but a crisp fifty-dollar bill was already tucked away in Meg's camera case. "Don't worry, Dr. Lowell. The bet's still on." She turned the gas on under the brand-new shiny wok that sat proudly on the old-fashioned stove. A plastic bag filled with shrimp, dark and unappetizing looking, rested on the counter next to it. "Now, tell me, Elly. What in hell do I do with all this shrimp?"

Elysse sighed long and loud, and Meg had to suppress a chuckle. "Well, once you've boiled and shelled them, you—"

Meg groaned. "Once I've what?"

It was Elysse's turn to groan. "I hope you have MCI, Lindstrom," she said. Meg could just imagine the look on her friend's face. "This is going to be a *long* afternoon."

It took a while, but Elysse led her every step of the way, no mean feat over the telephone, until the counter was neatly arranged with large bowls of cooked and cleaned shrimp, scallions and snow-pea pods, courtesy of the freezer, and a concoction of soy sauce, hot oil, ginger, garlic and assorted other unlikely ingredients that, combined, would dazzle even the most demanding palate.

Meg opened her third can of Diet Pepsi and sat down on the freshly waxed floor, resting her back against the counter. "I owe you one, Lowell," she said between long sips of soda. "Anyone who can lead me through a meal more complicated than scrambled eggs deserves an award."

"Just remember two things," Elysse said, her voice light with amusement. "Don't start stir-frying until you're ready to eat."

Meg thought of Elysse's warnings about limp pea pods and tough shrimp. "What's the second thing?" she asked. "Remedial rice making?"

"Don't get smart, Lindstrom. What I want is a full explanation about this dinner when you come home." She paused for effect. "And I mean *full*, Meg."

Meg, giddy with high spirits and fatigue, chuckled. "There's nothing to tell," she said, relishing the fact that her best friend was consumed with curiosity. "It's a simple dinner, nothing more."

"A simple dinner?" Elysse snorted, a decidedly unther apistlike sound. "And I'm the pope's wife."

"You are?" Meg's voice went high with feigned surprise "I'm shocked!"

"Just wait until you get home next week. I'll get the answers out of you."

Meg laughed. "What will you do—lock me in the garage and threaten to take away my driver's license?"

"If necessary." Elysse's voice suddenly grew serious "We've been friends for eight years, Meg," she said softly "I just want you to be happy."

Meg swallowed around the lump that rose in her throat "I am happy," she answered. "Very happy."

"The work is going well, then?" Elysse, Meg knew, had already deduced what was really going on and was gracefully offering her friend an out.

"Wonderfully," Meg answered. "It was a big surprise but we've managed to blend our differences and double our strengths." She told Elysse about their daily schedule, about the many arguments they'd had along the way and about how logic and reason usually provided a solution. For a loner like Meg, this was a revelation.

"Sounds serious," Elysse said when Meg finished. "Any chance things will continue after you leave Lakeland?"

Meg's heart fluttered. "Well, we *do* own this house together," she said. "I'm sure we'll see each other now and then."

Elysse's laugh was low and amused. "Anyone but me Meg. I've known you too long to buy that casual approach."

Meg managed to make her laugh sound equally low and amused. "No casual approach, Elly," she said. "Just the truth." Well, almost.

It wasn't until Meg hung up the phone and hurried up the stairs to shower and change before Joe got back from his afternoon of errands that she realized the full extent of what she'd said to Elysse. For the first time in her life, she was honestly happy. She was in her favorite place on earth, doing work for a woman she had loved and living side by side with a man whose talent was exceeded only by his goodness.

He seemed to embrace all of life with an intensity she'd forgotten was possible, an intensity she had once possessed herself but had let wither and die. He pushed her too far at times, crossed too many boundaries, but when she pushed back, he always respected her wishes.

He challenged her on many levels, seemed to demand an excellence from her that he demanded from himself, as well, and she rose to the challenge. The photos she'd taken during her three weeks at Lakeland House were among the best she'd ever done.

And, she admitted as she slipped out of her clothes and stepped into the steamy shower, the simple act of taking those photos was no longer enough. A long-hidden part of her was cracking through the shell of reserve she'd erected around her heart, a fledgling clawing its way into the real world, eager to try its wings.

Maybe it was time for her to admit that driving a limousine wasn't enough—had never been enough. Maybe it was time for her to admit that her ambition, her need to excel, had not died when her sister did.

She lifted her face toward the spray and let the warm water cascade over her head and shoulders, thoughts of Joe, his dark green eyes burning with desire, rising with the steam. Despite the challenges he hurled at her, despite the intensity that was as much a part of him as his voice or his physique, Joe would allow her room to expand as she regained her sense of her professional self. She knew that as well as she knew her own name.

And she also knew it was time for her to admit that she was falling in love.

JOE PRIDED HIMSELF on being a man of the eighties who neither sought nor expected a woman to possess any of the domestic skills earlier generations had prized so highly. He knew how to cook and clean and shop and fortunately had enough money now to delegate those responsibilities to someone else. So it came as an enormous shock to him when he discovered just how much he loved the fact that Meg, his Margarita of fantasy and flesh, had made the effort to prepare a complicated—and surprisingly delicious—Szechuan dinner for him that night.

Even now, as they lay curled together on the leather sofa in the study, watching the fire dance and listening to the strains of soft music filtering in from the other room, a feeling of intense, old-fashioned pleasure made it impossible for him to wipe the smile off his face.

"That meal really was fantastic, Margarita," he said, stroking her silky hair with his free hand, the one that wasn't securely wrapped around her waist. "You know I would have been happy bringing in pizza again. You didn't have to do it."

She leaned up on her elbow, glaring at him in mock annoyance. "That's the third time you've said that, Alessio. I'm beginning to wonder if my Szechuan shrimp was really such a success."

"It was fantastic," he said honestly. "I had no idea you could—" He stopped, feeling his face redden. "I mean—"

She laughed, a full-bodied laugh of intense enjoyment. "You mean, my scrambled-egg breakfasts were no indication of my culinary talents, right?"

He grinned. "I couldn't have put it better myself." He pulled her back against him, resting her head against his chest. "Are you sure you didn't hire someone to sneak in here while I was gone? Mrs. Fitzpatrick, maybe?"

"Close. Let's say I had some long-distance supervision of the project. But don't think I can pull something like that off on a regular basis. Franks and beans are more my style."

"Food isn't my biggest passion," he said, moving his hand up her rib cage until the sweet weight of her breasts, free beneath her silky dress, rested against his fingers. "I could live on franks and beans."

"Not as a steady diet," she said. "Wouldn't a man get terribly bored?"

He took a deep breath. "Never," he said softly. "I can't imagine ever being bored with you."

Joe had expected her to come back with a quick remark, some self-deprecating crack about scrambled eggs or burned toast, but instead she fell terribly silent. In the best of situations he'd found it hard to keep his emotions under control; feelings always translated themselves immediately into words, and those words had the most awful habit of popping out at the wrong time.

But he meant what he said, and it was only the beginning of all the things he wanted to say to her, all the wonderful things he had left to tell her before this month of magical beginnings was up. Gently, he pushed her away from him and got up to stand by the fireplace a few feet away. He felt vulnerable and much much younger than thirty-three as he pushed his tousled hair off his forehead and faced her, certain that she could see the pulsing of his heart beneath the fragile layer of skin and muscle that hid it from the world.

"I love you, Margarita," he said clearly, unable and unwilling to shield himself any longer from the truth of it. His chest opened, and his heart lay totally exposed and beating wildly before her. "I love you."

"You don't have to say that, Joe." Her voice was a whisper. "I know things like this don't have to mean forever." She looked away, her eyes straying toward the crackling fire. "I understood the risks going in."

Tension knotted the muscles of his shoulders and back. "That wasn't something said in the heat of passion, Meg."

"Look, Joe, you don't have to say anymore. Please don't think that because you were my first lover, you owe me some kind of undying devotion." Again she seemed to find it difficult to maintain eye contact. "This isn't one of your family sagas where the worldly young man is forced to declare himself to the wronged virgin."

Her words proved she didn't know him at all. He moved closer to her, hunkering down in front of where she sat on the couch, close enough to touch her but not quite touching. "Sex is everywhere, Margarita." She was watching him, her dark eyes unreadable. "And it comes cheap. Either one of us could walk into any bar in town and score within the first five minutes." He laughed harshly. "Hell, you wouldn't even have to exchange names, much less have a conversation." He'd been in too many bars in his day, known the pleasure of too many different bodies beneath his, too many mornings where he wondered about the night before, to underestimate the availability of quick satisfaction.

"But love," he continued, "love is something else again." His voice grew more gentle, and he let his body sway closer until his knees were pressed against hers, until he could catch the scent of her perfume. "I love you, Margarita. I love your mind. I love the talent you try so hard to suppress." He reached out and drew his hand lightly along the curve of her cheekbones, the chiseled perfection of her jaw. "I love your beauty, the way you give yourself to me each night. Everything you are is precious to me." He stood up and moved away from her again, knowing that it was imperative that she understand fully what he was saying to her. "Even if I never had the pleasures of your body again, it wouldn't change a thing. I would still love you, Margarita Lindstrom. I would still love you."

For Meg, twenty-six years of solitary living vanished like a long-forgotten dream. She wanted to take his words and tuck them somewhere deep inside her heart, for he had voiced what she had longed to say to him but hadn't dared. All of her life she'd dreamed about that kind of all-encompassing love, but she had never believed someone like

Joe existed. That he did, that he loved *her*, was a miracle of the highest order.

Joe was standing by the fireplace; his green eyes, dark and intense, were focused unblinkingly upon her as if his entire life hinged on her response to his declaration. She got up from the couch and walked toward him.

"I love you, Joseph Alessio, Angelique Moreau, Bret Allen and whoever else you are." She stopped in front of him and looked directly into eyes whose honesty and beauty took her breath away. She aimed her words at his heart. "I think I've loved you from the start."

His whole body seemed to relax; unguarded happiness lit up his face. She smiled, knowing her words had been right on target.

He opened his arms to her and drew her into the circle of his embrace. They didn't kiss; they didn't say anything at all. Meg simply wrapped her arms around Joe's waist and rested her forehead against him, letting the most profound sense of peace, of having reached the end of a long search, wash over her.

After a while—whether minutes or hours, she didn't know—Joe said, "Come with me," and they went upstairs to her room at the end of the hall.

WHEREAS THEIR LOVEMAKING of the past week had been fevered and urgent, their passion in the nights that followed their declarations of love was slow and luxurious, rich with the knowledge that it wasn't the last time, that there would be many many nights spent in a wide and welcoming bed. Their work was deep and fulfilling, and an endless line of days together stretched into the future, reaching almost to the edge of forever.

Promises were made in the night. Neither one was willing to pretend that what they'd found together was anything less than the kind of love and friendship that would take a lifetime to explore. Details hadn't been discussed, concrete plans had yet to be made, but the one reality was that they had pledged themselves to a future together.

Now it was the middle of their fourth week at Lakeland House. The yard below was filled with the sounds of night creatures scurrying across the hard earth in search of food and shelter. Meg and Joe lay together in their room, their bodies covered by the patchwork quilt, and watched the way the light from the stars and moon spilled through the unshuttered window and splashed across the glowing oak floor. She felt more incandescent than any star, more magical than the light from ten moons.

Her head rested on Joe's muscular, amazing chest. Strands of her long pale hair drifted across her face, and every now and then Joe would smooth them away from her skin, wrapping their silky length around his hand as if he could bind her to him forever. It was a revelation to her that intense physical pleasure could bring about intense spiritual joy.

She pressed a kiss against his hair-roughened chest. "We must have invented this," she said, her voice lazy with satisfaction. "I can't believe anyone on earth has ever been this happy."

He chuckled. Its low rumble tickled her ear. "When it's right, it seems that way." He stroked her hair; pinpoints of awareness tingled across her scalp. "We keep reinventing what we need to be happy."

She leaned up and looked at him. "I never knew you were a philosopher."

"All writers are to one degree or another. We just get to put our own philosophies into the mouths of other people, that's all."

She thought about the Angelique Moreau books that she'd read. Despite the high degree of sensuality and excitement in the sprawling sagas, family ties had been the strongest themes, the unbreakable bloodline linking one generation to the next.

"I'm surprised you never married," she said. "With your background, I would think you'd have a wife and six kids by now."

He was quiet for a moment. "I thought I'd have them by now, too."

Her curiosity suddenly grew intense. Not even her normal reticence to dig deeply was able to squelch it. "Have you ever been in love?"

"Before now?"

"Yes," she said. "Before now."

"I thought I was once." His eyes closed against a memory Meg almost feared. "Rita and I went together through high school. We got engaged right after I got drafted."

"What happened?"

He looked at her, all lightness gone from his face. "Time happened. Distance happened." He was quiet for a second. "Vietnam happened. When I came back, I couldn't settle down to be the nine-to-five breadwinner she wanted. Three-piece suits felt like straitjackets, and the idea of 'happily ever after' seemed like some psychedelic distortion of reality."

"What happened to Rita?"

"A nice accountant named Artie DeFalco. They live in Bayside now. A duplex with an eight-percent mortgage, a new car every year and two kids to send to college."

"You keep in touch with her?" He didn't seem the type to carry a torch for almost fifteen years.

He laughed, and her fears disappeared. "My mother keeps in touch with her every Christmas. Ma likes to let me know how respectable people conduct their lives."

"Poor Joe," she said, kissing the underside of his firm jaw. "Poor disreputable writer."

"What about you?" he asked. "Have you ever been in love before?" Just because a woman's body had been untouched didn't mean her heart had been.

"I've dated, if that's what you mean, but never anything serious." She chuckled softly. "When I was in school, I was one of those terribly artsy types who sublimated desire for unbridled creativity. You would have hated me.''

Joe, however, found that hard to believe. ''Where did you get the idea that celibacy promoted creativity?'' His six months of celibacy had done wonders for his soul but very little for his creativity.

''My sister. Kay was a workaholic, and dutiful little sister that I was, I followed suit.''

''You thought it would make your parents love you more?''

She shrugged. ''It couldn't hurt any. Besides, I don't think I was ready for anything heavy. I had enough trouble keeping my self-esteem afloat with my family. A love relationship might have done me in entirely.''

''So you protected yourself through college?''

''With the help of my trusty camera and tripod.''

''What about after you graduated? Wasn't there ever one man who mattered more than others? Another photographer, maybe?'' Damn, what was the matter with him? Why couldn't he control his insane writer's curiosity?

Meg, however, didn't seem to mind. ''When I got out of Stony Brook, I started a project on old whaling villages. *National Geographic* was interested in my work, and I didn't have time or energy for anything else.'' She was quiet for a moment, and he waited for her to gather her thoughts. ''Even my parents were impressed.'' She drew a hand over her eyes, brushing away a lock of blond hair. ''I was on Maui, at Lahaina, working on the series, when Kay was killed.'' She sighed. ''My parents were destroyed by it.'' God knew, Meg had reached out to them in their shared pain, only to be rebuffed. It had been concrete proof that her existence ran a distant second to Kay's memory. ''Then *National Geographic* fell through—I often wondered if Kay hadn't been behind the offer somehow. After that I traveled for a year, and well, you know the rest.'' She laughed, a bit nervously. ''World's most overqualified limousine driver.''

He thought of the photos he'd left with Renee, photos good enough to excite even his very difficult to excite agent. The idea that the woman capable of taking such incredible pictures was the same woman who spent her days driving a limousine to the airport was incomprehensible.

"Why do you do it? Do you need the money?"

"Who doesn't?" she tossed back. Both were aware her answer was too glib. "I don't need it desperately," she continued when Joe said nothing. "Kay left me a great deal of money, and Paine Webber sees that it keeps growing."

"Terrific," Joe said. "So why aren't you out there with your camera right now? Why hide behind the steering wheel of a Lincoln Continental?" He was relentless in his need to know all. "You must know you have the talent."

She pulled away from him, and he had to remind himself this was the Margarita of flesh and blood and not the woman of his own creation, a character whose actions he controlled.

"I can see that the pictures I take are good." A pause. "Damned good. I lost the ambition. When Kay died, it didn't seem so important anymore."

"I don't understand," he said. She looked away as if seeking out an avenue of escape. "I want to understand, Meg. Please."

"For a long time I was second-best, Joe." She laughed softly. "You know, like Avis. I had to try harder. When Kay died—" She shrugged, her slender shoulders bathed in moonlight. "Well, I lost my incentive. I had no one to pattern myself after, no one to look up to and—" She stopped.

Joe, however, was able to fill in the blanks. "And no one to try to beat." Meg nodded, her brown eyes filling with tears. He brushed one gently off her cheek.

"How could I top a sister who died a heroine?" Meg asked softly. "What kind of person would even want to try?"

"You weren't the one who died, Margarita. You still have the right to your own life, your own success."

He thought of telling her about Renee and her interest in the pictures of Hunt, but the moment was so special, so intensely personal, that he kept silent, afraid his attempt to help would be misconstrued as interference.

"What's the first step?" he asked instead, hoping to pick up a cue from her. "What's the first step in renewing your career?"

"Buying some more film." Her voice was cool and calm, but he thought he could detect a note of enthusiasm in it, the fire beneath the ice.

"Seriously, Meg."

"Oh, God, Joe, I have no idea. Look up some of my old contacts in Manhattan, maybe. A new portfolio." She groaned. "I just don't know."

"You could stay here," he said. "You don't have to go back to New York at all. You could work on that series of pictures you did on Hunt's imaginary village." He took a deep breath. "I could even contact my agent and have her take a look at them. Maybe she—"

Meg raised a hand to stop him. "Forget it." Her jaw was set in a tight line. She was all ice now. "Don't push me, Joe. I'll work everything out on my own. I always have before."

"There's nothing wrong with a few introductions," he said, feeling guilty and annoyed simultaneously.

"No, there's not," she answered. "But I'm not looking for any right now."

"Your sister helped you out. There's no reason I couldn't."

"Don't push, Joe." He must have looked more upset than he realized, because she suddenly thawed and reached for his hand. "I have to walk before I can run, don't I?"

"Why run when you can fly?"

She said nothing. He pulled her closer, and she tugged the quilt up over both of them against the draft that whistled through the cracks around the window. For days, as the pages of his Angelique Moreau novel began piling up beside his portable typewriter, he'd felt himself building speed, gaining strength, recovering his old agility. His future no longer seemed barren; he no longer felt he'd be forever trapped behind the pseudonyms he'd once willingly embraced. His own past didn't frighten him any longer; he'd even begun outlining the Vietnam story he'd put off writing for so long.

He could almost physically feel the barriers he'd erected so long ago breaking down as his heart opened toward the real Margarita as well as the fictional one. He wanted her to know that he, too, needed help sometimes.

He kissed the top of her head. "Thanks."

"For what?"

"For providing the inspiration."

She moved herself away from him and narrowed her eyes. "Inspiration for what?"

He laughed. "Don't sound so suspicious. The inspiration for *Fire's Lady*." She stared at him blankly. "When I got here, I was in the middle of the worst case of writer's block since F. Scott Fitzgerald."

"How bad?"

He rolled his eyes. "Terminal, I thought. For four months, two weeks and three days I didn't write anything more than a personal check. I thought Angelique Moreau was finished. A few weeks ago I would have asked you if there was room in your business for another limo driver."

"What was the problem?"

"Everything and nothing," he said. "Maybe I'm getting tired of hiding behind someone else's name. Maybe I'm tired of writing someone else's story." The story about Vietnam, about an American's coming to terms with death and new life, was Joseph Alessio's to tell. "Whatever it is, it was taking its toll."

"I still don't understand how I helped you."

"I'd been having a lot of trouble catching the spirit of the heroine," he began, feeling suddenly awkward about explaining the motivation behind his new spurt of creative energy. "For a long time now I've been wondering if I'd played out my hand. I knew I had to create a high-spirited, strong, beautiful woman to found the Franklin dynasty, but she never came to life." He hesitated. "At least not until I met you."

She moved slightly away from him and looked into his eyes.

"The second I saw you square your shoulders and go back into the church at Anna's funeral when all I wanted to do was run for the nearest bar and cry into a scotch, I knew you were the woman I'd been searching for."

"For your book, of course," she said, a smile teasing the corners of her mouth.

"Of course." They both knew it went far deeper.

"And what is this woman's name?"

"Margarita," he said, drawing her back into his arms.

He pulled her on top of him, then rolled over so his body covered hers and their mouths were just a breath apart.

"And what are you up to, Angelique Moreau?" she asked, her dark eyes twinkling.

"Research," he said, his lips meeting hers. "Research."

THEY WERE GOOD. *Very* good.

Meg stepped away from the prints lined up on the desk in the library and inspected her handiwork with a determinedly dispassionate eye. It had been so long since Meg had seen these photos of Anna and the Lakeland House alumni she'd taken three years ago at a Dartmouth fundraiser that she'd forgotten just how good they really were.

The contrast, the balance, the way she'd managed to catch the bizarre blend of awkwardness and grace so common at such gatherings, pleased both her artistic eye as well as her practical one.

She and Joe had been trying to find a photo of Anna at work to finish off the final portion of the history of the Kennedy Colony, and until last night Meg had stubbornly refused to consider any of her own photos. She knew it had taken all of Joe's self-control to stop trying to goad her into taking action, and she appreciated the fact that he'd been able to drop the subject against what obviously was his better judgment. He was a man who needed to guide, to control, and she appreciated his having curbed those instincts with her. To someone else it would be a sign of disinterest; to Meg it was a sign of love.

For a long time she'd been guided by needs that had little to do with her own talent and everything to do with her desire to be loved. However, last night, in the darkness and intimacy of her room, as she listened to herself tell Joe her reasons for resisting her own progress, the need to break free of the past had grown wings inside her mind.

While Joe slept an extra hour before embarking on his daily run, Meg showered and hurried to the library where she had spent the last three hours sifting through her photos that Anna had saved. Her stomach fluttered at the thought of taking this small step into her professional future. The years of having doors opened for her surfaced, and she had to actively force twinges of guilt out of her mind as she selected the best three shots and hurried downstairs to the study.

Joe was drooped over his typewriter, his dark hair flopping across his forehead, his glasses sliding down his strong nose. She stopped in the doorway and held an imaginary camera in front of her face.

"Click, click." She grinned at him when he started in surprise. "I call it *Writer in Torment*." She crossed the room to him, her photos securely tucked under her arm. "Is Margarita giving you trouble?"

He pulled her across his lap, and she laughed. The envelope fell to the floor near them, but it went unnoticed as he pressed kisses along her throat and shoulders.

"I know how to handle Margarita," he said, demonstrating with hands and mouth just how accurate a statement that was. "It's these damned biographies that are doing me in."

She leaned over and glanced at the piece of white paper sticking out of his portable typewriter. "'Thomas Preston was born in Manhattan in 1931. He attended the Parsons School of Design, and after graduation he—'" Meg stood up and looked at Joe. She shook her head.

Joe raked his hands through his already tousled hair. "Awful, isn't it?"

"Awful isn't the word for it," Meg said. "This stinks."

"Well, you're blunt, I'll grant you that." He reached for the cigarette resting on the edge of the nearly overflowing ashtray. "I've done so many of these the past few weeks that I can do them blindfolded."

"I know what you mean." Meg groaned. "It's gotten so I'm alphabetizing things in my sleep." She glanced at his empty coffee cup and poured him a refill from the carafe on the credenza behind the desk. "Here," she said, handing him the steaming cup. "Maybe some caffeine will rev your motor."

He took a sip and grinned at her, his good humor obviously restored. "I know a few other ways to rev my motor."

"Let's keep it in neutral for a while, Joe," she said with a pleased laugh. "I have some business to discuss with you." She picked the fallen envelope from the floor, opened it and removed the photos. "Take a look."

Joe took the photos from her, taking careful note of the way she seemed to find it difficult to meet his eyes. He spread the prints out on top of the desk and knew instantly they were Meg's—that kind of talent happened rarely.

"Where did you find these?" he asked, not looking up at her.

"With Anna's personal papers." She cleared her throat. "I thought they might be good for the opening to the final chapter."

Might be good? he thought. The photos were perfect. "This is the one." He gestured toward the shot of Anna and a group of young dancers. "That look of exultation on her ace—that's the essence of Anna.'' He looked up at Meg, rying to keep the sparkle from his eyes. "Who took it?''

Her smile was proud and nervous. "I did.''

"Did you take all three of them?''

She nodded. "I may have resigned myself to just being a footnote in the colony's history, but a photo credit would still be nice.''

His smile was amused, slightly self-mocking. "No pseudonyms?''

She smiled back at him. "No pseudonyms.''

"Good going, Lindstrom," he said, trying to cover up the feeling of excitement her decision stirred up inside him.

"It's just a start," she said slowly, as if she were carefully sorting out her feelings before she spoke.

He put the picture back down on the desk. "What do you expect to come of this?''

"Nothing." She laughed and spread her hands open wide. "Everything. God, I just don't know, Joe. I've been getting so restless these past weeks, so aware that time is slipping away.''

He stood up and took her in his arms as much for his own deep pleasure as to comfort her. "Time won't slip away from us, Margarita. We're going to have all the time in the world." He thought she understood that finishing their project did not mean finishing their relationship. Things had gone too far for that.

Her cheek against his was cool and soft, but he could feel the warmth beneath the surface. "I know that," she said. "I was talking about my work. There's no guarantee the world is waiting for me with open arms, you know. None of my old contacts are even in New York anymore.''

"We'll find out where they are and go to them," he said, thinking of Renee's positive reaction to Meg's series on Huntington Kendall. "I can always ask Renee to—''

She pulled away from him. "Forget it, Joe. I let Kay pave the way for me, and it backfired. Let me worry about my own career.''

She tried to soften her words with a smile, but still Joe fel
stung, more so than her words warranted. "I'm not talkin
patronage, Meg," he said, his voice louder than before
"It's called networking."

"I call it interference."

"Writers rely on contacts and intros all the time."

"I'm not a writer," she said. He could almost see he
stubborn Swedish side butting heads with the more volatil
Italian.

"Terrific," he said, embarrassed and angered by her re
fusal to accept his help. "Do it yourself." He turned his at
tention back to the unfinished biographies on his desk. H
wondered what she'd do if she knew he'd given her photo
to Renee.

She waited quietly for a few moments. He could feel he
dark eyes upon him, but he refused to look up.

"Have you had breakfast?" she asked finally.

He nodded, saying nothing.

"Want more coffee?" She was sounding less concilia
tory by the minute.

He shook his head, fully aware he was acting like a guilt
ten-year-old child but unable to stop himself.

"Fine," she said, storming toward the door. "Sulk all yo
want, Alessio. I'm going upstairs to the library."

Joe worked alone for the next few hours. The library wa
directly over the study, and he could hear the sounds of he
footsteps on the parquet floor as she obviously paced back
and forth while working on her final index. Six steps to th
left, six steps to the right, pause near the window. Then si
steps to the left again, six steps to the right. He even foun
himself typing up the rough draft on a bio to the same stac
cato rhythm of her heels against the wooden floor over hi
head.

Finally, around two o'clock, the footsteps stopped, and
he assumed she'd finally settled down at the desk like a
normal person. So when she popped up at the door to the
study around three-thirty, bearing a piping-hot pepperon

izza from the one pizzeria in town, he was taken totally by urprise.

"Enough sulking," she said, crossing the room toward im and letting him get the full benefit of the spicy aroma f the cheese-laden pie. "We've both sulked enough today o qualify us as honorary first-graders." Her smile was disrming enough—and the pizza enticing enough—to break rough the snit he was in. "How about we bury the atchet?"

He removed his glasses and rubbed the sore spot on the ridge of his nose. "Peace offering, is it?"

"If you kick in on half the price, it is." Her dark eyes ere twinkling, and he knew she had worked through her rritation with him.

"I still think you're stubborn as all hell," he said as he ood up, stretching his aching muscles.

"And I still think you're too damned pushy." She headed oward the door. "But the only important thing is this pizza. don't know about you, but I'm starving."

He was two sentences away from finishing the bio on a articularly important art critic. "Let me just finish this," e said, "and I'll be right there."

"Better hurry up," she said over her shoulder as she left he room. "I can't guarantee there will be anything left when ou get to the kitchen."

"I'll take my chances." He eyed her slender form as she isappeared down the hallway, feeling a mixture of love and dmiration for that stubborn, talented woman who'd comletely captured his heart.

The last two sentences practically wrote themselves, and e was just adding the finished bio to the folder containing he others when the telephone blared. He got it on the first ng.

"You're an anxious man, Joseph." Renee's husky New ork voice was instantly identifiable. "I thought country ving destressed people."

"There's no hope for a born New Yorker," he said wi[th] a laugh. "You should know that." He lit up a cigarett[e.] "What's up? Does Audrey have a problem with the pag[es] I've sent down?"

"No, not at all. She thinks they're great. I'm calling abo[ut] those photos you left with me." He heard her flippi[ng] through some papers. "The ones by Meg Lindstrom."

"Don't worry if something happened to them. She mad[e] up a new set of prints."

"That's exactly why I'm calling," Renee said. "I need [a] clean set of prints—in fact, I need everything she has on th[e] series."

His stomach clenched like a fist. "Personal curiosity?" he asked, hoping against hope.

"Professional interest. I showed them to a friend on th[e] staff of *People* magazine, and they'd like to run the series [as] part of a feature on new artists."

Joe took a long drag on his cigarette, then stubbed it o[ut] in a nervous gesture.

"They think Huntington Kendall is the hottest thing [to] come along in years," she was saying as Joe's mind ski[t]tered around, trying to absorb her words. "And Lin[d]strom's photos are attracting a lot of attention."

"For Kendall?" he managed.

Renee laughed. "For both of them. I'd like to talk wi[th] Ms Lindstrom about representing her work."

"No." The word burst out of him like gunshot.

"Has she already sold the series elsewhere?"

"No, no." Damn it to hell. Why had he ever shown tho[se] pictures to Renee? Meg would view this as the ultimate d[e]ceit.

"Has she left the colony?"

"No, she's still here."

"Then what in hell's going on, Joseph? Let me speak wi[th] her, unless you've suddenly become a business manager o[n] the side."

He managed to explain to Renee that Meg wasn't interested in getting back into photography professionally at the moment. Without going into detail, he hinted that she had a few things to work out.

"I don't understand it, but I'll take your word for it," Renee said. "What does she do for a living?"

"Drives a limousine."

"She's a chauffeur? A woman with that kind of talent is a chauffeur?"

It was the same reaction Joe'd had when he realized the scope of Meg's abilities.

"Tell her this assignment from *People* will put a lot of gasoline in her tank."

"I wish it were that easy."

Renee sighed theatrically. "Every time I think I've seen it all, I see a little more. You creative types are incredible. I think you all have this romantic notion that it's better to starve in a garret than compromise your talent with the real world."

"Come off it, Renee," he said with a laugh. "This is Angelique Moreau/Bret Allen/Alex Dennison, you're talking to. I'm the expert at compromising talent."

"Your words, not mine. Besides," she continued, her voice softening, "your time is coming. You won't be able to hide forever."

As usual, Renee was right on target. But the subject, this time, was Meg.

"I'll see how she feels about it, Renee, but I can't promise anything."

"The woman's damned good, Joe, and so is Kendall. Some national exposure could really get their careers rolling."

After he hung up, Joe lit another cigarette, savoring the jolt of nicotine to his system. What had started out as an impulsive act of generosity had suddenly escalated to the point where he held two careers—both Meg's and Kendall's—in the palm of his hand.

He'd been around long enough to know that coverag such as *People* could offer was a once-in-a-lifetime shot fo a new artist or photographer. His own career had taken a enormous leap into the ranks of best-selling authors after "Who is Angelique Moreau?" article appeared in the sam magazine a few years earlier. For all of Meg's righteous ir dignation about patronage—or networking, as he though of it—he couldn't help but wonder if even she would refus the chance to have her photos seen by millions of people coast to coast. No matter how hard she tried, she hadn' been able to extinguish the light of ambition from her eyes The photo credit she yearned for in the "Annotated His tory of the Kennedy Creative Colony" was nothing com pared to this.

But then the memory of how she felt in his arms, the scer of her hair, the sound of her soft voice greeting him ever morning, wrapped themselves around his heart. He be lieved the love they'd found was a forever kind of love, love that provided a firm foundation for a life together. Ye he wasn't fool enough to think that the foundation had set tled enough to weather this storm easily.

They were both stubborn, both volatile, both easily hur by slights real and imagined. Four weeks in an idyllic set ting was hardly enough to counter almost thirty years o solitary living.

"Come on, Joe!" Meg called from the kitchen. "Ther won't be anything left for you!"

"Be right there!"

He ground out his cigarette and pushed his hair off hi forehead with the back of his hand. There would be othe chances. Hunt was young and burning with genius; noth ing could keep his star from ascending. And Meg—hi Margarita—was gifted, as well. She was as logical as she wa talented, and Joe felt certain that when she wanted the righ doors to open, they would swing wide and welcome her bac inside.

Love was the one thing that couldn't be guaranteed, the one thing that could disappear within a heartbeat. A lifetime of loving and growing together couldn't compare with a fleeting moment in a magazine. Meg had said to stay out of her professional life, and now, at last, he was going to bow to her wishes.

He wouldn't tell her about Renee's call. She might lose a chance at stardom, but the future Meg and Joe could build together was far more important.

He'd waited thirty-three years to find her, and he wasn't about to lose her now.

IN THE END, though, it was *Casablanca* that was Joe's undoing.

If one of the late-night movie stations on cable hadn't picked that night to replay his favorite movie, he just might have been able to forget Renee had ever called with an offer for Meg's work. He just might have been able to pretend he made the right decision for both of them. But *Casablanca* was on, and the same sense of honor that made Rick send Ilsa away also made it impossible for Joe to give Meg anything but the truth. She deserved the right to make her own decisions—both about her career and about their future together.

It was nearly midnight. He and Margarita were curled up on the sofa, a bottle of Chianti next to him and a box of Kleenex next to her. Meg was already sniffling softly in anticipation of the moment when Rick saw the beautiful Ilsa again after so many years. He got up and lowered the sound on the television.

It was now or never.

Meg sat up. "Joe? What's wrong?"

He was beyond subtlety. "Do you remember that phone call this afternoon?"

She frowned. "The one from your agent?"

"That's the one." He jammed his hands into the pockets of his pants to keep them from shaking. "I didn't tell you everything she said."

Meg smiled. "You don't have to tell me everything she says, Joseph. I'm your lover, not your business partner. That's private as far as I'm concerned."

This was going to be even harder than he anticipated.

"Is something wrong with one of your books? A rewrite or something?"

He shook his head.

"Was she offering you a million-dollar advance on your next epic?"

"Not exactly."

"What, then?" Her face was relaxed and smiling, but he could sense she was picking up his uneasiness.

The movie started again. Ilsa and Victor walked into Rick's Place; Joe could feel Rick's pain.

He took a deep breath. "Remember those pictures you gave me?"

She frowned. "The ones of Hunt and us?"

Joe nodded. "And his imaginary village."

"Of course I remember them. What do they have to do with your agent?"

He raked his hand through his hair with the same nervous gesture he'd had since childhood. "Remember when I went down to New York and I took the photos along to look at on the plane?" She nodded. "Well, they were so terrific I showed them to Renee." He felt like a man with his neck poised, waiting for the blade of the guillotine to drop.

"And?" She wasn't smiling any longer. Her dark eyes seemed wary.

"I showed them to Renee. Renee showed them to an editor at *People* magazine. They want to use them in an article on up-and-coming artists." He swallowed hard. "It would feature both you and Hunt." If this were an old-fashioned movie, the heroine would toss aside her anger and throw herself into the arms of the hero just before the fade-out. However, this time fantasy wouldn't help him, and the "happily ever after" seemed more and more unlikely.

Meg said nothing. He decided to take it as a good sign.

"It's great publicity for both of you," he said. "Renee said they're offering two thousand dollars for the series."

She still said nothing. A close-up of Bergman, her face radiant with love, filled the television screen across the room. He was finding it hard to think clearly.

"Damn it, Meg, say something."

"If you're waiting for me to say thank you, you can forget it, Joe."

He sat down on the edge of the sofa.

"Come on," he said, battling now with annoyance, as well. "I didn't announce a second attack on Pearl Harbor. This is supposed to be good news."

"For you, maybe. Do you get ten percent on the deal, or will you and Renee split the fee?"

"What's that supposed to mean?"

He reached out to touch her arm, and she pulled away from him as if he were radioactive.

"You had no business showing those pictures to anyone, Joe. They were simply for your own enjoyment, nothing more."

"Maybe that's how you felt when you took them," he said, "but they were extraordinary. I was excited about them, and I shared them with a friend."

"A friend who happens to be an agent." The way she said the word *agent*, it suddenly became a four-letter word.

His fuse was growing shorter. "I showed them to my *friend* Renee, not my agent."

"Well, you can just tell your friend Renee to rip them up. They're not going anywhere."

"What about Hunt?" Joe said. "What about his stake in this?"

"They can send a photographer to take a new set of photos."

"It won't be the same, Meg, and you know it."

"I'm not Ansel Adams. I can be replaced."

"Damn it to hell, Lindstrom. Why are you being so stubborn?"

She was so cool, so calm, but he could tell by the rising color in her cheeks that her control was about to snap. "Don't try to turn this around on me, Joe. I'm not the one who violated a trust."

His laugh was sudden and sharp. "A trust? I didn't read your diary, Meg. I didn't peek at your bankbook or check your credit rating. Why don't you keep it in perspective? All I did was show Renee your photos."

"What you did was give personal property to someone I don't even know. That wasn't a submission to an editor, Joe. They were snapshots I took simply for my own pleasure."

"For *our* pleasure," he said, "and part of my pleasure was sharing those pictures with Renee."

"Showing them to her, yes, but why would you leave them with her? Didn't you wonder why she wanted them?"

She had him with that one. "Okay, I did wonder about it, but it didn't seem that big a deal."

Her anger increased. "Didn't you think to ask her what she was going to do with them? Didn't you think to ask me if it was okay?"

"Obviously the answer to both of those questions is no. Maybe I *was* hoping Renee would do something to help you—I don't know. I wasn't thinking that far ahead at the time."

"Maybe you should start thinking that far ahead."

"You seem to be forgetting one very important thing here. I didn't have to tell you any of this. I could have just told Renee to forget the *People* assignment and you'd never have found out. We could just go on the way we have been. Sounds nice, doesn't it?" He suppressed the need to step closer to her, to touch her. "It would have made it a lot easier on me, but I felt you had the right to make a choice."

"And that, Mr. Alessio, was your biggest mistake. Maybe this time you should have kept your mouth shut."

"Damn it to hell!" Joe slammed his fist down on the tabletop next to him in an attempt to hold back angry words he knew he would regret. Drops of Chianti stained the wood, and he watched, perversely fascinated, as they pooled at the edge, then began a slow trickling down the side. He was as unable to stop the progress of the wine as he was unable to make Margarita Lindstrom understand.

"Just tell me one thing," he said, crossing his arms over his chest to rein in his anger. "When are you going to stop getting in your own way?"

Meg suddenly had an overwhelming urge to pick up the bottle of wine on the table and hurl it at the wall behind Joe's head. The sound of breaking glass and the look of surprise on his face would be worth the cleaning effort afterward. But she managed to control herself—barely.

"You're wonderful at analyzing me, Joe, but have you taken a look at yourself lately?"

"What does that mean?"

"What about those notebooks you keep on the nightstand? What about all those times you wake up sweating after some nightmare and spend hours writing in the dark?" She saw his body actually jerk with surprise. "Did you think I didn't know about that? How would you like it if I took those pages and gave them to an editor? Are you ready for that?" She saw a flash of uncertainty in his eyes. Part of her reacted with love and empathy; part of her still needed to strike back. "You push too hard, Joe. Why can't you understand that I'll be ready in my own time?"

Damn it, that time was coming; it had been barreling down upon her since she returned to Lakeland House a month ago, afraid to face her former self. It had confronted her each morning as she evaluated other people's work; it had haunted her each night as she thought of all she wanted to do, all she could yet be.

"And maybe you'll never be ready," Joe said, anger and pain evident in his voice. "Maybe if you keep waiting for the right time, you'll wake up and find your life is over before you ever started." He lowered his voice. "Maybe all you need is a push in the right direction."

"Not from you, Joe." She remembered the uncomfortable feeling she always had when Kay's name opened a door for her. "Never from you." If she and Joe didn't each bring a separate entity into their relationship, they would each end up with nothing. Her sister had cast a large shadow, and for too long Meg had been happy to accept whatever sunshine filtered through. It wasn't a situation she cared to repeat. "If you really knew me, I wouldn't have to explain it to you."

"Maybe you do have to explain it." His beautiful green eyes glittered from the black-and-white glow of the television screen. Rick and Ilsa were reliving Paris, and Meg's heart was threatening to break right along with theirs.

"From the day we met, you've been probing every part of my personality. Don't you think I know how you watch every move I make? Don't you realize I can see that writer's mind of yours processing bits and pieces of my soul for your damned book? Do you think I like that? But I let you do it." A quick memory of the night they first watched *Casablanca* flashed across her brain, almost undermining all she wanted to say.

"I understand the creative process and all it takes to get to the end result. Do I harass you about doing your Vietnam book?" He flinched, and she was sorry, but she didn't stop. "You have your own boundaries, and I have mine. Why can't you understand that my methods are different and maybe my goals are, too. Let me find the path on my own."

"You're living in some kind of dreamworld, Meg. No one is going to track you down and leave a note on your windshield offering you the world."

"I don't want the world, Joe. I just want a part of it."

"Damn it, don't you know this has nothing to do with how I feel about you or what we have together? I shared your photos with a friend who happens to be a woman with business contacts. I didn't ask her to help you. She saw talent, and she acted upon it." He shrugged, and Meg wanted to smack him. "Maybe your real problem is with yourself."

"The hell it is. If I can't trust you to respect this part of myself that belongs only to me, how can I trust you with the rest of my life? Maybe what happened here was just a result of too many roaring fires and too much Cinzano."

"Terrific," he said. "Keep looking in from the outside. Keep yourself away from the life you really want. You can go on driving that goddamn limo the rest of your days for all I care. You can pretend to be part of Elysse's family until you're a hundred. You can pretend you don't want the photography and a home and everything else, but I won't buy it. I want more than that, Meg, and if you had half the courage I thought you had, you'd admit you want more, too."

Damn him and that uncanny writer's insight that stripped away all of the protective layers and exposed her vulnerable heart, which few had bothered to seek out. She wanted to draw those layers back around her heart and protect herself from any more pain. *I won't cry,* she told herself. *I refuse to cry.*

"You're going too far, Joe." *This hurts too much.* "Stop before we lose everything we had."

"We had nothing if so little can make it disappear."

"You can't control me like one of the characters in your book. I have a history—a past you didn't create."

"I know all about your past, Meg. Every time you come close to taking a chance, every time you come close to standing on your own, you put that past up in front of you like a shield." He paced the room, dragging his hand through his hair as he talked. "I'm sorry your parents didn't love you enough, I'm sorry your sister died, I'm sorry life hasn't always been kind to you, but those are the breaks. I've been there, Meg, I know what it's like to hurt." He stopped and looked at her, as if seeking a response, but she had none to give. She was a raw and aching wound.

"You can't let that ruin your life, Meg."

She stood up, surprised her legs were able to hold her. There was a kernel of truth in everything Joe had been saying to her, and the thought of facing that truth, coming to grips with a future she could control, rendered Meg speechless. She trembled as if caught in a vicious Arctic wind. On the screen, Bogart and Bergman were entwined in a cinematic embrace, their lips moving rapidly, comically, without the sound. Meg headed for the door, praying Joe wouldn't try to stop her and dreading the fact that he just might let her go.

Joe wanted more than anything to grab Meg and carry her upstairs to that wonderful bed where they'd shared such delight. Surely the magic they'd found together couldn't disappear in the wink of an eye. However, he knew he had pushed her as far as she could be pushed, and he hoped, instead, to win her back with words.

"I love you, Margarita. Don't turn away from me."

She stopped in the doorway and faced him. In her beautiful eyes he saw pain and fear and—please, God—love. "Let me go, Joe. If I don't leave, I may end up hating you, and I don't want to hate you."

Joe started to move toward her; he needed to touch her, to connect with her. She was slipping away from him, and he knew it. He also knew that this time he had to let go.

The sound of her footsteps on the stairs seemed to echo through the house. He glanced at the television where Bergman's incandescent beauty, so reminiscent of Margarita's own, hit him like a speeding railroad car.

He picked up the half-full bottle of Chianti and raised it toward the television set.

"Here's looking at you, kid."

No wonder he'd always preferred fantasy to reality. In a fantasy, the hero's heart never broke.

Chapter Twelve

Elysse Lowell pushed the crisp new fifty-dollar bill back across the kitchen table and into Meg's hands.

"Keep the money, Lindstrom," she said. "I'd rather have a few answers instead."

Meg took a sip of hot black coffee and prayed it would wake her up. The six-hour drive down from New Hampshire to Long Island had wiped her out. "Money's a lot easier to come by, Elly. If I had all the answers, I wouldn't be here right now."

How true. If things were different, she'd be back at Lakeland House with Joe just as she had been twenty-four hours ago. She'd be back in his arms, back in the place she most wanted to be. But the questions Joe had asked were the same questions she'd been afraid to face for so many years; questions for which she had no easy answers. This time she knew she had to find those answers.

"What happened?" Elysse pushed a buttered croissant toward Meg, who shook her head. "Did you two have a misunderstanding?"

"Oh, no. I understood Joe quite well. That's the problem." Quickly she outlined what had happened with Renee and the photos and the offer from *People* magazine. Elysse just listened quietly, her large blue eyes sweeping over Meg's face with the accuracy of an emotional mine detector.

"That's quite an opportunity, Meg. Forgetting Joe's part n it, how do you feel?"

Meg was quiet for a moment. "Excited, flattered, almost s happy for Hunt as I am for myself. But I can't accept the ontract."

"It could mean a lot for your career."

Meg looked down at her nearly empty coffee cup. "I now. Exposure like that could bring me back to where I vas before Kay died."

Elysse chuckled. "Exposure like that could take you light-ears beyond where you were when Kay died, and you know t."

Meg nodded and said nothing.

"You'll be giving up a lot."

"I'd be giving up much more if I let someone else open he doors for me again." She thought about Kay, about how vell-meaning assistance subtly kept one person subservient o another. It had haunted Meg all of her life, and she knew t could ruin her future with Joe.

Elysse got up and poured them each a refill of the coffee. t was so comforting to be in that familiar kitchen, but Meg vas sharply aware that it was Elysse's kitchen, not hers, that he had surrounded herself with the trappings of another voman's life, another woman's family, while she hid from ursuing her own.

Elysse sat back down. "And what about that young art-st—what's his name?"

Meg smiled. "Huntington Kendall IV."

"What about him? You may not want some friendly in-erference, but Kendall may welcome it with open arms."

Meg's eyes drooped closed for a moment. Great aching vaves of fatigue were washing over her. "I don't know, Elly," she said. "I simply don't know what to do." She sat up and took a bracing sip of hot coffee. "Either way some-ne gets hurt." Her thoughts focused in on Joe, on the look n his beautiful green eyes when she told him she had to eave. She had prayed he would stop her at the door; she had hoped he would let her go. Either way her heart was torn in two.

"Well, Dr. Lowell," Meg said, leaning back in her straight-back wooden chair. "Is there any hope for me?" Her attempt at lightness fell terribly flat. "Is there, Elly?"

Elysse, of course, knew exactly what Meg was talking about. "Did you leave him a note when you left?"

"Yes."

"What did you say in it?"

"I told him not to call me—I had to get away and think. I told him I would send Patrick the finished cumulative index by the end of the week. I told him I was still angry." Meg grimaced. "I told him much of what he said was true. I—"

Elysse leaned forward. Her large eyes never left Meg's. "And?"

Meg smiled, the first real smile since she left Lakeland House the night before. "And I told him I loved him."

"Do you, Meg?"

"Yes, I do." Physical fatigue and emotional exhaustion combined to lower her guard, and she began to cry, something she rarely did. "Damn it!" She brushed tears away with a white linen napkin. "I almost wish he hadn't told me about the offer. I would have been better off not knowing." Tears streamed down her cheeks quicker than she could blot them up.

"If he's half the man you say he is, he had to tell you Meg. You wouldn't want a man who didn't."

"So says Elysse Lowell, psychologist?"

Elysse got up and put an arm around Meg. "So says Elysse Lowell, best friend."

"I'm still angry, though, Elly. I still feel betrayed by what he did."

"You have every right to feel betrayed," Elysse said calmly, "but you have to try to understand his point of view. He saw it as nothing more than sharing photos with a friend."

"But I thought he knew me better than that—I mean, I've never felt so close to another human being. He should have known how I'd feel."

"He's only known you a month, Meg!" Elysse chuckled. "My God, it's taken me over eight years and a doctorate in psychology to begin to figure out what goes on inside that Swedish-Italian heart of yours." She reached out and patted Meg's hand. "Joe is a man—nothing more, nothing less. He may be a brilliant writer who understands a woman's deepest thoughts on paper, but the fact remains that real life is a far cry from fiction. He's only human. He can make mistakes just like you. If you expect a god, you'll end up disappointed every time."

"So what do I do now?" Meg stifled a yawn.

"Get some sleep."

"A professional opinion?" She stood up, almost swaying with fatigue.

Elysse put an arm around her friend's slender waist to steady her. "Definitely. Things will seem much better when you wake up."

"Is that a promise, Elly?"

Elysse draped Meg's coat over her shoulders and thought about the thousands of variables that governed human emotions. How could she possibly guarantee Meg that things would work out? But then Elysse remembered they were dealing with love, and love usually managed to make a monkey out of anyone foolish enough to doubt its power. "Oh, yes," Elysse said softly. "It's a promise."

IT WAS FIVE DAYS, four hours and twenty-seven minutes since Meg walked out the door of Lakeland House, and Joe was sitting in Patrick McCallum's office, doing his level best to get drunk.

"Is there any more Cointreau?"

Patrick held the heavy amber bottle up to the light. "No," he said, tossing the empty bottle into the wastebasket near his desk. "How about some Benedictine?"

Joe drained the last drop of Cointreau from his glass and leaned across the desk. "No Benedictine," he said, "but how about some of that Old Grand-Dad you keep stashed in the credenza."

McCallum's face, ruddy from the brandy and two glasses of port, registered surprise. "That's my secret hiding place," he said. "My last secretary had a penchant for liquid lunches. How would you be knowing about it?"

Joe, who was also feeling no pain, leaned back in his chair. "You took it out three times when you were looking for the address book with Meg's New York number in it." He grinned as Patrick took the bottle out from its hiding spot. "I also saw the schnapps right behind it."

"It's a fine thing when a man can't be keeping some of the better things in life for himself," Patrick groaned good naturedly as he poured them each two fingers of the Old Grand-Dad. "When Pegeen and I were courting, I can remember many a night when I'd be pouring my heart out to the local innkeeper, wondering what the Almighty had in mind when he created women."

"Does it ever get any easier?" Joe asked, accepting the refilled glass.

"We were married thirty years before she died—God rest her soul. It was wonderful and exciting and loving—but easy? That, my boy, it never got." Patrick quickly drained his glass and poured himself another. "If man and woman were meant to get along, God would have made them both the same sex."

Joe laughed into his drink. "What?"

Patrick, however, was nonplussed. "That didn't come out right, but you know what I mean."

It was probably a testament to how much alcohol he'd consumed, but Joe *did* know exactly what Patrick meant, and that fact gave him little comfort. He took a sip of Old Grand-Dad and let the liquor warm its way down his throat. He and Patrick had spent the last three hours discussing women in general and Margarita Lindstrom in particular.

trying to figure out exactly what Joe's next move should be. The five days since Meg left Lakeland House so abruptly seemed like an eternity to Joe.

On the first day, he had tried to drink his way through Anna's legendary bar. On the second day, he'd nursed a tremendous hangover. On the third day, he'd cursed and bitched about her pigheaded refusal to understand his position. On the fourth, he finished his work on the Kennedy Colony history and·finally admitted that magical Lakeland House wasn't magical without Margarita near.

Now, on the fifth day, he and Patrick McCallum, who took Meg's departure almost as hard as Joe himself, were sharing a boozy farewell lunch before Joe left for New Jersey and Patrick headed south to visit at his daughter's home.

"I think I should call her," Joe said, looking over at Patrick.

"The telephone's not a good idea, Joseph. Too easy to be misunderstood. Besides, I saw her before she left. Five days aren't enough for her to cool down."

"Will seven days be enough?" Joe asked. "Or eight or ten?" He shook his head. "She's going to slip away from me, Patrick, slip right back behind that shield of armor of hers. I can't let that happen."

Patrick remained unconvinced. "You've pushed Meg about as far as she can be pushed. Maybe this time you should bow to her wishes. Be a little more judicious in your actions."

Joe laughed. "If I knew how to be more judicious, I wouldn't be sitting here drinking with you, Patrick. I'd be back at Lakeland with Meg."

"You have quite a problem there, Joseph, my boy." Patrick polished off his glass of bourbon and poured himself another. "There doesn't seem to be any easy solution, does there? I wish Anna were here to help us out."

Joe held out his glass for a refill. "I wish Anna were here to explain Meg to me. I've never met anyone quite like her."

He grinned, thinking of his fictional Margarita. "Not ever on paper."

Patrick leaned way back in his leather swivel chair and put his feet on his desktop. "I had a friend once who was in a similar situation. He had a sweetheart who refused to listen to his explanation about why he was seen at the country club with a pretty little redhead. Betsy wouldn't even take his phone calls."

Joe took a long swallow of whiskey and prepared himself for an equally long dose of Patrick's blarney. "And how did your friend handle it?" Joe asked. "Did he send her flowers or write her a love letter?"

"Anthony Dowling do something that predictable?" Patrick laughed and crossed his arms behind his head. "Oh no. Anthony was a writer just like you, Joe, except he did children's books. I remember this particular one he did that—" Joe coughed politely, and Patrick stopped short. "Well, I was getting a bit off track. Anyway, what Anthony did was—"

Joe listened carefully to the story of Anthony Dowling and Betsy Ryan. By the time he landed at Newark Airport ten hours later, he knew exactly what he had to do to win Meg's heart once again.

Are you busy?"

Meg looked up from the final index she was working on. Elysse was standing in the kitchen door, looking extremely professional in a dove-gray suit and matching shoes.

"I thought you had office hours right now," Meg said, motioning her friend inside.

Elysse stepped over the pile of papers scattered on the kitchen floor and sat down at the table opposite Meg. "Lunch hour," she said. "Or have you been working so hard you hadn't noticed?"

Meg gestured at the stacks of photos, biographies and essays piled up on the table. "There's a ham and swiss on rye hidden around here somewhere. I'll get to it."

"How's the work coming?"

"Slowly. I'm almost finished—it only took four times as long as I figured it would. I just couldn't concentrate." That was an understatement. In the eight days since Meg had left Lakeland House and Joe, she'd found it difficult, if not impossible, to concentrate on anything besides the fact that she missed him more than she could have imagined. Yet when she tried to force herself to think about the solution to their problems, her mind skittered back to the index she should be finishing. And when she brought her attention to the index, her foolish heart skittered back to thoughts of Joe and all they had shared, and could share, if she could just see her way clear.

Each morning she slogged her way through another mound of papers. Each afternoon she drove out to Sunken Meadow State Park, searching out the swans she'd photographed before she left, but they, like her peace of mind, were elusive. What did it matter if she never saw the swans again, never took another photo? She had enough photographs stuffed in suitcases and crammed in file cabinets to last her the rest of her life. The sheer pleasure in the simple act of taking and developing the pictures was no longer enough; it had never been enough. Art needed to be seen; it needed to be brought into the sunshine so both its perfections and flaws were clearly visible. If Meg were to grow as an artist, and as a woman, she would have to face the sunshine, flaws and all.

Elysse got up and poured them each a cup of coffee. "Has Joe called?" she asked, sitting back down and handing a cup to Meg.

"I didn't expect him to, Elly," Meg said. Hadn't she made it abundantly clear she wanted time to think?

Elysse sat back down. "Have you thought about calling him?"

"Not really." *Only every hour on the hour.* "We never got around to exchanging phone numbers, if you can believe it."

"You could call Patrick."

Meg blushed. "I did. He's in Virginia."

Elysse grinned. "You could call Lakeland House. If Joe answers, you can always hang up."

"I already did that. The machine was hooked up. It said the Kennedy Colony was closed for the winter." Traditionally, Lakeland House was open only from April through October.

Elysse thought for a second. "Call Joe's agent. I'm sure she would help you."

Meg choked on her coffee. "And have to come up with a decision on that *People* magazine deal? Bite your tongue."

"I thought you didn't want any part of it."

"I don't," Meg said, putting her cup down. "Not this way. But every time I think of what it would mean to Hunt, I begin to wonder if I'm being selfish." She put her head down on her arms and sighed. "What in hell am I going to do with my life, Elly?"

"Well, I can't help you with the rest of your life, but I may be able to do something about the next seven days."

Meg looked up at Elysse, who seemed decidedly uncomfortable.

"God knows this is probably the worst of all times to ask this—I know you haven't decided if you want to drive again—but Al got sick and Marty still isn't back and—"

"You need a driver?"

Elysse nodded. "Starting Saturday, a one-week special. You know we wouldn't ask you right now if things weren't so difficult, but—"

"After you've opened your home to me, do you really think I'd say no?" Meg smiled. "Of course I'll do it."

Elysse still seemed on edge. "Maybe you should hear the rest of it before you agree."

Meg took a sip of coffee. "Not another Arab sheikh, please! The last one wanted me to cut my hair so he could have a wig made for his favorite wife."

Elysse shifted around in her chair.

"Elly?" Meg was getting nervous. "Tell me it's not another sheikh."

Elysse seemed to be finding it difficult to meet Meg's eyes. "I can promise you he's not an Arab sheikh."

"I don't like the way you're not looking at me," Meg said. "What is he? A sword swallower? A deposed potentate? An ax murderer?"

Elysse took a deep breath. "He's a writer."

Meg groaned and closed her eyes. "I'd rather an ax murderer."

"Jack was afraid you'd feel like that. That's why he asked me to ask you."

"Did he figure you could use some of your therapist's skills on me?"

Elysse laughed. "No, but he did figure I could call on eight years of friendship."

"Coercion?"

"Couldn't you find a better word for it, Meg?"

"I'm not the writer," Meg said dryly. "I'm just the chauffeur." She got up and poured herself more coffee. "You realize I'd be a lot happier if he were an Arab sheikh, don't you?"

Elysse nodded. "I'm really sorry, Meg, but you're the only one available. It won't be so awful."

One of Meg's pale brows arched. "How can you be so sure?"

"He writes children's books. Now tell me, how dangerous can a children's book writer be?"

DRESSED IN HER SOBER BLACK UNIFORM and high heels, Meg was standing in the waiting room of the Eastern Airlines terminal at LaGuardia Airport two mornings later, waiting for Flight 401 from Orlando to arrive. Usually there were a number of drivers waiting around the terminal, but the Orlando flight was usually short on business people and long on families who'd spent a week with Mickey and Donald at Disney World.

Two other drivers, older men who looked as if they'd seen quite a few decades from behind the wheel of a stretch Lincoln, were leaning against the railing opposite Meg, sipping coffee and idly watching her legs. She'd had her orange juice at the cafeteria, had her oaktag sign made up, but that once-familiar routine now seemed alien to her. In the fifteen short minutes she'd been there, Meg had come to realize once and for all that she couldn't go back to driving a limousine any more than she could go back to her old, insulated life before Joe. This would be her farewell appearance with A Touch of Class Limousine Service.

The PA system overhead crackled, sputtered, then blasted to life. "Flight 401, Eastern Airlines nonstop Orlando to LaGuardia, now arriving at Gate 19."

The other two drivers ditched their coffee cups in the trash, pulled at the tails of their suit coats, then pushed ahead of the milling crowd of family and friends near the gates. Meg ran a quick hand over her sleek French braid and smoothed the lapels on her jacket. Holding up the white sign that read Anthony Dowling in large black letters, she fastened a bright and businesslike smile on her face and waited for him to deplane.

Ten minutes later she was still waiting for him to deplane.

"Excuse me," Meg stopped a flight attendant who was pushing her luggage ahead of her. "Is that everyone?"

The attractive brunette smiled sympathetically. "Afraid so. Sorry."

The attendant hurried on to catch up with her co-workers. Meg's shoulders sagged beneath her well-padded suit jacket.

"Damn it!" she said aloud. A businessman hurrying by glanced at her, amused by her mumbled oath. Meg glared at him. In her heels she stood a full head above almost everyone in that crowd. There was no way Dowling could have missed her unless he simply hadn't been on that plane at all. Maybe Dowling called Jack and canceled, Jack called the airlines, and they had forgotten to page her. There had to be some logical reason. Meg turned to race to the ticket counter when someone tapped her on the shoulder.

"Touch of Class Limousine Service?"

Thank God. Meg spun around. "Mr. Dowling? I'm so glad to—" Her words died in her throat as she looked into the beautiful green eyes of Joe Alessio.

"Hello, Margarita."

She couldn't speak. Her heart was wedged firmly at the base of her throat.

"I know I said I'd never use another pseudonym, but this time it seemed appropriate."

He was smiling at her, but she found it impossible to smile back. She didn't want him here; she didn't want him to be part of this world she was about to turn her back on. This belonged to her alone; it had been her struggle, and it was to be her victory, and Joe Alessio, as much as she loved him, had no business being part of it.

She turned and started for the door a hundred yards away.

SOMETHING WAS WRONG HERE.

Somewhere between the hello and the fade-out, the hero and heroine were supposed to fall into a big screen clinch and vow their undying love for one another. Ingrid Bergman would not have done this to Humphrey Bogart.

"Meg!"

She didn't hesitate a moment. Her long legs were eating up the distance between herself and the door quicker than he could keep up. Just a month ago she had trouble walking fast in high heels, now it seemed as if she could run the 440 without even breathing hard. Thank God he only had an overnight bag with him; if he had any more to carry, she'd be merging onto the Grand Central Parkway before he even made the sidewalk.

Joe broke into a trot, elbowing past an elderly couple in matching tweed coats and a towheaded little girl wearing Mickey Mouse ears. Meg was just turning the corner near the flight-insurance machine when Joe caught up with her and blocked her path.

"We have to talk," he said. "I'm not going to let you walk away from me a second time."

"You should have thought of that possibility before you engineered this little stunt, Mr. Dowling."

None of this was going according to the plan he and Patrick McCallum had made up during that boozy lunch of theirs. At this point, Meg should have been in Joe's arms, weeping with pleasure at seeing him again. Instead, she was glaring at him with a fury Captain Kirk usually reserved for Klingons and Romulans.

"It's not a grandstand stunt, Meg. I wanted to see you; I don't have a car. What's so terrible about renting a limousine?"

She glanced over her shoulder at him as she exited to the sidewalk. "Nice tan you don't have, Alessio. You weren't even in Orlando, were you?" She waited for a break in traffic to cross to the parking area.

"Guilty," he said, darting around a curbside taxi in an effort to keep up with her.

"What did you do? Fly over from Newark?"

This was not going well at all. "I took a limousine," he admitted, deciding the truth was so absurd there was no point in attempting fiction.

"You took a limousine to LaGuardia Airport so you could rent a limousine?" She stopped in front of her sleek, freshly polished Lincoln. Her car keys dangled from her right hand, picking up the morning sunlight and flinging it back at him. "That's ridiculous even for you, Joe."

He shrugged. "What can I tell you? When Patrick and I came up with the idea, it seemed to have quite a bit of charm."

"You both must have been under the influence."

"We were," he said. "Courtesy of Cointreau and Old Grand-Dad."

She inserted a key in the lock of the limousine. "It's been an interesting morning, Joe. We'll bill you for the time."

"Of course you will," he said smoothly, stepping between Meg and the car door. "I wouldn't expect you to work a week for nothing."

"You don't intend to go through with this charade, do you?"

"It's no charade, Meg. The Franklin dynasty in America is based on the eastern end of Long Island." He rummaged in the breast pocket of his coat and drew out a scrap of notepaper. "In Orient Point. I have to do some research."

"I can give you the name of a wonderful limousine service. I'm sure you'll be very satisfied with them."

"I have the name of a wonderful limousine service."

"A Touch of Class is highly overrated," she said. "You can do much better."

"I don't think I can, Margarita."

Her civilized, cool composure incinerated at last. "Damn it, Joe! You just couldn't let things work themselves out, could you?"

"I couldn't risk it," he said. "Life is too short and we're too important to take chances like that." No subterfuge. He refused to be embarrassed by what was in his heart.

He saw a slight flush stain her throat and cheeks. "There are other drivers, Joe."

"Maybe. But there's only one you."

"It would serve you right if I drove off and left you standing here, cooling your heels."

"You wouldn't do that to me, would you, Meg?"

"You deserve it."

"Just take me out to Orient Point." He took a deep, steadying breath. "That's all I'm asking of you, Meg." *All I'm asking right now.*

She took her sweet time answering, and he was reminded of high school dances and the prime humiliation of rejection.

"I'll do it," she said finally, and he had to bite back a whoop of joy. "But only because I owe it to Jack and the company."

"Of course," he said. "Strictly business, right?"

She straightened her shoulders, and thanks to her high heels, looked down slightly at him. "Yes, sir, Mr. Dowling." With one smooth, practiced motion, she opened the door to the passenger section of the beautifully appointed limousine. "If you will, sir."

Joe frowned at her. "I can sit up front, Meg."

She gave him a plastic, professional smile. "Oh, no, Mr Dowling, sir. Paying customers never sit up front. I want you to enjoy all the amenities."

"To hell with the amenities. The front seat's good enough for me."

"Oh, no, Mr. Dowling. Only the best for you, sir."

"Dedicated to your job, Meg?"

"More than you know." She still held the door open for him.

"You're a lousy liar."

Those dark eyes of hers seemed to glow for a second. "Whatever you say, sir."

Muttering beneath his breath, Joe climbed into the backseat.

"If you have any questions, just push the intercom on your right. The bar is fully stocked for your enjoyment." She leaned inside the compartment and flicked on the small television. "We get all the metropolitan-area channels. We even have a VCR for your viewing pleasure. A selection of tapes is in the drawer beneath the bar. I'll let you know when we reach Orient Point."

"Mind if I smoke?" He tried to push her, get past this ridiculous pose of hers.

She was bland and professionally proper. "Of course not. You're a paying customer, aren't you?"

"Meg, I—"

She closed the door with a deep, resounding thud, then got into the front and slid behind the wheel. They were separated by a clear Plexiglas shield that might as well have been the Berlin Wall. She reached up to adjust the rearview mirror, and for an instant Joe met her eyes in the reflection.

Then she looked away.

He flipped on the television set, changing channels until he located an old Doris Day-Rock Hudson movie dedicated to the premise that true love always triumphs, no matter how silly—or serious—the obstacles.

A few hours ago he'd believed that. But then hadn't he always confused fact with fiction?

YOU'RE A FOOL, Meg thought as the big car kept pace with traffic on the Northern State Parkway. *A damned fool.*

The man she loved had come to her, willing to lay his heart at her feet, and she had taken one of her high-heeled shoes and stepped on it. When she first saw him standing there in the airport, his face naked with love and apology, she had wanted to fly into his arms. But years of guarding her heart had set up a pattern that was hard to break, and she allowed her stubborn pride to put up a barrier as effective as the one that separated them right now.

All her life she had longed for that kind of all-encompassing love, and here, when it was handed to her in the person of Joe Alessio, she turned and ran like a frightened child.

Love made you vulnerable. It was impossible to love the way Joe loved and not open yourself up to pain. He'd been wrong to give her photos to Renee Arden, but he'd risked everything to give Meg the right to make up her own mind about the magazine assignment. Even when it was likely their relationship would explode because of his honesty, he loved and respected her enough to take that chance.

He was human, and he made mistakes, same as she. But he also had within him that kernel of pure goodness she'd

always imagined he possessed, and it was that goodness tha
allowed him to risk everything to do what was right for Meg
Even with this absurd charade as Anthony Dowling, he'
proved himself a man who approached life head-on, ur
willing to sit back and hope that happiness would pop u
one day and knock at his front door.

Life didn't work that way. Joe knew that, accepted it an
set out to knock on a few doors himself.

Maybe it was time for her to do the same thing.

"JOE!" The woman's voice came from a great distance
"Joe! Wake up."

He opened one eye. She was blond and lovely. For a sec
ond he thought he was trapped in the middle of *Pillow Tal*
with Doris Day; then he saw the deep brown eyes with thei
flashes of gold, and he realized it was Meg and he had falle
asleep in the back of the limousine.

He sat up, feeling groggy and disoriented. "Are we a
Orient Point already?"

"Halfway," she said. "I thought we needed to stretch ou
legs."

He ran his fingers through his hair in an attempt to tam
it. The passenger door was open, and a chill wind ble
through the car. Meg was leaning inside the car, pale sur
light sparkled in her hair. It was hard to judge her expres
sion, because she was squinting against the glare, but h
suddenly felt a sense of irrational elation that knocked hir
for a loop.

The car was stopped in a parking lot that was ringed b
scrub pines. "Where are we?"

"Sunken Meadow State Park." She waited while h
climbed out of the deep back seat and straightened the leg
of his pants.

"Do they have coffee here?" he asked. "I could us
something to wake me up."

She chuckled. His elation heightened. "Not in the off
season, I'm afraid. How about a stiff sea breeze instead?"

"If it packs a jolt of caffeine with it."

She turned and started walking away from the asphalt
[pa]th he assumed led to the beach. She picked her way across
[a] bottle-strewn path that led into the thicket on the east side
[of] the lot.

"I'm not much on nature walks," he said as he caught up
[wi]th her. "Where are we going?"

She kept her eyes on the path. "There's a nice secluded
[sp]ot a few hundred yards up. It has a great view of the
[So]und. I think you'll like it."

What in hell was going on? He glanced at his watch. Two
[ho]urs ago she acted as if she'd rather transport toxic waste
[th]an take him out to the end of the Island. Now, despite
[ev]erything, a thin ribbon of hope was uncurling itself in-
[si]de his heart.

He followed her up a steep incline, reaching out once to
[st]eady her as she stumbled in her black high heels. Sharp
[bl]ades of brown dune grass jabbed at his ankles; cold, wet
[sa]nd slid into his shoes. The wind intensified as they reached
[th]e crest. But all of his discomfort disappeared when he
[st]ood beside Meg and looked out at the gray and wild Long
[Is]land Sound one hundred feet below them as it slapped
[ag]ainst the side of the cliff.

She wrapped her arms around her chest and looked over
[at] him. "Wonderful, isn't it?"

"Primitive," he said. "The kind of beauty that makes
[yo]u think of what it really meant to be man against the ele-
[m]ents."

She nodded, that secret smile he loved playing at the cor-
[ne]rs of her mouth. "I knew you'd understand."

He badly wanted a cigarette to calm his nerves, but he re-
[si]sted the urge.

She shielded her eyes against the glare and looked over at
[a] cliff about fifty yards away from them. "A pair of swans
[ha]d a nest over there," she said, pointing with her other
[ha]nd. "I used to watch them every day as they swooped out
[ov]er the Sound."

"Used to?"

"They're gone," she said. "I haven't seen them since went up to Lakeland House."

He couldn't stand this feeling of being poised on the edg any longer. "Meg?" Those deep brown eyes of hers met h held his gaze. "Why are we here?"

She motioned for Joe to sit next to her on an arrc shaped boulder that rested near the precipice. "This is n favorite place on the Island," she said slowly. "I thought might help me with what I want to say to you."

Any elation he'd felt shriveled and died. A gust of win salty and damp, sliced through his shirt and jacket a turned his heart to ice. "Is it that bad?" he asked. "May I should go back to the car and pour us each a drink."

She smiled. "No, it's not that bad, but it is that difficu for me." She looked out at the Sound and the faint outli of the Connecticut shore on the other side. "I've made decision about the *People* magazine offer."

"Yes?"

She turned back to him. "I'm going to take it."

"Meg! I'm so glad I—"

"Just listen, Joe. It's not for you or Renee or even for m exactly. It could be a big break for Hunt."

"It could be a big break for you, too."

She shook her head. "There's one condition—I dor want a credit on the pictures."

He started to protest, but she raised a hand to stop hir "My career," she said softly. "My decision. Too ma doors were opened for me before. I think it's time for me open a few myself." He was quiet, and she watched him f a few moments. "I stood in Kay's shadow for so long, Jo I don't think I want to stand in yours."

Pain, sharp and deep, tore at him. He stood up a jammed his hands in his jacket pockets. He'd pushed to hard, and this time he fell right over the edge. "The fat flaw," he said, looking away from her. "All classic hero have one."

Suddenly she was behind him, her slender arms wrapped ound his waist. The scent of her exotic perfume filled his ad with the craziest fantasies, the wildest hopes.

"Perfect people are fine in their place," she murmured, r breath tickling his ear, "but I don't think I'd like to be arried to one."

His heart slammed into his ribs. "What was that?"

She laughed and gently bit his earlobe. "Have you lost ur hearing, Joseph? A woman asks for your hand in arriage, and you demand a repeat performance! It was rd enough the first time."

He grabbed her by the waist and spun her around until her es were level with his, until he was able to lose himself in e warmth and beauty of her soul. "Writers are moody ople. Are you sure you'd like to be married to one?"

"Photographers happen to like challenges."

Take it slow, he warned himself. *Don't push.* "No more ousine driving?"

"Only for us."

"When did you decide?"

"I suppose I knew it the first day I returned to Lakeland use," she said, "but I was afraid to admit it. You just ppened to catch on to it faster than I did."

"I never meant to push," he said, his foolish heart urg-g him forward. "I have this habit of trying to make things rk out in real life the way they do in books."

"I've noticed," she said. "You *do* tend to try to domi-te a situation, Joe."

"I can't promise anything," he said, "but I'm working on ure."

She touched his face gently with her hand. He covered it th his own and pressed its softness against his cheek.

"I'm not perfect, either," she said. He laughed, and she de a face. "A gentleman would have denied that." She ntinued, "I'm stubborn." She paused. "I'm tempera-ntal." She waited. "Sooner or later you have to disagree th me, Joe, for the sake of our future together."

"Sorry, kid," he said, kissing her hand, then holding
next to his heart. "You are imperfect and stubborn a
temperamental." He laughed at the expression on her fa
"But you're also kind and generous and talented and
most beautiful woman—inside and out—that I've e
known." He saw in her a strength few human beings p
sessed.

Again that seductive smile that tied his emotions in kno

"Do you think you'll be able to stand living with a str
gling photographer?"

"It doesn't change how I feel about you, Margarita,"
said. "I want you to set the world on its ear, but if you
cide to throw your camera into the ocean and drive a
instead, I'm behind you all the way. Nothing can e
change the way I love you." He wanted her to know
would never stand in anyone's shadow again.

"Not even if I end up doing passport pictures all
life?"

He laughed. "Not even that."

Her eyes darkened. He drew her close to him and
about to kiss her when they heard a commotion, then
rhythmic sound of wings strong and steady on the wind.

Two adult swans, immense and majestic, arced upwa
then sailed out into the currents above the Long Isla
Sound. The pure untamed beauty of their bodies against
winter sky touched his romantic soul.

"That's all there is to it, Margarita," Joe said. "Son
times you just have to take the leap and try to fly."

She turned to him, her face wild and lovely, radiant w
the courage that was the real source of her beauty. "I m
never fly that high," she said. "There are no guarantees

"There never are any guarantees," he said, thinking of
own life, his own successes and failures. "But it's not h
high you fly that matters; it's that you fly at all." It h
taken him years, but he finally understood what Anna h
tried so hard to teach him. Real life was the biggest ch
lenge of all.

The swans soared higher, then disappeared from view, ~~lea~~ving just the memory of their beauty against the autumn ~~sk~~y.

Meg laughed, the sound pure and sweet against the rush ~~of~~ the wind. "Ah, Angelique," she said, kissing his jaw, his ~~ea~~r, his mouth. "Another happy ending."

Joe looked at the woman he intended to grow old beside, ~~th~~e woman in whose arms he wanted to die. He knew she ~~wo~~uld fly as high as she dreamed. "Are there any other ~~ki~~nd?" he asked.

Epilogue

Peace and quiet.

For the first time in three days, Meg was surrounded
peace and quiet.

"I've died and gone to heaven," she said as she sprawl
on the big couch in the library. "I never thought I'd hear t
sound of silence again."

"Quiet," Joe warned from across the room. "If Kris
wakes up, you won't hear silence again for quite a while.

For three days Lakeland House had been filled to capa
ity with friends and relatives, all of whom had come bea
ing gifts for the baptism of Kristen Anna Alessio. Elysse a
Renee had shared the godparenting honors, and it h
moved Meg tremendously to see their closest friends jo
together and pledge their responsibility for this new li
Patrick McCallum, beaming with an almost-fatherly pri
had ceremoniously taken pictures of each and every one
them with the baby. Everyone important to Meg and J
had been with them to share their joy in their daughter. On
Huntington Kendall, wildly successful now and curren
living in Paris, had been unable to make the christening, a
both she and Joe felt the loss sharply.

But now that all the excitement was over, four-week-o
Krissie, the focal point of the onslaught of family a
friends, was sleeping blissfully in her father's strong ar

What the press says about Harlequin romance fiction…

"When it comes to romantic novels…
Harlequin is the indisputable king."
— *New York Times*

"…always with an upbeat, happy ending."
— *San Francisco Chronicle*

"Women have come to trust these
stories about contemporary people,
set in exciting foreign places."
— *Best Sellers*, New York

"The most popular reading matter of
American women today."
— *Detroit News*

"…a work of art."
— *Globe & Mail*, Toronto

WORLDWIDE LIBRARY IS YOUR TICKET TO ROMANCE, ADVENTURE AND EXCITEMENT

Experience it all in these big, bold Bestsellers— Yours exclusively from WORLDWIDE LIBRARY WHILE QUANTITIES LAST

To receive these Bestsellers, complete the order form, detach and send together with your check or money order (include 75¢ postage and handling), payable to WORLDWIDE LIBRARY, to:

In the U.S.
WORLDWIDE LIBRARY
901 Fuhrman Blvd.
Buffalo, N.Y.
14269

In Canada
WORLDWIDE LIBRARY
P.O. Box 2800, 5170 Yonge Street
Postal Station A, Willowdale, Ontario
M2N 6J3

Quant.	Title	Price
_____	**WILD CONCERTO**, Anne Mather	$2.95
_____	**A VIOLATION**, Charlotte Lamb	$3.50
_____	**SECRETS**, Sheila Holland	$3.50
_____	**SWEET MEMORIES**, LaVyrle Spencer	$3.50
_____	**FLORA**, Anne Weale	$3.50
_____	**SUMMER'S AWAKENING**, Anne Weale	$3.50
_____	**FINGER PRINTS**, Barbara Delinsky	$3.50
_____	**DREAMWEAVER**, Felicia Gallant/Rebecca Flanders	$3.50
_____	**EYE OF THE STORM**, Maura Seger	$3.50
_____	**HIDDEN IN THE FLAME**, Anne Mather	$3.50
_____	**ECHO OF THUNDER**, Maura Seger	$3.95
_____	**DREAM OF DARKNESS**, Jocelyn Haley	$3.95

YOUR ORDER TOTAL	$_____
New York residents add appropriate sales tax	$_____
Postage and Handling	$___.75
I enclose	$_____

NAME _____

ADDRESS _____ APT.# _____

CITY _____

STATE/PROV. _____ ZIP/POSTAL CODE _____

WW-1-3